SAGAHAWK
by the Sea

A Love Story Changes History

JOHN F. BRONZO

ARCHWAY
PUBLISHING

Archway Publishing books may be ordered through booksellers or by contacting:

Archway Publishing
1663 Liberty Drive
Bloomington, IN 47403
www.archwaypublishing.com
1 (888) 242-5904

ISBN: 978-1-4808-5255-6 (sc)
ISBN: 978-1-4808-5253-2 (hc)
ISBN: 978-1-4808-5254-9 (e)

Library of Congress Control Number: 2017916074

Print information available on the last page.

Archway Publishing rev. date: 03/13/2018

Dedication

This book is dedicated to two service members. It is dedicated to Air Force Major Rudolf Anderson Jr., who, on the morning of October 27, 1962, took off from McCoy Air Force Base in Orlando, Florida, in his U-2 aircraft (AF serial number 56-6676) and never returned—sacrificing his life so that we could live ours in peace. He was the only US combat fatality of the Cuban Missile Crisis. In addition, this book is dedicated to my high school classmate, Peter E. Sipp, or "Dude" as he was known. He was killed in Vietnam, when he threw himself on a grenade to save his buddies – sacrificing his life so they could live out theirs.

This book is dedicated also to Christopher, who God created for a special reason, to Karen, Elayne, and Nancy, who died too young, and to Cliff, a true American farmer.

I want to thank my family: my mother, Gloria; my wife, Carole; and my children, Sandra, and her husband John J. LePino Jr.; John; Christine, and her husband Andy Okonkwo; and Joseph. I also want to thank my publicist, Laura Ponticello. Without their help and support, this book would not have been possible.

1961

one

The last thing I remember was looking at the clock on my desk. It read 3:08 a.m. I must've fallen asleep studying for my Latin exam. The next thing I remember was the feeling of sheer panic when I looked up and saw that same clock now showing the time to be 8:03 a.m. The sun had begun to stream through my bedroom window. Nevertheless, I did a double take because I still couldn't believe my eyes. Unfortunately, there was no denying it: The time indeed was 8:03 a.m. I had exactly twenty-seven minutes to be at my desk in school to sit for the exam or risk failing the course. Latin was the last test of the school year, and only a few students had taken it. Most chose Spanish instead. The date was Wednesday, May 24, 1961, a date that would change my life forever.

In 1961, Sagahawk was a small, sleepy farming community east of the town of Bridgehampton, a summer playground for the rich and famous on Long Island in New York. The New York City folks would pay us no mind as they drove by in their fancy cars on the way to East Hampton. Occasionally, our tractors would slow their progress until they could pass us on Route 27 with an annoyed and impatient look.

Dad was a Fordham University graduate who had hoped to become a classics professor before his plans were detoured by World War II and the unexpected death of my grandfather. A B-17 pilot in the United States Army's Eighth Air Force during the war, Dad met Mom in London, and he married her there. Soon afterward, I was born in 1946, and they returned to the United States in 1947. Dad was a newly enrolled graduate student in the classics at Columbia University a year later when my grandfather died of a heart attack while plowing the fields. Grandma asked him to take a leave from his graduate studies and come run the farm until she could sell it. She never did, and he never went back.

Mom was a university graduate and a writer who worked as a reporter during the war. She quickly became close with Grandma and adjusted to the quiet, rural life in Sagahawk. When she was not writing, she helped the family make ends meet by making jams and pies to sell at the family farm stand that Grandma ran.

Calling it a farm stand may be a bit of an exaggeration. It was more of a hodgepodge of two old tables, an equally old chair, and a covered cart that had fold-down sides, which could be locked but never were. Dad had made the cart and let my sister and me help him paint it. When I was too young to assist with the farm work, Grandma would make me sit there in the summers to collect the money from the city folks. In the off season, she went on the honor system and left a bowl out. People were pretty honest. But as soon as I became old enough to work with Dad in the fields, my younger sister was drafted into duty at the stand by Grandma. She still works there, especially when Grandma goes to stay with her sister who suffered a stroke.

After we made ten dollars at the stand in a day, Grandma let us keep one of every additional five that we made up to thirty dollars. Anything over thirty dollars but under fifty dollars that we made in a day, we got to keep. So if we sold fifty dollars worth of stuff in a day, we made twenty-four dollars, and Grandma made twenty-six dollars. Everything over fifty dollars that we made went to Grandma. Making fifty dollars or more in a day was a rare occurrence. It usually happened only on Memorial Day, the Fourth of July, or Labor Day if at all. It was a clever system on Grandma's part that was designed to keep us motivated and honest. If the truth be known, however, we loved her too much to ever slack off or cheat her. But it was nice to have the spending money, and I think she knew that and did it to help us.

My name is Joseph Christopher, but Grandma is the only one that calls me by that name, and it's usually when she's mad at me. Everyone else calls me Joe, JC, or Joey. I live on the family farm with my parents, John and Sally Carr, Grandma, my younger sister Kelly, and my little brother, Luke, who was born with a birth defect that has slowed his development. Mom is very religious and says that God made Luke that way for a reason, but it beats me what that reason might be. I just know that I love the little guy, and he follows me around like the tail on a dog. I can't say the same thing for my sister Kelly. I know why God created her—to make my life miserable, and boy is she good at it! Speaking of the tail on a dog, I almost forgot to mention our family pet: a black lab named Linus.

Dad was raised a mix of Catholic and Episcopalian. Mom was baptized an Anglican and reared in the Church of England. I guess it's no surprise that I'm a crucifer on most Sundays at Saint Ann's Episcopal Church in Bridgehampton, where Mom has become very close with Reverend Thompson, the rector. Dad doesn't seem to give too much mind to religion, although he does want me to go to a Jesuit college and study the classics.

We often listen to the Boston College football games on the New England radio station. Even though we live in New York, our old radio can pick up the New England broadcasts better than the New York city ones. Once in a while Dad and I take the Long Island Sound ferry to New London and drive to Chestnut Hill to see Boston College play Holy Cross. Yes, it is preordained that I will be going to Boston College to study the classics—that is, if I can pass my Latin exam.

And so it was in Sagahawk on the morning of May 24, 1961.

I jumped up and grabbed my books. My clothes were still lying where I'd left them on my neat and untouched bed. Putting on the clothes, I ran into the hall bathroom to splash water on my face and brush my teeth. Descending the stairs to the kitchen, I reached for an apple on my way out the door. Flying down the walk, I grabbed my bike only to find the front tire was flat. So I ran through the front gate, and onto Sagg Main, as Sagahawk's main street was called, toward our little white one-room schoolhouse about two miles down the road. Ten minutes had elapsed according to my watch. I had seventeen minutes to make it through the schoolhouse door before Miss Pickering closed the door at exactly 8:30 a.m. She was a stickler for punctuality. Once shut, the door would not be reopened. I would automatically fail Latin.

It would be close—very close. I decided to run. Discarding the partially eaten apple, I began to run faster and then faster still. I tried to keep up the pace, but after the first mile, fatigue set in. I began to slow down.

As I rounded the bend in the road, I saw Miss Pickering at the door. She had her back to me and was talking to Reverend Thompson, who was facing my way.

The old cemetery, with its split rail fence that made up the village green, along with the war memorial and flagpole, stood between me and the open door to the schoolhouse. According to my watch, I had a little less than a minute to make it through that door.

If I ran around the cemetery fence, I would not be in time. But if Miss Pickering saw me jump the fence and run through the cemetery, I would be inviting a different type of trouble. It was her cherished belief that the final resting place of the hamlet's dearly departed heritage ought to be shown the proper respect. I had no choice but to risk her wrath, so I jumped the fence.

Running with my eyes fixed on her and the reverend, I hoped that she would not turn and face me. Tripping and gathering myself, I prepared to leap the fence at the other side of the cemetery. I was almost there. But just as I flew over the fence, she turned to see me as I dashed toward her and the open door. It was 8:30 a.m. I saw her excusing herself and preparing to shut the door, when Father Thompson stopped her to ask something. I think he sensed my predicament and was trying to be of help.

I seized the opportunity to dash through the open door and crash land in my seat, sending it and my desk sliding several feet into the isle with me on board.

When she had shut the door, Miss Pickering came over to me as I was moving myself back into position. She said that I would be permitted to take the test, even though I technically had been late, but that I should stay to see her after the exam. Relieved, I was eager to oblige her and said okay.

The Latin test was grueling, and I was exhausted by the time it was over. My adrenaline had subsided and my lack of sleep the previous night was beginning to catch up with me. Nevertheless, I sat there patiently, telling myself that a reprimand from Miss Pickering was a small price to pay for my transgressions. However, what Miss Pickering had in mind for me was far more than a simple scolding. As I said earlier, it would change my life forever.

When the room had finally emptied, she and I were the only two people remaining. She walked over and sat in the desk in front of mine.

Turning in the seat to face me, she spoke. "Joe, you're a good boy, a serious student with a great deal of promise, and I know that you'll make something of yourself in the future. But that doesn't excuse what you did today. The people buried in that cemetery once had lives full of promise just like you. They loved and suffered, experienced great joy and sorrow, and had dreams and aspirations as well as disappointments."

She proceeded to say, "At your age, you may think that you're the center of the universe and that everything revolves around you, but as you'll come to realize, that isn't the case. You, too, will die someday, and you also may be buried in that little cemetery."

(The word in town was that the village elders wouldn't decide if you could be buried there until after you died because there wasn't enough room for everyone, so you had to earn the right during your life to be planted there.)

"I meant no harm, Miss Pickering. I was just trying to make it to the test on time. When I fell, it was because I lost my balance and tripped by accident. I'll go back and look, but I don't think I disturbed or hurt anything."

She smiled at me and said, "I know you meant no harm, but I want you to go back and do more than look. I want you to read the names, the epitaphs, and the dates that they were born and died, and try to imagine what their lives might have been like."

She took a breath and continued. "Then I want you to pick three grave stones to investigate, and I would like you to research the lives of the persons named on them and prepare a report on each of the three grave stones for me over the summer."

She paused momentarily before proceeding to say, "I will be here all summer and can meet with you any time you have any questions. If I receive three satisfactory reports by Labor Day, I will give you your Latin grade and promote you."

She finished by asking me, "Is that fair?"

I said yes, although deep down I wasn't sure that I thought it was fair. It seemed like a time-consuming and useless exercise to me. In the end, who really cared about these people---other than their relatives, of course? They were not famous or important historical figures. But anything was better than failing Latin. So, I resigned myself to the task and set about doing it.

two

It was Tuesday, May 30, Memorial Day of 1961. I awoke early, excited to get on with my day. I quickly bounced out of bed and ran to my bedroom window. I could see that it was to be a glorious day, filled with sunshine, cloudless blue skies, and the wonderful smells of spring. First there would be a parade that started at the firehouse, went down Sagg Main Street, and ended at the cemetery, where there would be a ceremony. The mayor would place a wreath at the war memorial. Later in the day, when the sun was not as strong and the afternoon breeze had been given a chance to pick up, there would be a tractor pull and picnic in town at the Bridgehampton Historical Society.

In the parade, I would be marching with my Boy Scout troop and with the Girl Scouts, behind my dad and the other volunteer firemen, who would be showing off their shiny red fire trucks along the route. Behind us would be the marching band, antique cars carrying the old soldiers, scores of marching younger veterans, army trucks towing large guns, and an amphibious navy vehicle with the mayor and the parade queen inside. Bringing up the rear, would be the local ambulance corps and the Coast Guard Sea Rescue Unit with their brand new white and orange helicopter flying high above.

As I gazed out the window, I saw my dad getting his old John Deere ready for the tractor pull later that afternoon. Kelly was by his side. I also smelled the pies cooling on the kitchen window sill that Mom had made for the picnic. Yes, it promised to be a magnificent day.

Since I would be at the village green for the laying of the wreath and I'd have several hours to kill between the end of the parade and the start of the picnic, I stayed behind at the cemetery after the ceremony to get started on Miss Pickering's assignment. The weather was nice, and my mood was good, so I actually didn't mind the homework task any longer. Kelly would be baking cookies for the picnic at her friend's house; I decided to give Mom and Dad a break and keep Luke and Linus behind with me.

After the ceremony, the crowd began to dissipate. Soon Luke, Linus, and I were the only ones left in the cemetery. Luke kept getting drawn to a headstone with three flags that the Girl Scouts had placed there for the veterans. At first I scolded him for not staying with me while I looked around the graveyard. I finally relented and walked over to where he was playing with the flags. It didn't take long for the headstone to catch my attention, too, not because of the flags, but because of one of the names engraved on the marker. It read:

Samuel Pierce Jr., beloved son and brother, member of the 3rd NY Regiment, born August 13, 1845, died July 8, 1864, at the battle of Bloody Bridge, John's Island, SC

August Pierce, beloved son and brother, born March 18, 1849, died January 30, 1868

Samuel Pierce, beloved husband and father, veteran of the Mexican-American War, born September 16, 1823, died October 6, 1881

Ernest Pickering, member of the 157th NY
Regiment, born October 10, 1844, died May 27,
1903

I had so many questions. Who was Ernest Pickering? Was
he any relation to Miss Pickering? Why was he buried with the
Pierces? What happened to the Pierces? I didn't know of any Pierces
still living in Sagahawk. Why did August Pierce die so young, and
what had become of Mrs. Pierce, if she isn't buried here?

Caught up in my curiosity, I decided that this would be my
first case. Over the next few days, I would check the records at
the Bridgehampton Library and at the Bridgehampton Historical
Society before going to speak with Miss Pickering. I wanted to
learn as much as I could on my own before seeking assistance
from her.

I gathered up Luke and Linus and began to head for home. As
I did, I took a backward glance at the grave. It was the one that
I'd tripped over and fallen on in my mad dash for the schoolhouse
door the week before. The realization caused a cold shiver to run
down my spine, but I decided to pay it no heed and told myself it
was just the afternoon breeze starting up.

The picnic and tractor pull proved to be every bit as exciting
and as much fun as I had anticipated. The pull itself came down to
a contest between Dad's John Deere and old man Foster's Ford, as
it had the last three years in a row. Much to my father's frustration,
the Foster tractor was the winner on each of those three occasions.
But Dad had tuned the old workhorse up that very morning and
refused to lose.

I was working on the antique steam-driven ice cream maker
that rattled and clanged from the vibration of the well-worn rubber drive belt and pulleys, but I could still hear the excitement and
commotion that the contest was generating. As usual, the line for
ice cream was long and full of anxious, happy faces. Nevertheless,
I had to excuse myself and go watch Dad fight back three years

of disappointing near misses and finally triumph for the first time since 1957.

People were rooting for Dad because he was the underdog, and when he finally got that three-year-old monkey off his back with a win, the crowd went wild. Even old man Foster seemed to be happy for my father. Or maybe he was just relieved to be rid of the pressure from the expectations that being undefeated brings with it. In any event, I was happy for Pop. It was glorious indeed to see him win!

Then I remembered the contraption that I was supposed to be working but had left unattended. I ran back to the antique machine as it continued to belch steam almost as if to protest my actions. The crowd was heading over to join the already longer-than-usual line the attraction was garnering.

Everybody seemed to be rooting for Dad! Nobody showed me any anger when I returned. They congratulated me as I got back into my work. Everything was forgiven when the ice cream began to flow again. One by one, they would swear to me that the ice cream from that noisy old thing tasted better than the store-bought variety, something I thought was more in their minds than anywhere else.

When Dad's turn in line came, he scolded me for leaving my post. It was only a half-hearted gesture that quickly gave way to a beaming smile of achievement.

Mom's pies did equally well. Her blueberry crumb won the award previously held by Mrs. Steffenbourg, and her cherry pie edged out Mrs. Mohair's. However, the best her Dutch apple could do was tie the one baked by Mrs. Foster. Mom was thrilled with two wins and a tie. After all, the last two years she had come out empty-handed.

It was fun to see my mother glowing with pride as she was interviewed by a reporter from the local paper. Even Grandma got into the act, posing for the newspaper photographer when he asked for a picture of the elder Mrs. Carr pinning the winning ribbons on the younger Mrs. Carr's blouse. Kelly had met a boy she was sure she had a crush on, although I don't think he knew about it yet. The ride home later was a joyous one all around.

The next day was a busy day on the farm as we tried to make up for the day before. On Thursday, Dad said I could have the morning off to go do my research in town, provided I take Luke and Linus with me. I quickly agreed because it was not as burdensome a request as it might sound. Mr. Carter, who owned the five-and-dime store in town, had a soft spot for Luke and would pay him a nickel to work in the store. Luke would take the small plastic cars out of their boxes and arrange them by color on the display shelf.

Miss Emily, Mr. Carter's daughter, had tutored Luke when he was younger and had used the cars to teach him his colors and how to count. Luke might have taken a little longer than most to learn things, but once he did, there was no stopping him. He never forgot a thing. He rarely would get the nickel because he usually would use it to buy one of the cars. His favorite was a yellow 1955 Chevy that he called Herbie. He also had a green 1950 Chevy pickup truck like Dad's that he called Sally Truck. Dad liked to tease Mom by calling his old, beaten-up wreck of a truck Sally because he knew how much she hated it. Much to Mom's dismay, Luke had innocently picked up on the name and it stuck.

Leaving Luke to his chores in the store and Linus resting in his usual spot on the sidewalk outside, I started about my work at the library. Mrs. Curtin had been the librarian for as long as I could possibly remember, and this morning she was her usual helpful self. We set out to check the obituaries from July of 1864, January of 1868, October of 1881, and May of 1903. We had no luck finding an 1864 obituary for Samuel Pierce Jr., but we did find one in 1868 for August Pierce. It seems he died from pneumonia after having rescued a child who'd fallen through the ice on Ellis Pond down by the beach. Mrs. Curtin suggested that we look for any related articles that might shed light on the details of the rescue, the child that was saved, or the funeral of the young Pierce boy. We did, and what we found was amazing.

August Pierce had suffered injuries to his head and spinal cord during birth that stunted his physical growth and coordination, but not his mental abilities. When he died at the age of eighteen, he was only three feet ten inches tall and eighty-eight pounds. He had been very close with his older brother and was devastated when he learned that Samuel had been killed in the Civil War. It was not until Ernest Pickering had come to live with the Pierce family and work on the farm that he began to come out of his depression.

Ernest Pickering also had a tragic background. By a twist of fate, he'd been the only one spared from dying in a house fire that claimed the lives of the rest of his family. When the fire started that night, he was out rounding up a cow that had escaped from the barn. By the time he returned, the fire had engulfed the house, and there was no chance of rescuing any of his family.

Brokenhearted, he joined the US Army when the Civil War broke out and was fighting alongside Samuel Pierce Jr. in the Battle of Bloody Bridge on John's Island, South Carolina, when Samuel was struck in the leg by artillery fire. That day the smoke was heavy on the battlefield from all the Confederate artillery and rifle fire being rained down on the Union troops from a nearby ridge, making visibility poor and breaking cover dangerous. Nevertheless, Ernest risked his own life to rush and get medical help for his comrade. But by the time he returned with help, infection and gangrene already had set in, and Samuel had lost a great deal of blood. Samuel knew that his only chance at survival, albeit thin, would be to have his leg amputated.

While lying and waiting for help, he mustered up all his remaining energy and wrote a letter to his parents. When Ernest Pickering returned, Samuel, fearing that he might not survive, made his friend promise to deliver the letter in person to his parents after the war. Samuel had lost a lot of blood. He was too weak to withstand the trauma and died during the amputation.

Ernest survived the war, and after it was over, he kept his promise to his dying friend and delivered the letter in person to the Pierce family. In the letter Samuel said his good-byes and sent his love to his family. He also told them of Ernest's tragic loss and asked his parents to please take his loyal friend in and give him a job on the family farm, which they did.

On the farm, Ernest Pickering quickly formed a strong bond with August Pierce and the two became inseparable, the older Pickering having taken the younger Pierce under his wing.

Ernest never forgot his tragic past. Burdened by the loss of his own family to a house fire, he insisted that his younger companion learn to hold his breath long enough to crawl blindfolded from his upstairs back bedroom, down the stairs, and out the front door of the house. He taught the young Pierce to hold his breath so as not to breathe in the hot smoke, and to stay close to the floor by crawling where it would be cooler. The blindfold was to simulate the dark, smoke-filled environment. Fortuitously, it was this very training that allowed Ernest Pickering and August Pierce to save the young drowning child's life.

According to the account, Pickering and Pierce had just arrived at the pond to check if the ice was thick enough for ice boating, a sport for which the two shared a fondness. Then they heard the panicked cries of a young mother. She had been momentarily distracted and turned back, expecting to see the cold, rosy face of the child she left playing in the snow on the bank of the pond. Instead, what she saw was an abandoned toy and a dark black hole in the ice.

Realizing what had happened, the big, strapping Pickering grabbed a rope from his wagon, picked up the lighter Pierce, and ran over to the distressed mother.

Once there, the war veteran tied the rope around the waist of the smaller Pierce, who was light enough to walk out on the ice to the hole where the boy had fallen in. Upon reaching the hole, August jumped through it and into the pond. Holding his breath, he set about in the dark, murky water below until he located the limp body of the boy. Then he tugged on the rope to signal to Pickering to pull them up. Back on the shore, August turned the limp child over to Pickering, who was able to revive him.

That the desperate attempt had succeeded was dubbed a miracle. But as the account went on to say, the ensuing days saw the joy of that moment give way to sadness and concern. It was only a matter of time before pneumonia would claim the young hero's life. August Pierce died a few days later.

Per the article, a wake was held at the Pierce home on Sagg Main Street. It was so well attended that the crowd spilled out onto the Pierces' front porch, and the line of mourners stretched past the white front gate and picket fence and onto the road.

I was particularly moved to read in the account that an elm tree had been planted by the family of the young boy who had been saved in memory of the two Pierce sons who had given their lives at the age of eighteen—one to save the Union, and the other to save their young son, John. The tree was situated in a spot along the Pierces' front walk that was eighteen paces from the front porch and eighteen paces from the white front picket fence. The copy of the article was very old and somewhat damaged, and the last name of the family whose son had been saved was not legible.

I felt it was a most productive morning, and I thanked Mrs. Curtin for her assistance. Then I walked outside to fetch Linus and Luke before heading back to the farm for an afternoon of chores. As I stepped out of the library and into the warmth of the late morning sun, I felt the same cold shiver run down my spine that I felt at the cemetery on Memorial Day.

It suddenly began to dawn on me that the route from August Pierce's room to the front door that he would have to crawl in the event of a fire seemed awfully similar to the route from my room down the stairs and out the front door of our house. Also, we had a big old elm tree in our front yard between the front porch and the white picket fence. *Could it be?* I asked myself. No, it was just a coincidence—but I wasn't sure.

When we got home, I paced the distance from the tree to the porch and to the fence. It was eighteen paces in both directions. *No, it couldn't be,* I reassured myself.

On Saturday morning, Dad took me to the safe deposit box at the bank, and we looked at the deed for the house and the other papers Grandma had stored there. Indeed, it was true. Great-Grandpa had bought the farm from the widow Pierce in 1905 when she moved to Philadelphia to live with relatives. It had become too much for her to handle once Ernest Pickering died in 1903.

As we headed home in Sally Truck, I turned to Dad and said, "Do you realize that I sleep in the same upstairs back bedroom that August Pierce once slept in?"

Dad smiled and replied, "Now don't go getting all weird on me. Next thing I know you'll be telling me that you're seeing his ghost."

Well, I hadn't yet seen his ghost, but it sure was strange that I'd run down that same escape route out of the house on the day that I tripped on his grave. I asked myself if he was trying to tell me something. If so, what it might be?

Those two questions would haunt me for the rest of the weekend until I could return to the library on Monday and look at the materials more closely.

Monday morning I awoke at first light and immediately set about my work without even taking the time to have breakfast. At nine in the morning, I stopped what I was doing, jumped on my bike, and rode to the library. I ran past Mrs. Curtin at the front desk and up the stairs to the place where the papers were still spread out. She followed behind me, curious to see what had me in such a tizzy. I was too preoccupied to pay any attention to her or to respond to her many questions. My eyes darted with a laserlike focus from one document to another.

Then suddenly, right in front of me in black and white was the name of the boy that August Pierce had rescued. I could not believe my eyes and rubbed them to be sure that they were not deceiving me. They were not!

The rescued four-year-old boy was John Carr. Grandpa was John Carr Jr., so John Carr must have been my great-grandfather. Then the significance of that find hit me full force: If it were not for August Pierce and Ernest Pickering, I would not exist; Dad, Kelly, and Luke would not exist; and Grandpa never would have existed! I sat there in stunned silence for what felt like an eternity. When I finally became aware of my surroundings again, I apologized to poor Mrs. Curtin for ignoring her and showed her my find.

The next day, I went to see Miss Pickering and told her what I had found. She was delighted with my work and accepted the case as satisfactorily completed. She told me that as far as she knew, she wasn't related to Ernest Pickering. And so it was.

Die in a War?

three

I said, "and so it was," but it really wasn't. In the days that followed, I continued to think about August Pierce. I was convinced there was more that he wanted to share with me, but what could it be? The more I thought about it, the more frustrated I became.

I stopped by the cemetery and visited his grave often. I owed him so much, yet I knew so little about him. I found myself wondering what his dreams may have been.

What might he have wished to do with his life, if he'd lived?

Was it a coincidence that I was a healthy and fit older brother like Samuel Pierce Jr. had been, with a younger brother Luke who idolized me the way he'd idolized his brother Samuel?

Would I die in a war and leave Luke behind the way Samuel had left him behind?

Would there be a loyal friend to help Luke the way Ernest Pickering had helped August?

My Dad was right: I was getting weird. After all, there was no war going on that I knew of. But then again, the Civil War had not been going on when Samuel Pierce Jr. had been fifteen. As scared as I was to admit it, I almost hoped that I would see the ghost of August Pierce. I had so many questions for the former occupant of my upstairs back bedroom.

The next Friday night, there was a dance at the firehouse in Bridgehampton. I hoped Mary Hurd would come. I met her last summer, when she was still recovering from a serious horseback riding accident. We instantly were attracted to each other and found that we had so much in common, as I helped her walk and ride her bike to rebuild her leg muscles.

She had missed two years of school because she was in a coma, needed numerous surgeries to repair broken bones, and had to learn how to walk again. I also was two years behind because of all the school I missed when Dad ran into financial problems and needed my help to avoid losing the farm. Self-conscious of the fact that I was so much older than my classmates, I felt especially awkward when meeting girls. But with Mary it didn't matter. We were in our own world from the beginning.

Her parents were summer people, and I hadn't seen her since she went back to the city last September. Dad watched their house on Hedges Lane in the off season, and he told me they were scheduled to be out by the night of the dance.

I made it my business to be in their driveway when they pulled in. The Ford wagon was loaded to the max with suitcases, grocery bags, golf clubs, tennis rackets, fishing poles, and gardening books, to name a few of the many things. After helping Dr. Hurd unload everything, I dropped some of Mary's things off in her room and finally had a moment alone with her.

It amazed me that we could be separated for so long, and yet when we got back together, it felt like we'd never been apart. We picked up where we left off, as if it was only yesterday that we'd seen each other. However, as we settled into an active and animated discussion of our exploits during the off season, Mrs. Hurd called us down for lunch. She had purchased fried chicken and potato salad in town at Pieper's market, along with ice cold lemonade. We sat out in back and ate. I asked Mary if she was coming to the dance and she told me she was.

Being with Mary at the dance was wonderful. For the first time in a while, my thoughts were on someone other than August

Pierce. We danced, went for a walk in town, and caught up further on what each of us had been doing.

The next day we met at the Candy Kitchen for an ice cream. I told her about my special summer assignment as well as about Ernest Pickering, August Pierce, and my great-grandfather. It fascinated her, and when I shared with her that I was on my way over to the cemetery to pick out my next case for Miss Pickering, she asked if she could come and help me. I said fine, and we rode our bikes over to the village green.

We were the only two living people in the cemetery. I found myself fascinated by her shiny hair rustling in the breeze and her soft, pink lips moving as she read the headstones. Her skin was a smooth, silky white, and her scent was as fresh and beautiful as the sea air. I was shy and embarrassed that she might catch me staring at her, but she was too busy with her efforts to notice my admiring gazes.

All that changed on a dime. Without warning, she suddenly turned her head toward me with exhilarating excitement to proclaim that she'd found the perfect case. In doing so, she caught me staring at her. Our lips were only inches apart, and before I could catch myself, I kissed her, hoping to consume some of that excitement. When our lips finally broke apart, there was total silence. All that could be heard was the soft sound of the afternoon breeze. I waited for my reprimand or perhaps a slap, but to my surprise it never came.

She said: "Now can we get on with Miss Pickering's assignment?"

Feeling somewhat embarrassed, I quietly replied yes.

She then proceeded to tell me she'd found the perfect candidate for my next case, and pointed to the headstone in front of her. It had the image of a small angel on it. Below the image was inscribed:

Captain Thomas J. Harding, US Army 8th Air
Force, beloved husband, born February 14, 1910,
lost at sea, July 7, 1951

"What is so special about this one?" I asked.

"His widow, Mrs. Harding, lives in the house next to ours. Captain Harding was working in his study over the garage when he came down around 6 p.m. that Saturday to see if he had time to go to the beach and take a quick swim before supper. Mrs. Harding was preparing dinner at the time, and only momentarily looked up at him to nod yes and say to be back by seven.

"He walked out of the house and she heard the car start. That was the last she ever saw or heard of him. They found his car parked at the beach and his keys and other belongings on the beach, but they never found his body. He is presumed to have drowned and been washed out to sea. She locked the door to his study later that night, on July 7, 1951, and she has never allowed it to be opened since then. I think I can talk her into letting us open it and go in."

"Why would she let you open it and go in?"

"She was younger than Captain Harding and pregnant at the time with what would have been their only child. The image of an angel that you see on the headstone is for that infant. The shock of suddenly losing her husband is thought to have caused her to have a miscarriage. The baby would have been a little girl, and they already had picked the name Mary Bernadette for a daughter. Mrs. Harding sponsored me for my confirmation a few years ago, and I took the name Bernadette as my confirmation name. She considers me to be the daughter she never had. I think I can convince her that it's time to open that door and that we should be the ones to do it."

"I see," I said.

But I mustn't have sounded all that convinced because she looked at me and exclaimed, "I don't think you do!"

"Why do you say that?" I asked.

"Because I don't think you understand. She has no other family.

She has told my parents that she plans to leave everything to me when she dies. That study probably will belong to me someday!"

"You're right, I didn't fully appreciate what you were saying. Now I do. One question: What were they going to name the baby if it was a boy?"

"Why do you ask?"

"I'm just curious."

"It wasn't Joe or Luke, or anything like August or Samuel, if that's what you're thinking. She told me a long time ago, but I can't remember what it was. I'm pretty sure it was a double name, and it may have been something like Brian George, or George Brian. For some reason those names stick out in my mind. I can find out if you want me to."

"No need to. It's not a big deal. I'd rather you let it go. Like I said, I was just curious."

"So are you okay with this being your next case? If you are, I will ask Mrs. Harding to speak with us."

"Yeah, sure. It sounds cool to me," I said, as we began to walk toward our bikes.

Walking past the Pierce grave site, I once again tripped and fell. Mary laughed, but I didn't think it was funny. I took a backward glance as we started to ride away on our bikes, and once again that same cold shiver ran down my spine. I didn't say anything to Mary, but it felt odd to me.

When we got to my house, I couldn't help myself and asked Mary if I was a good kisser. She smiled and said it was hard to say after just one kiss. As she waved good-bye and rode away, she looked back, and with a wink called out that today was a good start.

The next time I saw Mary was at the Lions Club fair the following Saturday night. We had a great time, and afterward Mary told me that she had spoken with Mrs. Harding, who wanted to meet me. The next day was Sunday, and Mary asked if I would be free to meet at around two that afternoon. I said yes and rode my bike over on Sunday. Mary and I then walked next door together.

Mrs. Harding was a small, thin woman and still very attractive for a person her age. She clearly liked Mary. For the first thirty minutes or so, I felt I was being interrogated, not for purposes of being allowed into the locked study, but to see if I was worthy of "keeping company" with Mary, as Mrs. Harding liked to say. Through it all, Mary smiled sheepishly as Mrs. Harding placed her on a higher and higher pedestal.

Finally, after about forty minutes, I was given a chance to explain the assignment and why Miss Pickering gave it to me. I could see that Mrs. Harding was moved by the reason for the assignment, and told me that she couldn't deny Mary.

She asked that we try hard not to disturb things any more than necessary, and that we not remove anything from the room. She also requested that I not go in without being accompanied by Mary, and that we not discuss our findings with anyone else until we've shown her what we've learned. I thought it was a lot of *thats* and *nots*, but I nevertheless agreed, whereupon she handed the keys to Mary. We made plans to open the study the next morning and get started. Dad already had given me the time off. I think he was as curious as anyone to find out what was in there.

We weren't prepared for what we would uncover when that door was opened for the first time in almost a decade. Nor would the world be.

four

Slowly and carefully we opened the door. Except for a small amount of dust that had gathered over the years, the room looked as though Captain Harding had walked out of it the night before. His reading glasses were still on the desk where he'd left them. His cigarette butts remained in the ash tray, accompanied by their ashes. His empty coffee cup, still stained by its former contents, stood guard, along with a half-empty pack of Lucky Strikes and an open book of matches, over the untouched top of his desk. Papers and pictures, some work notes, and other official-looking documents with stamp markings on them were scattered everywhere.

Textbooks were resting open on a sofa. A slide rule and a microscope were on a coffee table, and a portable blackboard had "1062" with an "X" through it, followed by a question mark, written on it in white chalk. Otherwise, the room was decorated as you might expect of a former military man. There were black-and-white pictures of people in uniform, of what looked like military bases or installations, and of tanks, fighting planes, and ships. There also were framed awards, medals, and a letter from President Truman.

Some items weren't as easily explained. For example, there were pieces of shiny silver material that weren't familiar to us. There were pictures of what looked like dead aliens or mannequins made for a Hollywood science fiction movie. And there was a model of a flying saucer that Captain Harding must have made.

Pinned on the wall behind the desk was a calendar for the year 1947, with the date July 7 circled, which I thought was strange. Next to it on the wall was pinned a map of Roswell, New Mexico. On the floor, leaning against that same wall, was a framed picture of an airborne B-17 with Eighth Air Force markings that had been taken down to make room for the calendar and the map. The plane had the name *Sweet Sally* painted under the cockpit window, which was odd. My Dad had named his B-17 *Sweet Sally* in honor of Mom. That same cold shiver ran down my spine again, as I began to wonder what Mary and I were getting ourselves into. The shiver was an entirely involuntary action on my part, but trying to hide from Mary the fear and concern growing in me took all the strength and determination that I could muster.

"Where do we begin?" Mary asked.

"I don't know," I replied. "I feel completely overwhelmed. Let's take a break and go down to the beach for a swim. I think it'll help us clear our heads."

Mary agreed.

We were careful to lock the door to the study behind us when we left. We changed into our suits at Mary's house and rode our bikes to the beach—the same beach Captain Harding had vanished from.

At first I walked the beach deep in thought about what I'd just observed in the study, oblivious to Mary and the many strangers who were swimming and sunbathing. Looking back and forth between the ocean on one side of me, the dunes on the other, and down both directions of the sprawling beach, I kept hoping for some inspiration—some clue or insight. But none came to me. Finally, feigning annoyance at me for ignoring her, Mary coaxed me into joining her in the water. It was my first swim of the season, and felt good.

As we swam and bodysurfed, a lot of the tension that had been building in me began to dissipate. When we finally had enough of the ocean, we sat on the beach and ate the lunch Mary's mom had prepared for us. Handing me a cucumber sandwich and a bottle of soda pop from the picnic basket, Mary smiled and asked what was bothering me.

"Bothering me? What makes you think anything is bothering me?" I said as I tried to spare her my concerns by throwing her off the scent.

A part of me found comfort and delight in realizing that she was that attuned to my feelings. I took a liking to Mary the first time I met her, but up until the kiss in the cemetery, I'd been too afraid of being rebuffed by her, to let her know. Now it seemed she knew me better than I'd realized.

"Is it that obvious?" I asked.

"Let me see," she said as she put her right index finger to her lips in an inquisitive pose.

After a brief pause she continued. "You completely ignore me as if I weren't even here, and you pace up and down the beach deep in thought instead of being the first one in the ocean as you usually are. What do you call that if not obvious?"

"I guess it was more obvious than I thought."

"Perhaps not to everyone, but certainly to me," she replied. "I don't think you realize just how well I know you," she added.

"I guess not," I muttered quietly as the significance of what she was saying sank into my dazed brain. Catching myself, I blurted out, "But I sure am glad to hear it."

"Are you really?"

"Absolutely! I've been crazy about you since the first time I set eyes on you."

"You sure have a strange way of showing it. Then why didn't you kiss me at the end of the summer last year when I was going away?"

"I was chicken!"

"You have nothing to be afraid of, Joe Carr. I made up my mind a long time ago that you're the boy I'm going to marry."

Feeling a mix of shock and exhilaration, I croaked, "I am?" then tried to calm myself.

In a feeble attempt to regain my suave and cool demeanor, I asked, "And I guess you've also made up your mind about how many kids we're going to have and where we're going to live?"

"I have, but you don't need to know all of that stuff yet."

With that, she stood up and packed up the picnic basket. Smiling, she began to walk to the bikes.

As she did, she looked back, and with the same wink she had given me the other day said, "For now, your best bet would be to practice your kissing."

"Oh, is that so?" I yelled as I jumped up and chased her. Grabbing her, I kissed her as we fell to the sand.

"Better," she commented as she got up and started to pick up the mess the picnic basket made when it fell and opened.

As I bent down to help her, I said to myself, "You're the luckiest guy in the world."

I must have said it louder than I realized because she whispered, "You are, and don't you ever forget it."

I knew then that I never would.

five

When I got home from the beach after accompanying Mary back to her house, Mom told me that Mrs. Curtin called from the library and asked that I stop by as soon as I could. Apparently she'd found something that she thought I'd be interested in seeing. She was right.

After taking a shower and getting dressed, I rode up to the library to see her. She'd found a newspaper article about an interview that Mrs. Pierce had given the now-defunct *Sagahawk Gazette* in 1905, when she'd sold the farm and was preparing to move to Philadelphia. The article said:

The End of an Era—Pierce Family Picks up Stakes, But Selma's Roots Remain Strong

> For the first time in living memory, there will be no Pierce family members domiciled in Sagahawk. Mrs. Mildred Pierce, the widow of Samuel Pierce, has sold the farm to John Carr, who as a young boy was saved from drowning in Ellis Pond by her late son, August, and her recently deceased farm hand, Ernest Pickering. When asked why she was selling the farm, she said it had become too much for her

to handle after Ernest died, so she decided to go live with relatives in Philadelphia.

I asked her if she was sad to see the farm leave the family. Her response was heartwarming. She said: "My boy died saving Johnny Carr, and he has never forgotten it. When he was little, he would often come calling on me. At first it was because his mother made him, but over time he came because he wanted to. When the time came for him to be confirmed, he asked me to sponsor him, and he took the name August as his confirmation name. I think he had to get special permission to do it. He's been like a son to me. He promised that he would farm the property until the day he died and see to it that his offspring did the same. I won't hold him to that promise, but it does give me a great deal of comfort to know that he feels that way and that his parents planted the elm that he named Selma in the front yard. The *S* in front of the elm stands for Samuel, and the *A* in back stands for August. Pretty creative of Johnny, don't you think?"

When I respectfully offered Mildred Pierce the opportunity to reflect on her two hero sons, her eyes welled with tears. She confided: "Naturally, I would rather have had them live to grow old with me, but I guess I always knew that young Samuel was destined for glory. He had such a strong sense of justice and fairness and never could understand how one human being could justify owning another. When the Civil War broke out, he was eager to go and save the Union and free the slaves.

"August was a different story. I always would tell him as a little boy, when I was putting him to bed at night, that God had created him small for a special reason, so he wouldn't grow up wallowing in self-pity. Afterward, I'd have to go into my room and pray to God to please not make a liar out of me. I guess you might say God answered my prayers."

I couldn't wait to get home and see Dad. I had so many questions for him. After dinner, I asked him if we could sit and talk alone on the front porch. He said sure, and went to get his pipe first. Once he had sat down and lit his pipe, I started to ask my questions.

"Did Great-Grandpa die working on the farm the way Grandpa did?" I inquired.

"I think it's fair to say that he did. Grandpa dropped dead while he was out plowing the back five." (The farm originally had consisted of fifteen acres, and then later another five were purchased that everyone called the back five.) "Great-Grandpa came in from a day's work on the farm, ate his dinner, and came out onto this porch to smoke his pipe, when he fell asleep in his rocker and never awoke. Great-Grandma found him when she came out to rouse him to come to bed."

"If Great-Grandpa was named John, and Grandpa was named John, and you are named John, why wasn't I named John?"

"Great-Grandpa was John Carr, Grandpa was John Carr Jr., and I'm John Carr III. If I had named you John, you would have been John Carr IV. I thought three John Carrs were enough. I didn't want you to be the fourth at anything. I wanted you to be the first. Why do you ask? Do you not like the name Joseph?"

"No, I like my name. I was just curious."

"What's your next question? I think I'm on a roll."

"Did you know that Great-Grandpa named this elm Selma?"

"Wow! You know, son, I had forgotten that fact. This work

you are doing for Miss Pickering certainly is putting you in touch with your past, isn't it?"

Aloud I simply answered yes, but to myself I thought: *In more ways than you might think.*

"Next!" Pop barked as he took a puff on the pipe.

"If the war in Europe ended in 1945, how come you didn't return to the United States until two years later?"

Sitting up in his chair and taking on a more serious demeanor, he replied, "That's a rather strange question. Why do you ask?"

Having promised to respect Mrs. Harding's privacy, I merely answered, "I was just curious, no big deal."

"Well, if it's no big deal, I would rather not get into it. What's your next question?"

"What happened to your B-17 after the war? Did it stay in England, or did it come back to the United States?"

Beginning to look visibly agitated, Dad put his pipe down and asked: "What's this all about? Does this have something to do with the room over at the Harding house?"

"Nothing, Dad. Like I said, I was just curious."

"Curious, my foot! What are you getting yourself into, son? I want to know, and I want to know right now!" he demanded in a loud voice.

Dad was not one to raise his voice, so it intimidated me when he did. I decided that I had better come clean with him. Leaning closer to him to speak in a whisper, I told him: "There is a framed picture in Captain Harding's study of an airborne US Army Eighth Air Force B-17 with the name *Sweet Sally* painted on the fuselage under the cockpit window. It had been hanging on the wall, but he took it down to hang in its place a 1947 calendar and a map of Roswell, New Mexico."

"What else did you see?"

"A model of a flying saucer, lots of papers and pictures spread around, and some photos showing what look like mannequins from a Hollywood science fiction movie. Plus a blackboard on which was written the number 1062 with an X through it, and some pieces of shiny silver material."

"Did Mary see all of this too?"

"Yes. I'm not allowed in the study without her. Why do you ask?"

"Well, son, perhaps it's time we had a talk. Before Tom Harding was a captain, he was my co-pilot on the *Sweet Sally*. Toward the end of the war, when we were on our bombing runs over Germany, we sometimes saw what looked like bright spots high in the sky. I dismissed them as the sun reflecting off the cockpit glass, but Tom was convinced they were something more.

"After the war, we were asked to become part of a group that stayed behind to study what experimental projects the Germans had been conducting to see if that might explain the bright spots we'd reported seeing. We found nothing, so our group was disbanded and we were sent home.

"In 1947, when I left to return to the United States and begin graduate studies at Columbia, Tom was promoted to captain, and the *Sweet Sally* was placed under his command. He and the *Sweet Sally* were eventually reassigned to what is now known as Carswell Air Force Base in Fort Worth, Texas. In July of that year, there was a mysterious crash in Roswell, New Mexico, and Tom was part of a group that was sent up there to investigate. At first it was said to have been a flying saucer, but later it was identified as a weather balloon."

"This mysterious crash—was it reported on July 7 of 1947?"

"Yes, what makes you ask?"

"The only date circled on the 1947 calendar hanging on the wall is July 7."

"I didn't have a whole hell of a lot of contact with Tom after the war. That is, not until he wrote to me in early 1951. In the letter, he told me that he'd gotten married to a lovely local gal and was planning to retire from the air force and accept a job with a government contractor on Long Island.

"I suggested they consider living in Sagahawk and arranged for them to look at some houses through a local real estate agent I knew. The house on Hedges was the first and only house that they looked at. Beth Harding fell in love with it, and they bought it.

"They had just moved in when Tom vanished, so I didn't have much of a chance to become reacquainted with him. And of course I didn't know Beth Harding at all because they'd met and married after we'd lost contact with each other.

"Over the years, I've looked in on her from time to time. We've run into each other in town or while I'm next door checking on the Hurd house. I've done a few small repairs on the house for her, but I certainly had no idea that Tom had this sort of thing going on in his study."

"Was he a UFO nut?"

"No, not when I knew him. He was an engineer by training, Michigan graduate I think, and level-headed."

"Dad, do you think there is anything to this UFO and alien stuff?"

"Joe, I spent a lot of time in the cockpit of the *Sweet Sally*, flying high in the night skies over Europe and the Atlantic. On a moonless night, it is pretty dark and expansive up there. It is just you and the stars to keep you company, and they're as numerous as grains of sand on a beach.

"Here, stand up and look up there at them. The odds are that there is intelligent life of some kind up there somewhere. But do I think it has come here in flying saucers and crashed in our desert?

"No I don't. It is far more likely to have been a weather balloon or some secret project the military was working on and didn't want the public or the Russians to find out about."

"Why would they use mannequins that look like aliens?"

"What do you mean?"

"Some of the pictures in the study are of mannequin-like figures that look like Hollywood props for a UFO movie."

"They were probably dummies that got damaged in the crash.
Listen, it's getting late, and I have a busy day tomorrow. Perhaps
we should be thinking about hitting the sack. What do you say?"

"Thanks, Pop."

"No problem," Dad said as he mussed my hair. He put his arm
around me as we walked back into the house.

For the first time in my life, I wasn't sure Dad was leveling with
me. Even when I pressed him about Santa Claus, he tried his best
to dodge the question but eventually came clean with me. It was a
little unsettling, and as I tried to shake off my uneasiness, I felt that
same cold shiver run down my back again. What more was there?
The answer would have to wait for another day. It was time for bed.

six

The next day was a busy one on the farm. By the time I got back to the house, I was so sweaty that the dirt was caked on me. Mom wouldn't even let me in. She told me I had to use the outside shower and tossed me a clean towel through the door. "And leave your dirty cloths out there!" she shouted as I heard the screen door shut behind her.

Even though the water was warm from sitting in the pipes, it felt cool against my steamy body. Soon the shower was drawing from deeper in the well, and the result was truly refreshing. As my tired muscles began to relax under the falling drops of man-made rain, my mind started to wander back to the study in the Harding house. After I got dressed, I would give Mary a call to see if Mrs. Harding would let us return.

Anticipating my call, Mary had already obtained Mrs. Harding's consent to our coming back over to visit the study. She even said she would have lemonade and freshly baked cookies for us. Anxious to get going, I thought I'd skip dinner since it was too hot to eat anyway. However, Dad had different plans for me and made me sit and eat.

At dinner, the conversation got as hot as the weather when Dad said that I would have to take Luke along with me.

"Why?" I asked.

"Because you have virtually been ignoring him since Mary's

family came out east, and I don't think it's right that you're not spending any time with your little brother."

"But Dad, I can't!"

"Nonsense, there's no reason why you can't. Bring his toys with you. I'll give you some money to get him an ice cream afterward, and it will be fine. Anyhow, your Mom and I are going to the movies. The alternative would be that you stay home with him."

"But Dad, can't Kelly stay with him?"

"But Dad nothing, son. Kelly has a sleepover to go to, Grandma is away helping her sister, and your Mom deserves a little time off, too!"

Mom smiled, and I knew I was sunk. "All right, I'll give Mary a call and ask her to check with Mrs. Harding."

I wasn't holding out much hope and began to resign myself to spending the night at home alone with Luke and Linus.

However, much to my surprise, Mary called back to say that Mrs. Harding said, "By all means bring Luke, and please bring the dog too."

I was surprised but thrilled. Even though I was only fifteen, I'd been driving tractors and potato trucks since I was eleven. So Dad said I could take Sally Truck as long as I stayed on the back roads and went directly there and back. Since Mrs. Harding had baked cookies, we could save the ice cream for another time. I loaded Luke and his bag of toys into the front seat, and let Linus jump in the back where he preferred to ride, and we rumbled off to meet Mary at the Harding house.

Once Luke was settled and playing with his toy cars on the kitchen floor, and Linus had found a comfortable spot to lie down on the cool slate in the entrance hall, Mary and I went about our business in the study. We decided to start with the coffee table and work our way over to the couch. First we looked in the microscope and saw that Captain Harding must've been observing something when he'd stopped to go to the beach because there was a glass slide in place. The contents had long since evaporated, but the stain it left behind was still visible.

On more careful examination, we saw that there was an injection needle on the table, along with a tiny bottle with a rubber stopper, like what the doctor uses when giving an injection. Some remnants of the clear liquid remained in the bottle. When I tilted the bottle, some of the liquid spilled on me. The bottle had no label, so we had no way of knowing what it was. Hoping that the textbooks on the couch might shed some light on what Captain Harding was observing, we began to look at them. We didn't have to look far. The text was titled: *Modern Advances in Chemical and Biological Weapons Research.*

"Don't touch any of the stuff on the coffee table," I told Mary. "We better have it checked out. Chemical and biological weapons research sounds scary. I'm a little worried because I got some of that clear liquid on me when I tilted the bottle. We should scrub our hands when we get back downstairs."

"Don't be silly, Joe. Why would Captain Harding be doing something dangerous here? Plus, if this stuff was bad for you, don't you think Mrs. Harding would have gotten sick by now? My Dad is a doctor for Pfizer. Maybe we can ask him?"

"Okay, but please don't touch anything until after we speak with him."

"Oh, fine. But do you think I can pick up that bottle lying under the coffee table?"

"What bottle?"

"This one," Mary said and picked it up from the floor before I could say anything.

"What's in it?"

"It looks like a chicken's foot suspended in a solution."

"What could Captain Harding possibly want with a pickled chicken's foot?"

"I don't know. Maybe he was into voodoo!" she exclaimed as she shoved the bottle in my face and started to laugh.

"What a chicken *you're* turning out to be—no pun intended," she added as she laughed harder.

"It's better to be safe than sorry. Go ahead and laugh, but we'll see who's laughing after we speak to your father. Now give me the bottle, please."

"Here," she said as she handed it to me.

Upon examining the contents more closely, I realized that this wasn't a chicken foot. It was a thin, boney hand with long fingers that had fingernails on them. It looked like the hands on the mannequins in the pictures. Reaching for one of the many pictures spread around the room, I compared the hands on the mannequin in the picture with the object in the jar, and Mary had to agree that they looked the same.

No longer laughing or in a joking mood, she said, "This is starting to get creepy. Put that thing down and let's go."

I agreed, and once again we were careful to lock the door to the study behind us when we left.

When we got back to the kitchen, we asked Mrs. Harding if we could use the sink in the mudroom off the kitchen to wash our hands before we had the lemonade and cookies. She told us to use the powder room in the hall instead. Taking turns, we carefully scrubbed our hands and then our lower arms just to be safe.

In the kitchen, Luke had his toy cars lined up by their colors the way he'd been taught to do it at the store: two red, two blue, two yellow, two white, and two black. He was waiting for me to tell him what a good job he'd done, so he could have some of Mrs. Harding's homemade lemonade and chocolate chip cookies. His face lit up when I made a big fuss, praising him on his outstanding accomplishment. His reaction reminded me of what an important part of my life he was. Dad was right—I had been ignoring him.

While Luke was eating his cookies, Mary and I began to put

the toys back in the bag. Suddenly a squirrel jumped onto the bird feeder that was on the deck outside the kitchen. In his excitement, Luke ran to the sliding glass door that leads to the deck. His chocolate-covered hands left handprints and smudges all over the glass.

I went to yell at him, but Mrs. Harding stopped me, putting her hand up and saying: "Don't worry, Joe. I can clean it up after you leave. I've been enjoying him so much. Let him have fun with the squirrel."

But when I saw tears welling in her eyes, I started again to apologize for Luke's behavior.

Putting her hand on my arm, she said, "My tears have nothing to do with Luke's actions. I was just reminded of what it would mean to me if just once I could see my little Mary Bernadette's handprints and smudges on that glass."

I didn't know what to say, so I just put my head down. Luke was uncharacteristically quiet as he tried to figure out whether he was in trouble, and then blurted out, "Look, squirrel!"

With that the silence was broken, and everyone began to laugh. Mrs. Harding wiped the tears from her eyes and put her arms out for Luke to come give her a hug. He came to her with a smile of contentment on his chocolate-covered face, and now Mrs. Harding's dress matched her sliding glass door.

But she truly didn't care. Looking at Luke, she said, "It's my fault, son, for making chocolate chip cookies on such a hot day. Next time you come, I will make sugar cookies."

"With sprinkles?" Luke asked.

"With sprinkles," Mrs. Harding replied.

I put Luke and Linus in the truck and asked Mary to watch them for a minute. Mrs. Harding was still standing at her front door, so I ran back to speak with her.

"Can you tell me where Captain Harding worked?"

"When we were in Texas, he accepted a job with Grumman.

I think he said they were building a facility in Calverton where he was going to work. But when we got here, he started spending a lot of time on Prune Island. Sometimes he would stay there and come home only on the weekends."

"Did you ever meet any of the people he worked with?"

"Not really. Captain Harding kept his work to himself, and we didn't socialize with anyone from his job. We had been here only a short time when he drowned."

"Did anybody from the office try to contact you after he went missing?"

"I tried to call Grumman, but they told me they had no record of him working there. I suspect he was so new when we lost him that the papers never got processed. But one man did stop by to ask about him and express his condolences to me. I don't remember his name, but he spoke with a German accent. That was it, and I never saw or heard from him again. Why do you ask?"

"I was just curious. No big deal."

At that point somebody, probably Luke, blew the truck's horn, and Mrs. Harding said, "Perhaps you had best be going. Goodnight."

"Goodnight," I said and walked to the truck. I watched Mary walk through her front door and started for home. I made a note to have another talk with Dad. I just couldn't believe that it was a real hand in the jar or real germs in the bottle. There had to be a reasonable explanation for all of this. But what could it be? If I could find the mysterious German, he might be able to explain everything. However, first I wanted to talk to Dad because a voice inside me was saying that I might have been getting in above my head, and Dad would know if I was.

It suddenly hit me as I pulled Sally Truck into the farm's drive-way. If you applied Luke's method for displaying his row of toy cars, paired by color, two per group, to the number 1062 that was written on the blackboard, the 10 and the 62 would be different colors. Maybe 1062 comprised two numbers—10 and 62—and referred to something like October of 1962. But what would be so important about that date? I believed that if I could find that out, I could solve the riddle.

By the time Mom and Dad returned from the movies, Luke had gone to bed, followed by Linus, who'd taken up his usual spot on the floor next to the nightstand. I was sitting on the front porch with only Selma and the stars to keep me company. Mom asked how things had gone with Luke, and when I told her they went fine, she kissed me goodnight and walked inside to get ready for bed. Dad took out his pipe and came over and sat next to me.

"Your mind seems heavy with thought, son. What's the matter?"

Seizing the opportunity, I asked, "Where is Prune Island, and what's going on there? Do you know?"

"It's in Gardiners Bay, a little east of Orient Point. The island is small, only about three miles long and a mile wide. During the war it was used as an anti-submarine base because there'd been so much German sub activity right off our coast. If I recall correctly, one German U-boat was sunk only 150 miles off Montauk. After the war, the island was assigned to the Army Chemical Corps. Why do you ask?"

In my haste to get more answers, I completely ignored Dad's question, and asked, "What would Captain Harding be doing working there?"

"Well, he was a chemical engineer by training, so maybe he was working with the Army Chemical Corps. Again, why do you ask?"

This time I answered. "I found some pretty strange stuff in his study, Dad."

"Like what?" he hastened to ask.

"Like a jar of fluid with a weird-looking hand in it; an injection needle and a bottle of liquid with a rubber top, like a doctor would use to vaccinate someone; a microscope with a glass slide left in it with the stained remains of something on it; and textbooks about chemical stuff."

"What do you mean by a weird-looking hand? A human hand?"

"I don't know. Mary thought it was a chicken's foot, but when we looked closer, it looked more like the hands on the mannequins in the pictures—like a human hand but longer and thinner."

"I don't know what to tell you, Joe. Are you sure that you and Mary aren't letting your imaginations get away from you?"

"I don't know, Dad. I'm afraid that I'm getting into something that's over my head."

"I'll tell you what. I still have a high security clearance from the work I was doing in Europe on the bright spots, and I also have many friends in senior positions in the military. Let me do some checking about Prune Island for you."

"Thanks, Pop."

"Promise me you'll stay out of that study until I check things out. If there are chemicals up there, they might be harmful."

"I promise," I said, but I wasn't sure it wasn't already too late. I had decided not to tell Dad about the liquid I'd gotten on me, even though I was still worried by what had happened. There was nothing that he or anyone else could do about it at this point, and I was still feeling fine now that several hours had passed.

"I'm going to be using the John Deere to pull up a big stump tomorrow and could use your help," Dad said.

In a strange way, I was almost glad to have to go do a miserable job in the fields to get away from the Harding situation. Pulling up stumps in ninety-degree weather was not fun, but it beat having to worry about human hands in jars.

Then I remembered. "Dad, just one more thing. Could you ask your friends if there are Germans working on Prune Island?"

"What makes you think Germans are working there?"

"After Captain Harding disappeared, the only person that came to see Mrs. Harding was a man with a German accent, but she can't remember his name."

"A lot of German scientists came to America after the war, and some even became American citizens. So that might not be so unusual, but I'll check it out for you."

"Gee, Pop, I just realized that you never got to smoke your pipe. I'm sorry about asking you so much stuff."

"No problem. You go on up to bed. I'm going to sit out here for a bit. Goodnight."

"Goodnight," I said as I got up and walked into the house. Relieved that the matter was now in Dad's trusted hands, I knew I would finally be able to get some sleep.

seven

Dad found out more than he was willing to share with me. He still had a top security clearance and friends in high places in the military. They were more than happy to bring him up to speed and would've anxiously welcomed him back into their fold if they could've talked him into it. It seems it was a tangled web of lies that our government was weaving about Prune Island, all in the name of security, of course.

In the early days of the war, the Germans boldly sent their submarines to hunt US ships off the eastern seaboard of the United States, including the coast of Long Island. It wasn't out of the ordinary to see the night sky lit up by the soaring flames from a torpedoed oil tanker, or to find debris from the sunken ships or the charred bodies of seamen wash up on the shore.

As the US eventually began to organize its defenses and fight back, several German U-Boats were sunk. One sinking in particular raised a lot of concern. On the floating body of one of the dead German sailors who was recovered by a US destroyer was found what appeared to be a recently used ticket stub to a movie theater in a nearby coastal town.

Two days later, a German sailor from the same doomed submarine who managed to survive the sinking was rescued by the US Navy. He subsequently was taken to Prune Island for interrogation. At the anti-submarine base, he revealed that he had studied in the

United States and obtained a degree in chemical engineering from the University of Michigan. He explained that some of the crew of the submarine had gone ashore and attended a movie to see how easy it would be to conduct sabotage operations, including releasing dangerous chemicals and pathogens in crowded areas such as a movie theater. He also provided the FBI with information that led to the capture of several other teams of saboteurs. His name was Max Werner.

Although most of these captured German saboteurs were tried, convicted, and imprisoned or executed, some, like Max Werner, were secretly taken to Prune Island. While there, they cooperated with their US captors in helping to foil other Nazi sabotage attempts on US soil, or to provide information on German submarine operations, especially details related to the German Enigma code. Max Werner also provided valuable information on German chemical and biological weapons development.

Many such German prisoners were returned to Germany after the war, but others were secretly allowed to remain and in some cases seek and obtain US citizenship. Max Werner was one of those who was allowed to stay and become a US citizen. When Prune Island was assigned to the Army Chemical Corps after the war, he stayed on and joined them.

Captain Harding and Max Werner had been classmates at Michigan, so the captain was asked to come to Prune Island and work with him and the rest of the team after the war. The position at Grumman was designed to provide a cover for the true nature of Captain Harding's work. The two men quickly rekindled their friendship and were working well together—that is, until Captain Harding disappeared without a trace while going for a swim in the ocean.

The man with the German accent who called on Mrs. Harding after her tragic loss had been none other than Max Werner.

Born in Heidelberg, Germany, in September of 1916, he moved

to America at the age of fifteen, when his father accepted a job in the spring of 1931 with the Upjohn Company in Kalamazoo, Michigan. Dr. and Mrs. Werner, together with their son Max and his sister Heidi, settled into a quiet life in the company town.

Max's first foray away from his new home came when he entered the University of Michigan to pursue a chemical engineering degree. It was there that he and Captain Harding first met and struck up their friendship. The Werner family moved back to Heidelberg, Germany, soon after Max had graduated from Michigan in 1938. Captain Harding and Max Werner had little or no contact after that point until Max was rescued at sea, brought to Prune Island, and reunited with his former Michigan classmate.

Trapped in Germany by the war, and caught up in the turbulent political currents that fueled it, Max, like so many young men his age, was pressed into military service. Never truly having the stomach to harm the country he was introduced to as a teenager, the country he more fully identified with and considered to be his own, he had no problem cooperating completely once he was back on American soil. Fearful of retribution against his family back in Germany, his capture and whereabouts were kept secret until well after the war had ended.

German naval records had him as being lost at sea, along with the rest of the crew of the submarine. It wouldn't be until many years after the sinking of the sub that Dr. and Mrs. Werner would learn that their son had survived the sinking and was alive and well and living in America.

The reason for the prolonged shroud of secrecy had to do with the highly sensitive and top secret nature of the project to which he and Captain Harding had been assigned and which he continued working on after his friend had been lost.

eight

There had indeed been a crash outside Roswell, New Mexico, in early July of 1947. The crash was not of a weather balloon or of a secret weapon being developed or employed by the United States military. Nor was it the crash of an extraterrestrial visitor in an alien flying saucer. Rather, it involved the crash of visitors from our future who were trying to make contact with us and warn us of something. This much our government had been able to ascertain. Solving the rest of the riddle, including what they were attempting to warn us about, was the assignment that had been given to Captain Harding, Max Werner, and the rest of their thirteen-man team. That team was assembled on Prune Island and at two other locations when Captain Harding disappeared.

Recovered from the crash site was debris of what appeared to have been a metallic circular or disk-shaped craft and what looked to be four small, deformed human bodies, three of whom were dead, and one of which was still alive, but barely so. The debris, the corpses, and the struggling survivor were transferred from the base at Roswell to other military installations, one of which was Prune Island.

Because of its secluded and inaccessible nature, Prune Island was chosen as the destination for the struggling survivor, who was kept in a specially constructed germ-free controlled environment. A sample of what was surmised to be the thin metallic skin used on the outer surface of the craft was also brought to Prune Island for study and analysis, as was a small amount of liquid recovered at the crash site that was thought to be the fuel source for the craft's propulsion system. The bulk of the wreckage was taken to a large hangar by a dry lake bed near what is now part of Edwards Air Force Base in Nevada, there to be reconstructed and reverse engineered by other members of the thirteen-man team. Max Werner and Captain Harding also made periodic visits to this location.

The autopsies that were conducted on the three corpses in a third location revealed that they were of human origin but had evolved or undergone mutations. They appeared to be relatively young in their lifecycle, and had larger heads, brains, and eyes than today's humans. On the other hand, they were much smaller than their present-day ancestors. They stood only about three feet tall and weighed about ninety pounds. Their bodies appeared to have been exposed to and able to tolerate high levels of radiation. They didn't seem to be armed or threatening to us in any way. There was no evidence to indicate that they'd anticipated a hostile reception.

After the 1947 crash, the surviving member of the crew was in a coma and in no position to communicate. It wasn't clear what language they spoke, because all recovered documents appeared to be encrypted. The one exception was a map of the western hemisphere that had the number 1062 with an *X* through it superimposed on the geographical area that comprised Cuba. Immediately to the right of that notation was the image of a mushroom cloud, also with an *X* through it. From these meager signs it was concluded that they'd come in peace to warn us.

However, in 1947, as well as in 1951 when Captain Harding disappeared, Cuba was a resort destination. It also was home to numerous sugar cane plantations. There were no atomic weapons there. So what were these visitors trying to warn us about? This is the question that still had the team stumped in 1951 when Captain Harding joined them and then disappeared not long thereafter.

After Captain Harding's apparent drowning without a trace, Max Werner and the rest of the team continued to persevere in their struggle to understand the so-called warning but with no luck. When the one surviving occupant of the craft died in 1952 without ever regaining consciousness and nothing sinister had happened, the government decided to close the file on the Prune Island part of the investigation. As a result of that decision, Max and the rest of the Prune Island contingent were relocated to Nevada.

The prevailing view at the time was that the warning must have been not to house atomic weapons on the US base at Guantanamo Bay. This made sense since the location was deemed too vulnerable to an irregular warfare attack or sabotage, and a nuclear incident or accident would be devastating so close to the US homeland. Since there were not any known plans to place such weapons there, the decision was made to concentrate the focus of the investigation going forward on benefiting from technology that could be garnered from our future.

In the intervening decade, the reconstruction and reverse engineering of the wreckage continued to provide a wealth of technological advances for the military and remained ongoing. It also revealed that the occupants hadn't been piloting the craft but were merely passengers. The disk appeared to have been remotely controlled in some way, but it wasn't yet clear how this was done. The thinking was that it might've been controlled by a computer similar to the ones IBM was developing but far more advanced and compact—something the team found hard to believe.

The four corpses, together with their body parts (except for one right hand that couldn't be accounted for) were properly buried. The documentation and small amount of debris that had been brought to Prune Island was either stored or transferred to Nevada. And in 1954, Prune Island was turned over to the Department of Agriculture to be used for the research of animal diseases.

Or so it was thought. No one knew about the documents, the

metallic sample, the pickled hand, and the vial of liquid that remained locked in Captain Harding's study. That all would change in 1961 when Mary and I unlocked the door to that study for the first time in almost a decade and unwittingly stumbled onto what had been going on.

It would change the course of history.

nine

When I came in on the John Deere from working in the field and saw Sally Truck parked in the driveway, I hardly could contain my excitement. Dad was back, and I couldn't wait to find out what he'd learned about the work Captain Harding was doing when he disappeared.

I went to ask Dad what he found out, but Mom cut me off. "Hurry up and get washed up. Dinner will be on the table in five minutes," she said.

"But Mom!"

"But Mom nothing! Get going!"

"Go ahead, listen to your Mother. She has made your favorite—pork chops. We can catch up afterward on the front porch."

"All right," I capitulated, but only reluctantly, and trudged up the stairs to my room while choosing to ignore Kelly, who was sticking her tongue out at me.

At dinner I had mixed feelings. The chops were delicious, but my appetite wasn't there. I played with my food nervously while my mind tried to glean hints from Dad's table conversation. Finally it was time to go out on the front porch. As usual, I went first while Dad took the time to get his pipe.

"So what did you find out, Dad?"

"Captain Harding was part of a team that was investigating that July 7, 1947, accident in Roswell, New Mexico."

"I knew it!"

"Wait now, son. Don't go jumping to conclusions. It wasn't a UFO, and the pictures you found weren't of extraterrestrials or aliens."

"Well then, what were they?"

"They were advanced human-like test dummies."

"And the craft?" I asked.

"It was the futuristic type of thing you might expect the government to try to take a secret look at."

"Okay," I said, "but how do you explain the pickled hand in the jar?"

"It likely belonged to an accident victim and may have been deformed or mutated as the result of excessive exposure to radiation."

"And the metallic sample," I asked, "what is the story on that?"

"From the fuselage skin that is being examined by the government."

I smiled inwardly, for finally Dad said something I viewed as truthful.

"Have I answered all your questions?"

"Not really. What about the injection needle and liquid in the bottle?"

"Right, I forgot about that. It's being examined as a fuel source."

"And the model of the flying saucer?"

"What about it? It's a model."

"All those documents that are in code—what are they about?"

"I don't know what they say, to be honest with you, but I suspect they are confidential and in code to protect their contents should they fall into the wrong hands."

"Any explanation for the number on the blackboard?"

"No one seems to be able to make heads or tails out of that number 1062. I get the feeling you think you know something. If you have any ideas, I'd be interested to hear them."

My father wasn't being totally forthright with me, but I suspected he had no choice in the matter. I could see that he had mixed feelings, struggling on the one hand to be as truthful with me as he could, on the other hand honoring any obligations of confidentiality he'd made. So I wanted to be careful how I answered him. I had to let him know that I wasn't buying what he was telling me without leaving him with the impression that I thought he was being dishonest with me.

"Dad, I don't think it's one number. I see it as two numbers: 10 and 62, and I think it might stand for October of 1962. What's more, I think it's a warning of some kind, and we shouldn't ignore it. If I'm right, we have only a little more than a year to figure it out. This craft that crashed may not have been an extraterrestrial UFO, but it was nevertheless a UFO. I don't think your friends are telling you everything."

Pausing momentarily to give Dad a chance to absorb what I was saying, I continued. "If you saw Captain Harding's study, you would appreciate what I'm saying. He was striving to understand what we were being told. The evidence in the room is overwhelming. There were open books all over the place, documents and pictures scattered about, cigarette butts piled high in the ash tray, writings on a blackboard, and stuff left open and under a microscope. It all points to a man consumed by a mission, working feverously, desperately trying to figure out the meaning of something. I wish you could come see his study. Actually, I wish he could be here because I know he would back me up."

Dad smiled, took a puff on his pipe, and said, "I'll get to see Tom's study tomorrow. They are sending one of the men he was working with, a fellow named Max Werner, to collect all the stuff in the study."

"Does Mrs. Harding know about this? Has she agreed? She made us promise not to remove anything."

"Max has spoken with her and she agrees with his coming to collect the stuff that belongs to the government."

"Great. Tell me: is Mr. Werner of German descent? Does he speak with a German accent?"

"Yes, why do you ask?"

"I think he may be the one who called on Mrs. Harding to convey his condolences after Captain Harding disappeared. Will I be able to come with you and meet him tomorrow?"

"I suspect you're right. He most likely is the person who contacted her when Tom vanished. And yes, I don't see why you can't come with me, but I must warn you in advance that Max Werner has not been well. So please don't start hitting him with lots of questions."

"What's wrong with him?"

"I don't think he knows for sure. He started to develop a lot of pain in his joints, and he thought it was arthritis. Now he has double vision, headaches, and unexplained personality changes. The doctors are doing all kinds of tests on him, but so far with little to no success. I understand from him that they think it might be neurological. He contracted these problems after he went back to Prune Island in 1958, and he thinks it may be connected to the animal diseases that the Department of Agriculture is researching there now."

"Wow, that's scary! Do you think it's some unknown stuff that came from what they're doing there?"

"I guess it's possible, but it sounds like a bit of a stretch to me." With that Dad looked at his watch and said, "Listen, we'd better think about getting to sleep. I want to get a decent amount of farming in tomorrow before we have to quit early to get ready to go over to the Harding house."

"Okay, Pop," I replied as I prepared to stand up and walk inside. Dad put his left hand on my right arm to stop me as he took his pipe out of his mouth with his other hand.

When he finished exhaling, he said, "I don't often take the time to say this, but I wanted you to know that I'm very proud of you and the way you've been conducting yourself."

I smiled and told Dad thanks before quietly walking into the house. It meant a lot to me to hear those words from him.

ten

The next morning Dad and I were up with the sun. When we came down, Mom had my favorite breakfast waiting for us: bacon and farm fresh eggs, toast with a generous portion of melting butter smeared on it, and that wonderful combination of ice cold orange juice and piping hot coffee. Enticed by the smell of the sizzling bacon, Linus abandoned Luke's bedside to follow us down the stairs. Mom, being the soft touch that she is, paid no heed to Dad's protests of spoiling the creature, and gave Linus a slice. Licking his jowls to catch every morsel, Linus looked up at Dad with contentment and what I saw as a sense of triumph. I knew then that it was going to be a good day.

We worked tirelessly in the fields until almost one o' clock in the afternoon, then headed back to clean up, grab a quick bite, and meet Mr. Werner at Mrs. Harding's place by two thirty. I was filled with anticipation to meet the German, hoping against all odds that he would tell me more about what was going on. When we arrived, he was already there, sitting and talking with Mrs. Harding and Mary. Mrs. Harding wanted to know where Luke was, but we explained that he had an appointment with his tutor.

"Remind me to send the sugar cookies home with you. They have sprinkles on them just for him."

"Thanks," Dad said to her, then turned to greet Mr. Werner, a tall, good-looking man, but visibly not well. He labored and held his left knee from the pain as we climbed the stairs to the study. When we entered, I saw the look of disbelief on his face. As much as he tried to mask his reaction, I saw that he was shocked that so much highly sensitive material had been overlooked and remained unaccounted for. Almost immediately he set about cataloging and packing up the photos, the encrypted documents, the map of Roswell, and the 1947 calendar.

When he wasn't watching, I took one of the documents, folded it up, and put it in my pocket. It was the one that was spread out near the coffee table. Judging by the cigarette burns on it, Captain Harding had pored over it. My conscience warned me that I was stealing, and that I shouldn't take it. But I felt an overriding sense that Captain Harding would have wanted me to do it. I told myself that I was picking up where he'd left off.

The next items to be noted and packed were the jar with the hand, the bottle of liquid (the injection needle couldn't be found), and the microscope with the glass slide still in it. The metallic sample followed. Next he wiped the blackboard clean, but didn't request to have it cataloged and packed. It was allowed to stay along with the model of the flying saucer.

I was a little surprised that he showed no interest in the saucer. I guess he assumed it had been the personal property of Captain Harding and was a harmless model with no special connection to the matter at hand. Dad, too, was taken back that Mr. Werner didn't want the flying disk cataloged and packed. I suspect that it didn't resemble the craft that had been reconstructed at the hanger in Nevada and so was thought to be of no particular value, other than as a decorative piece.

Giving the room one last glance as he prepared to leave, Mr. Werner was surprised when Luke came running up the stairs and burst into the study. Spotting the model of the flying saucer, Luke made a beeline for it. Dad was about to stop him when Mrs. Harding, who'd been following Luke, appeared at the door and insisted that he should be allowed to have it. Dad looked at Mr. Werner, who nodded his head in agreement, and allowed Luke to take the saucer.

At that point, Mom also appeared at the doorway. She explained that Luke had performed so well with his tutoring that he'd finished early, so she'd rewarded him by letting him come.

Again Mr. Werner's face gave his thoughts away, as it appeared that he thought Luke was being overindulged. Nevertheless, he politely smiled and started down the stairs, wrenching with pain as he went. Dad motioned to me, and I ran to take the packages and carry them for him. Meantime, Luke found the missing injection needle on the floor under the table. No one noticed when he hid it in his little book bag.

As we walked to his car, Mr. Werner asked me if I'd been the one that discovered all this material. I replied that my girlfriend and I had been the first to enter the room since it had been locked in 1951 following Captain Harding's death.

"What do you make of all this?" he asked.

I think he was looking for reassurance that the secret was intact and was hoping I would plead ignorance by saying something like, "I don't know."

Instead I seized the opportunity, looked him in the eye, and replied, "I think we've been warned of something bad about to happen, and if we ignore it, we'll be doing so at our peril."

My response stopped him in his tracks.

"What do you mean?" he asked.

"I think Captain Harding thought something bad is going to happen next year in October unless we figure out what they were trying to tell us and can stop it."

"How old are you, my boy?"

"Fifteen."

"You're a most impressive fifteen-year-old, but you have a very active imagination."

With that he took the packages from me and put them in the trunk of his car. As he was preparing to get into the vehicle, he seemed to have second thoughts. "Why October of 1962?" he asked.

"Because I think that what Captain Harding wrote on the blackboard is not the single number 1062, but that he wrote two numbers: 10 and 62. I think the 10 stands for October, and the 62 represents 1962."

"And why do you think it is warning of something bad?"

"Why else would Captain Harding have superimposed an X on it?"

"I see. Makes sense to me. Do you have any thoughts as to what the bad thing might be?"

"I wish I did, but I have no idea. Maybe an earthquake or something like that. I don't know."

He appeared relieved that I didn't seem to know about the mushroom cloud and the reference to Cuba.

As he was saying good-bye to me, Dr. Hurd walked over to introduce himself.

"Hi, I'm Dr. Hurd, Mary's father"

Mr. Werner hesitated for a moment, so I jumped in to help him by saying, "Mary is my girlfriend and was with me when we opened the door to the study. You met her upstairs."

Mr. Werner recovered nicely and said, "Oh yes, of course. How are you?"

"I'm fine, but I understand from Beth Harding that you are having a lot of joint pain, some double vision, mood changes, and headaches."

"Yes, that's correct."

"I wanted to mention to you that I have a friend who works with me at Pfizer and lives in Lyme, Connecticut. I tell you this because he had similar symptoms, and was surprised when they went away after his physician placed him on antibiotics for an ear infection."

"Really?" asked Mr. Werner. His whole demeanor changed, and he became eager to speak more with Dr. Hurd.

"What do they think it is?"

"We don't know yet, but whatever it is, it seems to be concentrated in the Lyme, Connecticut, area. And it appears to react to a course of antibiotics."

"I thought it was something I picked up on Prune Island because of all the research that's being done there on infectious disease. But I also was in Lyme, Connecticut, recently, so maybe I contracted it when I was there."

"I can see how hobbled you are. I recommend that you see your physician and ask him to treat you with an antibiotic. If your experience is anything like that of my friend, you should see positive results within fourteen days. Would you like me to give you my friend's phone number?"

"Yes, I think it might be helpful to talk to him about this Lyme disease experience he had."

"Not a problem. Let's go inside and I'll get you his number."

Dr. Hurd and Mr. Werner went into the Hurd residence. Dad, Mom, Mary and Luke emerged from the Harding house with Mrs. Harding carrying the sugar cookies. Luke was playing with the toy flying saucer, a fun sight to see.

The Fourth of July would be coming up soon, and I wanted to get my second report into Miss Pickering beforehand so I could relax and enjoy the holiday with Mary and my family. This July 4 would be our nation's one hundred eighty-fifth birthday, and while it would be only my sixteenth, it already had become a favorite time of year for me.

I told myself that I would try to start the report that night if I wasn't too tired. I wanted to make sure that I captured all the facts while they were still fresh in my mind. Then I began to have second thoughts about just how much detail I should provide. In the end, I decided to be as general as possible while still providing enough information to satisfy Miss Pickering.

eleven

After dinner, Mom and Dad decided to go up to town for an ice cream at the Candy Kitchen. Grandma and Kelly had plans. They asked if I would keep an eye on Luke. I said fine, since I was in my room anyway, working at my desk and finishing my report for Miss Pickering.

Luke wandered in not long after—sleepy-eyed, with the flying saucer in one hand, his thumb in his mouth, and Linus following him. When I finished Miss Pickering's report, I took out the encrypted document I'd hidden in my pocket earlier in the day, and replaced it with the report. I began to pore over the encrypted material in much the same way I imagined Captain Harding had. It wasn't long before Luke was sound asleep atop my bed. I picked up the flying saucer, placed it on my desk, carried Luke to his bed, and tucked him in.

When I came back, I had the shock of my life.

The toy flying saucer possessed a clear glass center. When I put it on my desk, I'd placed it on top of the encrypted document. On my return from putting Luke in bed, I noticed that when the encryptions were viewed through the glass on the toy, they were transformed into understandable words. The toy wasn't a toy, nor was it a model that Captain Harding built. It was a critical tool for deciphering the warning.

As I began to run it slowly over the encryptions, I soon realized that what the glass did was to highlight some portions and ignore others. It took a degree of concentration to read the highlighted portions and put them together to obtain a coherent message. Even a slight movement of the device moved letters out of focus or completely out of sight. It was much like trying to fix the antenna on Dad's TV to pick up the Boston College football games or the Red Sox games. Like with the TV, even when you thought you had found the sweet spot, it would move, and an entire new series of adjustments had to be undertaken.

Miss Pickering was leaving for the airport the next morning after meeting with me, and made me promise to be on time. It wasn't a problem, I had all night. I didn't have to meet with her until eight thirty the next morning. The report was already finished and safely tucked away in my pocket. I saw no harm in continuing to work on the encrypted document and started to read it painstakingly. The process was tedious and tiring. I had to adjust the saucer, read, stop, and write down what I had seen. Then I would readjust the disk, read some more, and stop and write that down. And so on, and so on—until I was bleary-eyed.

The last thing I remember was looking at the clock on my desk. It read 3:08 a.m. I must've fallen asleep studying the document because the next thing that I remember was the feeling of sheer panic when I looked up and saw that same clock now showing the time to be 8:03 a.m. The sun had begun to stream through my bedroom window, but I still did a double take, because I couldn't believe my eyes. Unfortunately, there was no denying it: The time was indeed 8:03 a.m., and I had exactly twenty-seven minutes to be at school to meet with Miss Pickering. She was doing me a favor, squeezing me in, and I knew she would be angry if I let her down.

I jumped up and grabbed my things, which were still lying where I'd left them on the bed. I ran into the hall bathroom to splash some water on my face and brush my teeth before descending the stairs to the kitchen where I reached for an apple on my way out the door. Flying down the walk, I grabbed my bike only to find the front tire was flat once again. Ten minutes had elapsed, leaving me with seventeen minutes to make it there. Discarding the partially eaten apple, I ran as fast as I could. As I rounded the bend in the road, I could see Miss Pickering at the door. She once more had her back to me and was talking to the Reverend Thompson, who was facing my way.

The old cemetery, with its split rail fence, stood between me and the open door to the schoolhouse, as it had the time before. If I ran around the cemetery, I'd be late. But if Miss Pickering saw me run through the cemetery, I'd be inviting another round of reports and my summer would be shot. I had no choice but to risk her wrath, so I again jumped the fence. I hoped that she wouldn't turn and face me.

Tripping once more on the Pierce grave and gathering myself, I prepared to leap the fence at the other side of the cemetery. I was almost there. But just as I flew over the fence, she turned to see me dash toward her and the open door.

It was 8:30 a.m., and I saw her excusing herself when Father Thompson stopped her to ask her something. I think he again sensed my predicament and was trying to be of help. In any event, I seized upon the opportunity to dash through the open door, but this time Miss Pickering reached out her arm and grabbed me.

Winking at me and smiling, she said, "I saw what you did. It was very nice of you to take that moment from your harried schedule to stop and say hello to Sam and August Pierce and the Pickering fellow. I know it must have meant a great deal to them. They don't get many visitors these days."

Relieved, I nodded to her while Reverend Thompson smiled at me. As he walked away and we started inside, I heard him say, "Hope to see you in church on Sunday."

I nodded and told myself Yogi Berra knew what he was talking about when he said, "It's déjà vu all over again."

The report went well. I didn't get into any stuff about the warning and Captain Harding's study. I discussed only his assumed drowning and how Mrs. Harding had made a life for herself and was friends with my girlfriend's family, who lived next to her.

She wanted to hear all about Mary and how we'd met. When we were done, I couldn't believe how fast the time had gone by. I was enjoying it so much.

She accepted the report by saying, "Two down and one to go. I can't wait for your last one because these two have been so interesting."

I smiled nervously, knowing she had to go and Dad would be growing inpatient, waiting for me to show up to work. As we said our good-byes, I realized that I was becoming very fond of Miss Pickering. In her own soft manner, she was quietly shaping my future in a good way. That is, of course, if we were smart enough to heed the warnings and change the course of our history.

Speaking of that, I told myself that I'd better get back to work on deciphering the message. First I had a day's work on the farm to do, and Dad was waiting for me.

twelve

As I walked toward the house, I saw Mom's car sitting in the driveway with the motor running and the driver's door open. I heard
but could not see Luke screaming and carrying on. Mom's back was
to me, and she was bending down. I figured she was comforting
Luke. I knew from his uncontrollable crying that he was extremely
upset—something that didn't happen often. Running up to the
porch, I asked, "What's the matter?"

"I accidently ran over his new toy when I was backing out of
the driveway."

"New toy? Not the flying saucer, I hope?"

"Yes, I'm afraid so."

"No!" I yelped. And then ran into the house and up the stairs
to confirm my worst fears. *It was gone.*

Mom called up from the bottom of the stairs: "Is everything
okay? I expected Luke to be upset, but not you. I don't understand."

"It's nothing, Mom. I'm sorry if I worried you. I'll be right
down to help you with Luke. What did you do with the broken
toy? Maybe I can fix it for him."

"Not a chance. I'm afraid I did a job on it. The glass shattered
into a thousand pieces, and the metal body is mangled. I was really
surprised to see that the inside was full of wires. You would have
thought it was a transistor radio or something."

"Where is it now?"

"I threw it in the garbage."

When I came downstairs, Luke was still sobbing but had started to calm down. He heard me say that maybe I could fix it for him. Hugging my legs, he looked up at me with those tear-soaked eyes and asked, "Will you fix it, Jo-Jo?"

"I'll try," I said as I took his hand and went over to the garbage.

The saucer was a mess. I carefully picked the pieces out of the pail one by one. I was happy to see that Mom was wrong about one thing. There was one decent-sized piece of glass left intact. I hoped I might be able to use it. But Mom was right: the metal part looked like a broken radio. There were wires and a board with lines on it that looked strange to me.

I carefully put the one piece of glass and the contents of the inside of the disk in a bag and took the metal shell into the workshop with Luke in tow. Linus wandered in as I tried to hammer the disk into shape, probably to find out what all the noise was. It came out pretty well. Then I tried a black plastic cap from one of Dad's old gas cans. It fit perfectly into the circular hole left by the missing glass. Luke was happy and ran out of the workshop flying his disk with Linus giving chase.

I wasn't as lucky. When I got back up to my room, I soon learned that the glass had lost its magic. Whatever had been inside the disk was what gave it the ability to decode the encryptions. I would have to work from what I transcribed the night before. First I needed to get out to the field. Dad would be wondering what was keeping me. If he only knew!

He was doing irrigation work when I caught up with him on the back five. We'd gone without rain for a while, and he was worried because we were just coming into the hottest part of the summer.

When he saw me, he yelled: "About time you got here. What kept you?"

"Mom ran over Luke's new toy flying saucer, and I had to fix it

for him before I came out. He was giving Mom a hard time because
he was so disappointed."

"Well, thanks for doing that."

"No problem," I said, as we got down to serious work.

Concentration is crucial when working with heavy equipment,
and idle conversation can lead to accidents. We worked late into
the evening to make up for the time we'd lost earlier. Mom and
Luke had already eaten, and Luke was in bed by the time we got
back. Mom was watching TV and thumbing through a magazine
but stopped what she was doing to warm up our dinner for us. I
wasn't all that hungry and ate quickly so that I could get upstairs
to my room and work on the encryptions.

Alone at last in my room with all night to work on the warning,
I started to piece together what I'd transcribed the night before.
The letters and numbers from the first series of encryptions were:

C_R__NT Y__R I_ 2038

Playing with it, I came up with:

CURRENT YEAR IS 2038

Since we were now in 1961, instead of 1947, when this message
was delivered, I figured in the future the year was now 2052. I
didn't know if that would turn out to be important, but I wanted
to keep it in mind.

The second series of encryptions was more challenging:

T_M_ W_R P __ _U L_ 7 C__A T__ W__D_W
TO _O B__K 91 Y__R_

I struggled and struggled with this one, but after two hours, I
finally came up with:

TIME WARP ON JULY 7 CREATED WINDOW
TO GO BACK 91 YEARS

I wasn't sure what a time warp is, but it was the only word that made any sense to me. July 7 was easy. It had been circled on the 1947 calendar. But I did wonder if it applied only to that July 7 in 1947/2038 or if it occurred every July 7. I needed to keep that in the back of my mind, recalling that the headstone in the cemetery said that Captain Harding vanished on July 7 of 1951.

We found the model flying saucer on the table near where he'd been working, and maybe he'd come to the same conclusion as me. It wasn't lost on me that July 7, 1961, was only a few days away.

I was exhausted and decided to call it quits, even though I couldn't wait to find out more. It wouldn't be fair to Dad if I wasn't rested and ready to work in the morning. Moreover, I wanted to be done with my work early so I could go to the movies with Mary that night.

The next day came and went, as did the one after it, and I didn't work on the encryptions. I was too busy with farm chores and seeing Mary. It was July 2, two days later would be July 4. We had the parade in the morning, and then the Hurds had invited us to a Fourth of July picnic and bonfire on the beach at the Bridgehampton Club. It was one of my favorite events. I didn't want to miss it because the irrigation work on the farm wasn't finished.

I also wanted to have my time free between the parade and the beach picnic to spend a few moments visiting with Sam and August Pierce and with Ernest Pickering. If it weren't for them, I wouldn't be here, and I didn't want to forget them. The future would have to wait.

At the Fourth of July picnic, when Mary and I were alone on the beach, I told her that I'd kept the encrypted document Captain Harding had been working on. I also told her about the flying disk and what I'd learned so far. She was excited and asked if she could come over and work on it with me the next day. Being a normal, red-blooded fifteen-year-old boy, I wasn't about to say no to the girl of my dreams if she wanted to come and be alone with me in my bedroom. The distant future might have appeared bleak, but the next day wasn't looking too shabby!

The next morning at breakfast, I told Mom and Dad that Mary would be coming over to help me with my project for Miss Pickering, which technically was true, since Captain Harding had been one of my subjects. To my surprise, neither of them objected. They welcomed Mary when she arrived.

We immediately went upstairs and got to work. I showed Mary what I'd uncovered so far, and she agreed with my conclusions.

Then we started working together on the third series of encryptions. These letters and numbers were as follows:

WA___NG _C_O__R 1962 _U_A ___S S_V__T
M__S____ AT U_ _AS_ C__ST _OS_

I was fairly certain that the first word was WARNING, and Mary agreed. Because of the sign in Captain Harding's office, we both concluded rather quickly that the second and third words were OCTOBER 1962.

Then it got harder. I thought the next word was _USA, but as Mary noted, the blank in front of the *U* made no sense. In desperation, Mary started going down the alphabet. She hesitated at *C* because CU_A caught her attention. Doing the same with the other blank, she stopped at *B*, and asked me if it could be CUBA.

"Cuba? What could possibly be so dangerous about Cuba?" I asked her. But we couldn't come up with anything better and decided to go with it for the present.

Figuring that the next word had to be a verb, we started thinking of all the five-letter verbs that end in *S*. After almost an hour, we had narrowed it down to SAILS or FIRES, and since FIRES seemed more ominous, we decided to go with it. So now we had:

WARNING OCTOBER 1962 CUBA FIRES

But fires what? The answer would have to wait a little while longer because our brains were fried and we needed a break. We decided to bike into town for a soda.

Riding along, Mary was quiet. Then out of the blue she said that she thought she had the next word. I wanted to protest that we were supposed to be on a break, but my curiosity got the better of me, and I asked what it was. "**SOVIET**," she replied, and it hit me like a ton of bricks that she was right.

Feeling light-hearted about our apparent success, I asked kiddingly, "I suppose next you're going to tell me that they fired Soviet missiles?"

Smiling, she simply nodded yes, and I found myself rethinking my position.

"But the Cubans don't have Soviet missiles, do they?"

"Not now, but who's to say that can't change by next year?"

When we arrived at the store, I asked her what kind of soda she wanted. She asked for root beer, and I went in to get it. When I came out with the two sodas, she told me she had figured out the next two words: **AT US**.

"Let me see if I have this straight, what we have so far is this:"

WARNING OCTOBER 1962 CUBA FIRES SOVIET MISSILES AT US

"Yes."

"Wow, that's pretty scary stuff. I doubt anyone is going to believe us. I'm not sure I do."

We walked our bikes through town and sat under a big old oak tree by the library. She gently leaned her head against my shoulder and told me that all this stuff was beginning to scare her. She wished we'd never opened the door to Captain Harding's study. I told her it wouldn't have changed anything. Whatever was going to happen in 1962 was still going to happen.

"Yes," she replied, "But at least we could've enjoyed one more year of normal life. Look at all these people walking through town, shopping and eating. They're carefree and having fun while we're living with this horrible warning we can't do anything about."

"I know. Ignorance is bliss. Anyhow, who says we can't do anything about it?"

"I'm not saying ignorance is bliss, but we've been robbed of our future a year ahead of everybody else. And for what reason?"

"To save the world. Isn't that reason enough?"

"You really think you're going to save the world—a fifteen-year-old farm boy with nothing to his name other than the dirt beneath his fingernails?"

"I don't want to make things worse for you, but I don't own even the dirt beneath my nails. It's my Dad's."

A smile broke out on her face that was as welcoming as the sun now breaking through the clouds on this overcast day. She sat up and playfully hit me. "Stop it; don't be silly," she said. "You know very well what I mean."

"I know what you mean, and I might agree with you if I was going to be doing it alone. I'm not. With you at my side, there isn't anything I can't do. So are you with me, or are you going to wimp out on me, Mary Hurd?"

She leaned over, gave me a kiss, and whispered, "I'm with you. I'm with you always even if you don't have any dirt of your own."

"Good, then let's get back to work."

As I started to get up, she stopped me and said, "I wrote the last part of the series on my hand. Do you want to work on it here?"

"Why not?" I said and sat back down. "Let's see what you've got."

She showed me her hand. The writing read:

_AS_ C__ST _OS_

We decided to go down the alphabet again and came up with many possibilities for the first word. Eventually we narrowed it down to three: **BASE**, **EAST**, and **LAST**. As much as we tried to cast a wide net, we kept coming back to one choice for the second word: **COAST**. With the last word, we started out thinking it was **COST**, but settled on **LOST**. We ended up with:

EAST COAST LOST

The smile was gone from Mary's face, and the sun had gone back behind the clouds. Gloom was setting in even for me. I just kept hoping it was only a bad dream and I would wake up from it. But it wasn't.

As we were getting on our bikes, I asked Mary, "Have you had enough? We can call it quits and go to the beach if you like."

"No, let's go back. The sooner that we're done with this, the better."

With that we got on our bikes and rode back to the farm. When we arrived there, Mom was gone and nobody was home, not even Linus. As we started upstairs to my bedroom, the temptations that arose from knowing that I was alone with her in an empty house were calling to me. I knew she was not there with the same thing in mind. I might lose her trust in me if I tried to take advantage of the situation.

Almost as if she could read my mind, she turned and said to me at the top of the stairs, "You do realize that we're all alone, and this may be the best chance you're going to have all summer to do something more than kiss me?"

I stopped in my tracks and turned to ask her, "What are you saying?"

"I'm saying that I'm really mixed up. I want to be the good girl that Mom tells me I should be, and not the bad one she's always warning me against becoming. I'd marry you now if we were old enough. I don't see myself with anyone else. Should we have only a year to live a lifetime, maybe it's time to make the most of what we have left."

"I'd be lying to you if I told you the same thoughts haven't crossed my mind. As much as I want to, right now it just doesn't feel right. You mean too much to me to take advantage of you when you're upset like this. Let's go save the world. When the time is right, we'll know it."

"I love you so much, Joe."

"I bet you say that to all the guys with dirt under their nails."

"Nope, only the ones who are superheroes. We must come up with a name for you. An ordinary Joe can't save the world. Let's see, how about Mighty Joe? No, that's too much like Mighty Mouse. They might want to make you a Mouseketeer and put you on the *Mickey Mouse Club*. Then Annette Funicello will get her paws on you. Maybe Jump'n Joe is better. What do you think?"

I leaned over, put my two hands on her arms, squeezed her like an accordion, lifted her up to me, and gave her a great big kiss. When I was finished, I said, "*That's* what I think!"

"Wow, that was your best kiss yet. It had a real jolt to it. That's it, I've got it: Jolting Joe!"

And Jolting Joe it was.

At that point we noticed that Mom must have come in the back door and had been quietly standing downstairs watching our antics. Mary was visibly embarrassed, but Mom put her at ease by asking with a smile, "Tell me, Jolting Joe, how does this fit into what you're doing for Miss Pickering? It's hard for us mere mortals to see the connection."

"I'm sorry, Mrs. Carr. I hope you don't think poorly of me."

"Not to worry, Mary; I was fifteen once, too."

"So you won't tell my Mom."

"My lips are sealed. Now why don't you and the superhero come down to the kitchen? I brought home some of Mrs. Harding's freshly baked cookies and some milk. I don't want you saving the world on an empty stomach."

"You're the best, Mrs. Carr!"

"Mom, can't you bring them up to my room? We have to get back to work."

"You're pushing your luck, superhero, but okay—just this time."

As we turned and walked into my room, I said to Mary, "You've created a nightmare for me with this superhero stuff."

"Sorry, Jolting Joe."

"Can't we wait until I save the world to call me that?"

She didn't answer, and we got back to work. The next series of encryptions were:

US ___ALI_TES _S_R _UB_ __P_D OU_

Maybe it was because we were reinvigorated, but this one seemed easy based on what we already knew. We quickly concluded that this read:

US RETALIATES USSR CUBA WIPED OUT

Mom came in with the cookies and milk, and we stopped to talk with her. She looked over my shoulder and asked how it was going. I replied that we were making progress, and she nodded and left.

We turned to the next encryptions:

___T CO__T __ST _O_K_T __ _IDW__T
S___IV__

Considering what we already knew, and looking at these letters in that context, we concluded that the beginning read:

WEST COAST LOST

But then the rest stumped us. No matter how hard we worked, we came up with nothing. We were about to give up when Mary noted that the warning had talked about the two coasts but hadn't mentioned the middle of the country. With that perspective in mind, we decided that __IDW__T was **MIDWEST** and S____IV__ was **SURVIVES**. Going down the alphabet, we eventually figured out that the missing word was **POCKET**. Consequently, we concluded that it read:

POCKET OF MIDWEST SURVIVES

Finally, a little bit of good news, we told ourselves.
The next series of encryptions were:

____NA _UR__V__ + RIS__. D__K _OL_
NUC____ WI___R

We weren't sure of the first word, but we were fairly confident from looking back at the previous series that the next word was **SURVIVES** plus something. Going down the alphabet, Mary stopped at *E* and said it's **RISES**.

Turning back to the first word, we now realized that it had to be a country or a region. We then narrowed it down to **CANADA** or **CHINA**, and assumed that there would be more concern about China rising than there would be with Canada rising. Furthermore, **CHINA** fit in the blanks. So we concluded that the message read:

CHINA SURVIVES + RISES

Mary's instincts told her that the next part read:

DARK SOMETHING NUCLEAR SOMETHING

Going down the alphabet once again, she stopped at *C* for the first letter and at *D* for the last letter, which gave her **COLD** and made her realize right away that the last word was **WINTER**. Thus, we figured out that this part was:

DARK COLD NUCLEAR WINTER

We were tired and glad to see we were on the home stretch. The last encryptions were:

D__CON___T PR___D__T _H_T _163

We played with it for about twenty minutes, but Mary had been fairly sure from early on that the first word was **DISCONTENT**. Then Luke came in and distracted us for a few minutes, and when we went back, it jumped out at me that the last word and number were **SHOT 1163**.

"Could it be that they shot the president?" Mary asked. When we looked at it, **PRESIDENT** was the right word. We concluded that it read:

PRESIDENT SHOT NOVEMBER 1963.

Could it really be true that President Kennedy was going to be shot in 1963? It seemed hard to believe because he was so popular. However, no matter how many ways we tried to look at it, our conclusion was always the same: Yes.

Exhausted but glad to be done, we decided to hit the beach. The clouds were gone and the sun was out. We biked to Mary's so she could change into her bathing suit, and then off we went. We spent the rest of the day trying to put the future out of our minds and enjoy the present. It was amazing to my young mind how precious life becomes when you think you only have a little of it left to live. As Dad likes to say: *Carpe diem*. And we were indeed seizing the moment.

thirteen

I decided to come clean with Dad and tell him what I'd found. That night after dinner we went out on the front porch and I told him everything. He was in shock and asked me if I would be all right to repeat what I'd told him in front of Mr. Werner. I wasn't thrilled with the idea, but I reluctantly agreed.

Two days later, on July 7, Mr. Werner pulled up in front of the house. He and Dad spoke for a few seconds by the hood of his car and then walked through the gate, up the front walk past Selma, and into the house. When I came downstairs, they were sitting at the kitchen table waiting for me. I came in, shook hands with Mr. Werner, and sat down. Trying to be professional and businesslike, I began to speak.

"Mr. Werner, I would like to give you this encrypted document. It's the one that I think Captain Harding was working on when he drowned. You can see all the cigarette burns on it. I know it was wrong of me, but I kept it when you were here recently. I wanted a little more time to try and work on the encryptions. I planned to turn it over to you eventually."

"You realize that you could be in a great deal of trouble for what you did?"

"Yes, sir. I know and I'm sorry."

"Your dad and I have spoken and I'm not going to do anything out of courtesy to him. But if you ever do anything like this again, I will not be as lenient. Do you understand?"

"Yes, sir, I do."

"How did you make out?" he asked, with a tinge of sarcasm in his voice.

"Very well. I accidently discovered that the flying disc wasn't a toy or model but a device that can be used to decipher the encryptions. When you run the disc over the encryptions, the glass center highlights certain markings and ignores the others. The other night I stayed up and started working on deciphering the document. Unfortunately, I didn't get all that far before I fell asleep. However, what I did get, I am fairly sure translates as follows:

CURRENT YEAR 2038

TIME WARP ON JULY 7 CREATED WINDOW TO GO BACK 91 YEARS

WARNING OCTOBER 1962 CUBA FIRES SOVIET MISSILES AT US

EAST COAST LOST

US RETALIATES USSR CUBA WIPED OUT

WEST COAST LOST POCKET OF MIDWEST SURVIVES

CHINA SURVIVES + RISES

DARK COLD NUCLEAR WINTER DISCONTENT

PRESIDENT SHOT NOVEMBER 1963

"Can you get the flying saucer and show me on this encrypted document how you did it?"

"Unfortunately, I can't. You see, Mom accidently ran over the disc with her car and broke it. It no longer works. The glass is shattered. I tried to use the largest chunk of glass that I could find to see if it would still translate. But it doesn't function without being a part of the disc. Luke still has the shell, but I placed the contents of the disc in this bag that you can also have."

As I handed him the bag, he asked, "So let me get this straight. You translated the document using the disc, but now you have no way of duplicating what you did?"

"I'm afraid that's correct."

"I have no way of verifying what you're telling me?"

"I'm afraid that, too, is the case."

"What's to say that your eyes weren't tired and playing a trick on you?"

"What can I say, sir? I guess it's possible, but I know what I saw."

"The mind is a funny thing. It sometimes sees and believes what it wants or expects to see. There is a famous case of a law professor who wanted to show his class how unreliable eye witnesses can be. He had a fellow professor come in and pretend to rob him using a banana. Afterward, there were students who were prepared to swear that the man had a gun and even described the type of gun. This is not all that unusual, my boy, especially when you're tired and under the kind of stress you've been experiencing."

"Mr. Werner, you've got to believe me! This isn't my mind playing tricks on me. I think Captain Harding was onto the same thing when he disappeared. I even went as far as to confirm with Mrs. Harding yesterday that her husband disappeared on July 7, 1951, so I suspect that the portal was not unique to the ninety-one-year gap between 1947 and 2038, but may be available on July 7 of any year."

"Are you saying that you expect Captain Harding to come walking through that door today in a wet bathing suit?"

"I don't know, but I think it's possible, sir. In fact, I think you will find that the bright spots that Captain Harding saw over Germany from the cockpit of the *Sweet Sally* occurred in the July timeframe."

Turning to Dad, I asked, "Was it July, Pop?"

"I don't remember, Joe. I always thought they were nothing more than reflections of the sun on the cockpit glass. I was too busy trying to keep the *Sweet Sally* in the air and getting us all home safely and in one piece. Listen guys, I think this has probably gone as far as it can. I've got a farm to run."

"I'm just trying to be helpful, Mr. Werner. I hope you will listen to what I'm saying, because I honestly believe we're all going to be in a lot of trouble next year if you don't."

"I know you are trying to be helpful, and I promise you I'll take what you've said under advisement. I'll even have the stuff you gave me in this bag examined. Thank you for your efforts, Joe."

"You're welcome, sir."

With that I got up, gave him a backward glance as I walked out of the room, and reminded him, partly in jest, not to forget that today was July 7. Seizing upon the opportunity, he called me back to ask that I please keep quiet about what I'd concluded because it could create unnecessary alarm. And then he repeated what he'd told me last time, namely that I was a most impressive fifteen-year-old but that I had a very active imagination. I once again let the comment slide and kept walking. When I got outside, Mary was waiting for me.

"How did it go?"

"He gave me the same old bullshit about being very impressive but having an overactive imagination. I'm really getting tired of it."

"Don't take it personally. He's probably just trying to throw you off the trail."

"I know, but it doesn't make it any easier, especially when you believe the world is going to incinerate in a little more than a year. It's just so damn frustrating!"

"I'm sure that they're going to be secretly working on it behind the scenes, feverishly trying to do all that they can."

"Well, Mary, at least you got your wish. The monkey is off our backs, so I guess we can go up to town and stroll around in ignorant bliss like the rest of the folks. The dark, cold nuclear winter is now Mr. Werner's problem."

"Come on now, stop being so dramatic! It's Friday, and tonight is the carnival in town. Let's go to the top of the Ferris wheel, and if you play your cards right, maybe I'll let you kiss me. I've never been kissed by an unemployed superhero!"

"You don't know, maybe I'll try to make it to second base while we're up there."

"You do, Joe Carr, and you'll get smacked back to 1947."

That night we went to the carnival and rode the Ferris wheel. Mary let me kiss her, but when I tried to steal second, I got thrown out with a left-hand slap from home. Even with the rebuff, I relaxed for the first time in a long while and enjoyed myself and forgot all about the warning and Captain Harding. Fortunately—or unfortunately, I'm not sure which—July 7, 1961, faded into history without incident. Dad told me to put the Harding situation behind me and leave it to the pros to handle. I did with surprising ease.

Not long thereafter, in late July, Mr. Werner came to the house with a shiny new toy flying saucer for Luke. With a little bit of effort, he was able to coax Luke into trading his old one in for the new one. Before he put the old saucer in his bag, he gave the gas cap I'd borrowed to replace the broken glass center back to Dad. He then asked Dad if he could speak with me alone.

Dad said, "Sure, why don't the two of you use the front porch?"

Mr. Werner replied, "Fine, sounds like a good idea." With that we went out front and sat down.

"I would like to speak to you in confidence. I feel you have earned the right to know what is going on. The flying disc that crashed in Roswell was not from our future, and the occupants weren't trying to warn us of anything. They weren't even operating the craft they were in. We think they were involuntary occupants at best."

"Well, then, what were they?"

"We think the Soviets were attempting to test our defense system. The disc was not self-propelled. It was attached to a high-altitude balloon that was being controlled remotely. The occupants were children who were a little younger than you, about ten to twelve years old. They were severely deformed, either because of an accident such as exposure to radiation, or as the result of cosmetic surgery of some kind that gave them a larger than normal head, big eyes, and elongated fingers. The encrypted documents were unintelligible nonsense."

"But why would the Soviets do that?"

"If they could successfully penetrate our air space undetected with the balloon and the disc, they could attach an atomic weapon or a canister filled with germs or gas to the balloon, and they could release it over the US the way they did the disc."

"Is that why Captain Harding was looking at the liquid under the microscope?"

"Yes, we think he was checking to see what it was and whether it posed any danger to us. It did not. It was nothing more than distilled water with a trace of dye in it."

"Hearing you say that is a relief to me because I got some of it on me at one point."

"You've nothing to worry about. It's harmless."

"What was Captain Harding doing with the metal sample?"

"We think he was trying to ascertain why our radar didn't pick it up. Frankly, we still aren't sure, although we would never admit to it as I'm sure you can understand."

"Yes, sir, I understand. But you must have some ideas about why we couldn't detect it?"

"It may be that there is a special coating on it that we haven't been able to identify yet. Your dad thinks it may have something to do with the fact that the balloon and saucer had no sharp edges. Trust me, we'll eventually figure it out."

"What was their reason for putting the deformed kids inside? It seems like a really mean thing to do."

"We think they did it in case something went wrong and we detected it and shot it down, or they couldn't retrieve it and it crashed."

"I don't understand."

"The Soviets wanted us to think they were aliens from outer space. And we did for a brief time. But then we realized we were being had, but we didn't want them to know that we knew they were behind it, so we said it was a weather balloon."

"Weren't the Soviets afraid that if the kids survived they would tell us where they were from?"

"Unfortunately, they couldn't speak because their vocal cords were not functional, and they had preexisting brain damage that made them severely retarded."

"I see. It now makes sense to me. Well, all except for two things."

"What things?"

"What was the purpose of the miniature saucer that Luke kept and that Mom accidently ran over with the car?"

"It was battery powered and transmitted a signal periodically that we think was being used to track its whereabouts. It also may in some way have aided in the remote control of the balloon and disc. We're still working on that aspect. What's your other question?"

"Why did Captain Harding write the number 1062 on the backboard and put an *X* through it?"

"I was afraid you were going to ask me that. We don't have a good explanation for what he was doing with that one."

"I see. But if the Soviets were trying to throw us off, why would they draw attention to 1962, or October of 1962?"

"Joe, 1062 is a random number. If it refers to a date, it could just as easily be the year 1062, which occurred almost 900 years ago. You seem to have forgotten that you're the one who has interpreted 1062 to be the two numbers 10 and 62 and concluded that it refers to October of next year. No one else has gone there with you."

"That's true, I see your point."

"Well, I'd best be going. While I'm here, I want to visit with Dr. Hurd for a few minutes. I feel like a new man since I've been on the antibiotic regime that he suggested, and I want to thank him. Please remember that everything I've told you is in confidence, and if you ever repeat it, I'll deny having said it. Do you understand?"

"I do," I said and stood up. He did too, and we shook hands. As he walked down the porch steps, he looked back and said, "Please say good-bye to your dad for me, and tell him I'll be in touch with him."

"You got it," I said and walked into the house after I saw him pass through the front gate, get into his car, and drive away.

Inside, I had a chance to sit quietly and digest all that I'd heard. A part of me said everything he told me made sense—at least as much sense as what I'd concluded about it being our future coming back to warn us. Maybe he was correct that my eyes had played tricks on me that night. A side of me wanted in the worst way to believe that he was right: that it was just a Soviet prank, and we weren't in any imminent danger. But a voice inside me said that in believing him, I was no different than the students in that law professor's evidence class. I was seeing and believing what I wanted to see and believe rather than what really had happened.

More importantly, however, he'd given me the peace of mind of knowing that he was still working on the matter. Maybe nobody could stop what I thought was going to happen in October of 1962 and November of 1963, but at least I knew someone was looking into it.

As July gave way to August that summer, I found myself thinking less and less about the Harding situation. It began to seem more like a bad dream and less like a reality. Mary and I had been spending all our free time together. We would swim in the ocean at least once daily and sometimes as often as three times in a day. She was a beach attendant at the Bridgehampton Club beach, and I would try to sneak down for an early morning swim before they got busy setting up the chairs and umbrellas and before we started work on the farm.

Dad would cut me a little slack whenever he could, and I was grateful to him for it. Very often I would meet her there again in the evening after work, and we would surf together along with some of our friends. Linus frequently would come with me and take a swim or run up and down the beach, barking at us as we tried to ride the waves. From time to time, when we just couldn't get enough of the ocean and its salty sea breeze, we also would go back down after dinner, make a fire on the beach, and swim under the stars or in moonlight.

We biked every chance we could. On Saturday, August 12, 1961, Dad gave me the afternoon off, and Mary and I biked all the way out to the Montauk lighthouse. We kept to the side roads where we could because of the traffic on Route 27. This made the trip more interesting, since we could ride slowly alongside each other and talk without having to yell. It also allowed us to enjoy the beauty of the passing scenery, whether it be the farm fields or the distant ocean views.

However, it added greatly to the time that it took, which got our parents worried about us. As evening approached and we hadn't returned, the four of them came out looking for us in the Hurds' Ford wagon. They found us biking back as we were passing the

Lobster Shack on a long, lonely stretch of the Montauk highway. Tired and happy to see them, we put the bikes on the wagon's roof rack and gladly accepted an offer to join them for dinner. The lobster rolls were every bit as good as they were reputed to be. Dad had supplied the owners with tomatoes in season for years, so they were more than happy to accommodate us on short notice.

And of course, besides biking, swimming, and surfing there was the drive-in up in town where we occasionally went to catch a movie, and the Candy Kitchen to hang out in afterward. I was having lots of fun, but I still hadn't gotten to second base with Mary. The truth is, I hadn't even gotten up the nerve to try again after having been shot down in flames the last time around.

However, the summer was more than half over, and I still had one more project to do for Miss Pickering. I told myself it was time to get started on it. Riding home from the Lobster Shack in the Ford, Mary said that she would help me, and we agreed that the next day would be a good opportunity to visit the cemetery and pick our final case.

I wasn't at all prepared for what I was about to find.

fourteen

Sunday, August 13, 1961, dawned a beautiful day. Dad and I were up at dawn and took Luke and Linus with us when we went out to the fields. Dad wanted to let Mom sleep in until we got back around 8:30 a.m. to get ready for church. He told us we would take the rest of the day off if we could finish before church what we hadn't completed on Saturday.

He and Mom had been invited by the Fosters to go on their boat, and I knew how much Dad enjoyed being out on the water. We worked hard and finished with time to spare. After church, Luke and Linus went to stay with Mrs. Harding while Mom packed two picnic lunches, one for them to take on the boat, and one for Mary and me to take to the village green.

The afternoon was even more beautiful than the morning had been. There wasn't a cloud in the rich blue sky. The only sounds were a soft breeze rustling Selma's deep green leaves and the chirping of a bird on one of her strong old branches. Mary had come to meet me, and it was from these surroundings that we set out together on our bikes for the cemetery with our picnic lunch in hand. The whistling of the gentle wind in Selma's branches almost made me think for a moment that she was reminding me to say hello to Sammy and August Pierce for her, but then again, it was probably nothing more than what Mr. Werner would call my overactive imagination at work. Whatever it was, it didn't matter, because I was planning to visit with them anyway.

When we got there, Mary started to lay out the picnic blanket by the Pierce grave. Their resting place enjoyed the shade of an old oak tree in the afternoon, making it a wonderful location to picnic. While she was doing that, I decided to walk around in a part of the cemetery that I hadn't previously explored and read the headstones. There was a bevy of familiar names, many of whom also had streets in town named after them. There also were names that I'd never seen before. One caught my eye: William Duxbury. Buried with him were his wife Sarah and a child named Peter and a woman by the name of Emily Wells.

At that point, Mary called to say that lunch was ready, and I turned and went to her. Mom had made us ice cold lemonade, deviled eggs, southern fried chicken, and a fresh tomato and cucumber salad. For dessert she had packed slices of watermelon. I hadn't eaten anything other than a cup of coffee and a buttered roll at 6 a.m., so I was starving.

While we were eating, I told Mary about the Duxbury headstone. She wasn't as keen on it as I was, fearing that it wouldn't be all that different from the Pierce story. I was surprised by her reaction and asked her why she felt that way.

"Sarah Duxbury probably died before William, possibly giving birth to their son Peter. Maybe Peter died during the birth as well. In any event, Emily Wells most likely was his second wife, although they may never have formally married."

"Wow, you have their lives all figured out, and you haven't even seen where they are buried."

"How much do you want to bet?"

"I'll bet you five dollars."

"Don't you want to make this interesting?"

"Five dollars is plenty interesting to me. What did you have in mind?"

"How about if I win, you have to sneak on to Prune Island with me?"

"Are you crazy? I'm already in trouble with Mr. Werner for having held on to that document. If I get caught, my ass will be grass."

"All right, may be that wasn't such a good idea. You think of something."

"If I win, we go skinny dipping in Ellis Pond on a moonlit night."

"And what if I win?"

"We go skinny dipping in Ellis Pond on a moonlit night."

"Maybe we better stick with the five dollars."

"I have an idea. If you win, I have to pay you five dollars. But if I win, you have to go swimming topless with me in Ellis Pond on a moonlit night."

"Oh, sure, it's no big deal for you to go swimming topless."

"All right, I have to skinny dip. What do you say?"

"If I win, you have to take me to dinner at the 1776 House. And if you win I will go swimming with you."

"You want to go to dinner at the 1776 House! Do you know how long it will take me to earn enough money to do that?"

"I'm serious. I can wait all the way up until you are ready to put that diamond ring on my finger. Just how badly do you want that moonlight swim?"

I knew then that I was in trouble. If I said no to the bet, in some crazy way she would twist it to mean that I didn't care enough about her. If I said yes, she had an uncanny way of always being right. Betting against her instincts rarely ended well for me. I had a bad feeling that this time would be no different. But in my heart I didn't care because I knew now what would make her happy. If the world didn't end first, I would take her there someday to get engaged. She was all that I wanted. She was the girl of my dreams, the person I wanted to spend the rest of my life with.

"All right, you're on," I reluctantly agreed.

"Let's go look," she said as we shook hands.

My worst fears were confirmed when we got to the Duxbury headstone. Mrs. Duxbury had died at the age of twenty-eight, on the same day that Peter was born. Peter in turn lived only one day. Mr. Duxbury lived to be eighty-three, and Emily, who was younger, outlived him by three years.

Mary was milking it for all it was worth. Smiling, she said, "I think I'm going to have the pheasant under glass."

I was about to answer, but then I saw something that stopped me in my tracks. There, three plots to the right, was a headstone with the name Carr.

Mary had started to walk back to the blanket when I called to her. "Mary, come here! The name on this marker is Carr, and it lists two sons named George and Brian."

She stopped with the kidding and came quickly. The headstone read:

> George Michael-Xavier Carr and Brian Angel Carr,
> beloved sons,
>
> born June 9, 1945, died July 26, 1945, and June 9,
> 1945

"Mary, I don't understand. We already have a Carr family plot in this cemetery where my grandfather and my great-grandparents are buried. Can it be that these are my twin brothers, and if so, why are they buried here?"

"I don't know. I would think you would've known about it."

"I would think so, too. But Mom and Dad have never said anything about it."

"Why don't you ask them?"

"I'm a little nervous. Perhaps they don't want me, Kelly, and Luke to know, or maybe it's just too painful for them to talk about."

"Why don't you ask your grandmother?"

"She's away this week taking care of her sister."

"You have a right to know, and you certainly are old enough to handle it. If I were you, I would raise it with your father during one of your front porch get-togethers. Tell him that you would like to make it your last case study for Miss Pickering, and see what he says."

"That's a good idea. I think I will. Do you think I should do it tonight?"

"Well, that's up to you, of course. But I was hoping to find someone to go for a swim with me in Ellis Pond tonight."

"Are you serious?"

Leaning over and giving me a kiss, she whispered in my ear: "Dead serious."

We both broke out laughing at the irony of choosing that expression while picnicking in a cemetery. There may not have been any clouds in the sky that afternoon, but somehow I was walking on one.

I know this is going to sound farfetched, coming from a fifteen-year-old boy, but it was more about the feeling of our becoming more intimate than it was about the expectation of seeing her topless. That's not to say that I wasn't looking forward to that part, too. But this was different. It was even more wonderful! And I hoped it always would be.

fifteen

Sunday night, August 13, 1961, was a moonless night. The stars glistened like diamonds in the jet black sky. The weekend visitors had migrated back to the city, and the local folks were home getting ready for another day on the farm. When Luke was asleep and Mom and Dad had gone to bed, I snuck down the stairs and out the front door, which we always kept unlocked. Even Linus didn't bother to leave Luke's bedside to see what I was up to. Nodding to Selma, I mounted my bike and rode into the dark August night.

When I got to Mary's house, she was already outside waiting for me. We both had a nervous excitement about us as we started for the pond. Soon our eyes adjusted to the lack of light, and our ears became attuned to the sounds of the night, which included the dull hum of the Long Island Railroad train as it clicked and clacked westward, its whistle occasionally crying out in the dark as it crossed a lonely road. And there were the peepers, who insisted on serenading us as we rode ever closer to our rendezvous with our sexual awakenings. Nervous, scared, excited; pedal, pedal, pedal; nervous, scared, excited; pedal, pedal, pedal. So it went, on and on, until finally we arrived at Ellis Pond. No one was there, not even a deer attempting to sneak a drink.

I knew deep down this had to be hard for Mary, and I appreciated so much that she was willing to subject herself to this for me. She was giving of herself to please me, and I wanted her to feel comfortable and at ease. Without hesitation I stripped off my trunks and jumped into the dark abyss that was Ellis Pond, the same pond that had almost claimed Great-Grandpa and had cost August his life. Mary made me turn and not look as she took off her top and slowly waded into the calm water. When she said I could turn around, I did. Her breasts were beautiful—perfectly white and perky. The nipples were hard from the coolness of the water. I tried not to stare, but I couldn't help myself. With all the strength she could muster, she asked in a calm voice: "Do you like what you see?"

"Magnificent! But more importantly, so are you." Moving closer to her, I began hugging her in a way that told her I never wanted to let her go, and then I kissed her. Gently, we caressed, and I knew that she could tell how excited I was to be with her. We swam and frolicked as we laughed and splashed one another until we no longer were aware of our nakedness or our surroundings. Then we thought we heard someone coming. She quickly covered herself with her crossed arms and retreated into the tall cattails. It was only a doe coming for a late drink. As scared of us as we had been of her, the graceful creature leaped and ran at the notice of us.

"I'm sorry, Joe, but this is all a little too new for me," Mary whispered.

"I understand," I said and swam away to give her some time to collect her thoughts. Floating on my back, I became engrossed in looking up at the stars. They were beautiful, and in short order Mary joined me, as we floated together and admired them. We amused ourselves by trying to name as many stars and constellations as we could.

It was peaceful, and before long we found ourselves embracing and kissing one another once again. I was so content that I never wanted that moment in time to end, and I knew she felt the same. But it was almost one o'clock in the morning, and the farm and Dad would be waiting for me with the arrival of the sun. I accompanied

Mary home, and after giving her an extra-long kiss and thanking her for the best night of my life, I headed for home. As I tiptoed up the stairs, I could hear Linus stirring and hoped he wouldn't come to investigate. He didn't budge, and soon I was fast asleep in my bed.

Monday morning came quickly as usual, and Dad was up with the dawn. He expected me to be bright-eyed and ready to go. If I could just make it through the day, I would be set for the rest of the week. When I was slow to breakfast, he came up to fetch me.

"What's the matter with you, son? You went to bed nice and early last night. I expected you to be the first one at the table."

"Just a little slow getting going. I'll be fine once I'm up and about."

"Well hurry up. We've got to dig up a trailer load of potatoes for shipment to Puerto Rico, and Mom wants you to have a good breakfast in you."

When I came down, Mom handed me a fried egg and ham sandwich and a thermos full of black coffee.

Smiling, she said, "Last night must have been quite a night for you."

"What do you mean?"

Holding up the wet swim trunks I had left on the bathroom floor, she said, "I'm sure this didn't happen from sweating in bed. Did you have a good time?"

"I couldn't sleep, so I went down for a quick swim."

"Alone?" she asked.

"I've got to go, Mom. You can give me the third degree later." With that, I rushed out of the house before she could ask me again.

The day was long and hard. A trailer truck full of potatoes brings with it a lot of dust to swallow, a ton of sweat to wipe from your brow, and a great deal of digging. It also means plenty of east end dirt beneath your nails and down your perspiring back, and a laborious amount of washing, bagging and loading. But most of all it's a *shitload* of potatoes to deal with in one long, hot, grueling day. At least the night before had been more than worth it. The memory of Mary's clean, wet, soft milk-white body dripping with droplets of crystal clear pond water in the cool night breeze that carried her magnificent and refreshing scent kept me going. I would gladly do it all over again. And Mary and I did—sneaking off to Ellis Pond whenever we could that summer.

sixteen

When we came in from the fields that day, I was exhausted. I hoped a shower would perk me up. When it didn't, I told Mom that I was too tired to eat and planned to skip dinner.

"Is this because you were out late swimming?"

"No, Mom, that isn't the reason. I had something on my mind that has been bugging me."

"Would you care to share it with your father and me?"

"I don't know if this is the right time and place."

"There is never a good time or a bad time, only the present time. What's on your mind, Joe?"

"Yesterday when Mary and I were at the cemetery, we came across a headstone with the name Carr on it. Twin boys named George and Brian are buried there. Are they brothers of mine, and of Kelly and Luke?"

"Oh my Lord, the day has come, John."

"I always knew that it would, Sally. I just didn't expect it this soon. I guess I should have when he got this assignment."

Turning his attention to me, Dad said, "Yes they're your brothers. Like you they were born in Europe and when they didn't survive, the military shipped their remains home for us. Grandma buried them in a separate grave thinking it would only be temporary, and we would move them to their final resting place when we came home."

"Why didn't you ever tell me about them?"

"We planned to tell you about them when we thought that the time was right. You obviously have moved that date up to now. I knew that you weren't yourself out there in the fields today, but I thought it was something else. I never dreamt it was this. As I said, I guess I should've known."

Feeling a little dishonest about letting that misconception stand, I soothed my conscience by mumbling, "This was a part of it, anyway." Fortunately, neither Dad nor Mom noticed what I'd said, as they were preoccupied trying to decide how and what to tell me.

"Son, do you know what a chromosome is?" Dad asked.

"Yes, Miss Pickering taught us about them in science class last year."

"Well, the boys had a chromosome disorder known as trisomy 13. We didn't know that much in 1945."

"Can you tell me a little about it?"

"The disorder was first observed as far back as the 1600s, but last year a man named Dr. Patau identified the chromosomal nature of the condition. He named it trisomy 13, which means that each cell has three instead of two full copies of chromosome 13. It's this extra material that disrupted the normal course of George and Brian's development and left them to be born with many problems."

"What sort of problems did they have?" I asked.

"Some were physical and easy to observe. For example, George had a cleft palate. I think you know what that is, don't you?"

"Yes."

"The boys also had extra fingers and toes and things of that nature."

"I see."

"But the truly serious and life-threatening problems were the internal ones that you couldn't readily see."

"What were they?"

"Their brain stems and spinal cords were not properly formed and connected, and there were times when their brains either didn't tell them to breathe or the message didn't get through to their lungs and hearts. Brian was stillborn, but George managed to live for a little less than seven weeks."

Mom interrupted to say, "It was heartbreaking to hold him when he would start to turn blue from not breathing and to be helpless to do anything for him."

"What did you do, Mom?"

"I did the only thing that I knew how to do, the one thing that kept me from coming unglued. I prayed that he would start breathing again. He always did, except for the last time, of course. And I knew in my heart that there eventually would be a last time, for the doctors had warned me. I must confess, though, it didn't make it any easier. The only thing that gave me solace was knowing that he was with his brother in a better place where their problems would no longer plague them."

"That had to be so hard for the two of you. I can't imagine what it was like."

"We didn't know why it happened to us because the condition is more common with the offspring of older women, those who give birth later in life. I was so young. We were afraid that maybe we shouldn't try to have any more children."

"What happened that made you change your mind and decide to have me?"

"The military put us in touch with some of the best doctors in London. The doctors there went over our entire history with us to figure out what caused us to have this problem."

"And what did they conclude?"

"I was having problems with my back before I realized I might be pregnant. I went to see a chiropractor who took several X-rays of my lower back. They think those X-rays may have damaged the recently fertilized eggs."

"But not the rest of your eggs. Is that right?"

"Obviously not. Otherwise you and Kelly wouldn't be the bright, healthy children that you are!"

"I guess you're right. Do they think that is the reason Luke has the problems that he has?"

"No, they don't think so. Luke's situation is unrelated in their view, but no one can be one hundred percent sure."

"I understand. But what do they have to say about his issues?"

Dad jumped in and said, "These memories are very hard for your mother, Joe. I think we've covered enough to answer your questions for now. Luke's problems are best saved for a discussion at another time. Suffice it to say that we decided to call it quits after Luke and not have any more children, not so much because we were afraid of birth-related problems, but because we knew Luke would need our care to one extent or another for the rest of our lives. You and Kelly will grow up, marry, and probably start families of your own. I'm not sure that Luke will be able to do the same."

"You know I will always be there for Luke, don't you?"

"Well, Joe, your future wife may have something to say about that and so might your children."

"My future wife lives down the road, and she doesn't have a problem with it. And neither will my kids."

"That's comforting to hear, son," Mom said as she patted me on the knee. "You sure you don't want some dinner? I'm making lamb chops with string beans and roasted potatoes."

"Well, all right, you talked me into it."

"Good, go relax on the front porch with your father, and I'll call you when it's ready."

"Thanks, Mom," I said as I started to walk out of the room.

"Are you and Mary really that serious about each other, son?"

"Yes, she's the girl for me. I have no doubt about it. I knew it the first time I set eyes on her. And what's more, she feels the same way about me."

"That's wonderful. She's a good girl. Make sure you do the right thing by her. Be a gentleman."

"Of course, Mom, what do you expect? Why are you telling me all this?"

"Mrs. Hurd called me this morning. She found Mary's two-piece bathing suit on her floor."

"She went swimming with me. Is that a federal offense?"

"The bottom was wet and full of cattails. The top wasn't. It was clean and dry."

Stunned, I stood there in silence as my brain tried to absorb the question, process the implications, and come up with an answer. Then it hit me, and I said with a degree of satisfaction at the cleverness of my answer, "She only waded in up to her waist."

Choosing to ignore me, she asked, "You went skinny dipping with her, didn't you?"

"Mom," I yelped, "You shouldn't be asking me those kinds of questions! A guy doesn't talk about that stuff with his mother."

"Would you rather be having this discussion with your father? I can call him in if you like, but it might end in a trip to the woodshed."

"No, I'd rather not be having it with either of you."

"You should have thought of that before you decide to take that nice young girl skinny dipping."

"Anyhow, my bathing suit was wet. You said so yourself this morning, remember?"

"I will give you credit for thinking about wetting it in the sink. But there were no cattails or the usual pond debris in them."

"When you were in England, did you work for Scotland Yard or something?"

"MI5 at your service, Master Carr. You may be able to keep something from Mr. Werner and the federal government on Prune

Island, but you are no match for the mommy patrol. Mrs. Hurd and I are on your trail, and we always get our man—or boy! Come clean and we may show some leniency."

"Fine, we went swimming and I was skinny dipping, but Mary wasn't. Can we leave it at that?"

"Yes, and I'm proud of you for standing up for her in that way. I hope you always will. I can see that the two of you really do have something special, and I'm happy for you."

"Thanks, Mom."

"Should she become your wife someday, Dad and I certainly don't expect you and Mary to be Luke's keeper any more than we would expect Kelly and her future husband to be. Luke's well-being is our responsibility, and we are planning for it. But as I said, it is comforting and heartwarming to know how you and Mary feel. The important thing is for you to realize that, God willing, you will experience the full blessings of life: a wonderful wife and children, and the success and satisfaction that come with hard work in school, on the playing field, and during your career.

"Every time you score a touchdown, kiss Mary, get a hug from your child, or earn a promotion, you will be doing it for the four of you because George and Brian will never have that opportunity, and it's possible that Luke may not either. Go out there and live your life to the fullest, but be responsible. And make sure you do the right thing by that young girl. She's a keeper, and someday she may be the mother of your children."

"I promise, Mom. You can trust me when I tell you I will never do anything to hurt Mary or Luke, and I won't ever forget George or Brian or, for that matter, August and Sammy and the Pickering fellow. I will live my life to the fullest for me and for them."

"Oh, gosh, I think I've burned the lamb chops. Please go call your dad and tell him that dinner is ready."

"Okay."

"I'm sorry if I embarrassed you. That wasn't my intention. I was fifteen once, and I went skinny dipping, too. You can always come and talk to me about anything, son. I'm a big believer in communication."

"I want you to know I love you very much, Mom."

She took the sizzling lamb chops and the roasted potatoes out of the oven and put them down on top of the stove. Then she undid her apron, placed it on its hook, and came over and gave me a big hug. As she did, she told me, "I can't say it enough: I'm so proud of the fine young man you are becoming and the love and respect that you have for that young girl and your brother and sister. I love you very much, too."

Giving me a smack on the rear end, she continued, "Now, go get your dad before I get really mushy on you."

I didn't answer, and walked out to the porch to fetch him.

seventeen

Mary and I tried to make the most of the remaining days of summer, before she would have to head back to the city for school. The more we tried to slow it down, the faster the time went. And finally the day came for her to leave. I stood by as Dr. Hurd tied the suitcases to the rack on the family station wagon. Then with a wave from the back window of a disappearing car, the girl of my dreams signaled her good-bye to me and was gone—until Thanksgiving.

The next day I went and presented my final case to Miss Pickering. I think even she was shocked by what her assignment had uncovered for me, and she gave me an A-plus. More importantly, she promoted me. I had a newfound respect for the lives that had been laid to rest in the village green and in cemeteries everywhere, a respect I was sure would stay with me for the rest of my life.

The fall was filled with football, school, and farm work. Even though I was only in the eighth grade, they drafted me to play on the Bridgehampton High School team. I was as fast as the wind, and just as hard to bottle up. Mom and Dad together with Kelly and Luke would come to cheer me on, as did Miss Pickering from time to time. If only Mary could have been there too.

When Thanksgiving finally approached, I anxiously awaited Mary's arrival. We had a game on Thanksgiving morning, and I was hoping she would come, but she never did. It seems her family decided to spend the holiday in Aspen instead. Devastated, I tried to keep a stiff upper lip, but I fooled no one as I moped about. We nevertheless won the game, but it had little if anything to do with me.

Then on the Friday night after Thanksgiving, there was a knock on the front door. It was Mary. She hadn't gone with her parents but stayed behind with Mrs. Harding. They'd spent Thanksgiving together in the city and gone to the Macy's Day Parade. Standing there in her tan camel hair coat, deep red sweater, and plaid skirt, she was a sight to behold. I gave her a three-month hug and kiss, and almost knocked the wind out of her.

"Careful," she half-heartedly protested and then gave me a kiss back. Suddenly it felt as if we'd never been apart. The three months seemed to evaporate faster than the raindrops from a summer shower on a hot tin roof.

"Let's go up to town. I'll get the keys to Sally Truck!"

"Are you sure it will be okay?"

"Dad won't mind."

"Well all right."

And off we went into the cool November 1961 night. It was almost 1 a.m. when I finally coasted back into the driveway with the lights off. It'd been a spectacular reunion. Under the stars and in the warm glow of a fire that I made with driftwood on the beach, we'd caught up on three months of separation. It was so nice to have Mary by my side again—to feel her soft hair, smell the sweet scent of her perfume, and taste her warm breath and inviting lips.

But something wasn't right. The lights were on in the kitchen. Walking in, I saw Mom sitting at the table crying. Dad was nowhere to be seen.

"What's the matter?" I asked.

Sobbing, she said, "Luke is missing."

"Luke is missing!" I exclaimed. "He was asleep when I left,

and you guys and Kelly were next door at the Lynches. What happened?"

"He lost that toy flying saucer that Max Werner gave him when we were at the store today."

"And?"

"And I got a call from someone before we went over to the Lynches who said he'd found it."

"How did they know how to reach us?"

"I left our number with the store manager in case somebody turned it in. When the man called and found out where we lived, he said he could drop it off because he would be passing by here. I thought nothing of it and asked him to leave it on the front porch because we were going out."

"Where's Linus?"

"Dad took him to the vet. He must have caught the man by surprise and taken a chunk out of him before getting hit over the head with a pipe. We found the pipe and a bloody piece of clothing on the porch."

"Is he going to be okay?"

"Yes, Dad says Labs have thick skulls. I wouldn't worry."

"What about Luke?"

"The police were here earlier and took all the necessary information and evidence. They have put out an all-points bulletin for a wounded man and a child with a flying saucer. They have a roadblock and checkpoint set up at Canoe Place by the Shinnecock Canal in case he tries to leave. They have notified the hospital and most of the doctors on the South Fork to be on the lookout for them. They're confident they'll find him. No need for all of us to stay up. Why don't you go up to bed? We'll wake you if there's any news."

And then she lost it.

Crying profusely, she kept repeating, "I hope my little guy is okay. I don't think I can take losing a third child. I'm a good mom, why is God doing this to me?"

I gave her a hug and told her she was a great mom, and we'd find Luke unharmed. I stayed with her until she eventually sobbed herself to sleep out of shear exhaustion. Linus needed emergency surgery and the vet decided to keep him overnight for observation. Dad never got back home until almost 5 a.m. Then I walked out of the house, got back in Sally Truck, and drove to the village green.

Unconcerned about Miss Pickering, I hopped the fence and went to the Pierce grave. Bending down, I pleaded, "August, you've got to save one more Carr, do you hear me?"

Then, I went over to George and Brian Angel and told them to please look out for their younger brother and to put in a good word with the Big Guy for him. I sat down and started to pray. The moist, chilly night air slowly penetrated my clothing like a quiet fog rolling in over the water, but I refused to succumb to it. Blocking it out, I was still there praying when the sun finally started to come up. As I stood to leave, I stopped to take a backward glance. A warm feeling ran down my spine. Somehow I knew then things would work out okay.

Back at the house, there was a police car in the driveway. When I went inside, Dad told me they'd gotten a tip that Luke and the man were on the early morning ferry to New London. The coast guard stopped and boarded the ferry. Soldiers from Prune Island were flown out by helicopter to help them with the search. It wasn't long before the man was found on deck. His leg wound gave him away when he was ordered to roll up his pants leg. Seemingly resigned to his fate, he led the police to his car where Luke was in the trunk. Luke's hair was dyed red and his clothing had been changed. He was tied up and gagged and dressed in a Cub Scout uniform. His flying saucer toy was lying beside him.

Luke was taken to the hospital where a thorough examination showed that he hadn't been physically harmed. Dad and Mom brought him home and tried to explain to him what had happened. In the end, the best therapy proved to be the sugar cookies with sprinkles that Mrs. Harding baked and brought over to him to-gether, of course, with the return of Linus to his side.

Later in the day, when Luke was napping, Dad and I went out on the front porch. As we sat there, he asked me how I was doing.

"I'm not sure, Dad," I replied. "I've always felt so safe here. Now I don't know how I feel. Nothing like this has ever happened before."

"I know. Your reaction is very normal and common. Kelly told Mom the same thing. The world is not as safe as we sometimes think. Parents try to shield their kids from upsetting news stories on TV, but sooner or later reality seeps into everyone's life. We do live in a very safe area, but bad things can happen anywhere. It's that they're more likely to happen in some places than in others."

"What made this man single out Luke?"

"The police think he was hanging out in the store, looking for a victim and picked out Luke because he could see that Luke is im-paired. Mom tells me that Luke was giving her an unusually hard time and may have drawn the man's attention. It's their opinion that Luke didn't lose the toy. Rather, the man took it when Luke was distracted and planned to use it to get to Luke."

"What do you think made someone call in a tip about the man? Luke wasn't with him, and the police said he had changed into a clean pair of pants. How was he any different than any other guy on the boat? I doubt you could see the bandage on his leg under his new pants."

"The tip was called in from Prune Island."

"Prune Island? How can that be? How would someone who wasn't even on the boat know to find Luke and the man on it?"

"They *didn't* know where to find Luke or the man. They knew where to find the toy flying saucer."

"I don't get it."

"Max Werner is the man who called in the tip."

"I still don't get it."

"Max Werner knew where the toy was because he had put a secret, experimental signal-sending device in it. The device operates on a battery that is powered by sunlight and automatically shuts down unless it receives a set signal. When it receives that signal, it turns on and replies with a signal of its own. We live well outside the relatively short range of this experimental signal, but the boat must have passed within it. When it did, the device activated and sent back the reply signal. Max Werner received it on Prune Island and immediately called the police when he realized what it meant. I had called Max from the vet's office to tell him that Luke and the toy were missing."

"Wow, that's interesting. The toy saved Luke?"

"I think so. If the man had gotten to New London with him, I don't think we'd ever have seen Luke alive again."

"A little too close for comfort, don't you think, Pop?"

"I think we owe Max Werner and Tom Harding a debt of gratitude."

"Why Captain Harding?"

"Tom either was working on building or understanding the device when he disappeared. After you gave Max the bag of parts, he reverse engineered what he'd found in that bag to build the toy he gave Luke. I understand that as we speak, they are still working on building an improved version that will have a stronger signal and longer range."

"But why would Mr. Werner give Luke a secret experimental device to play with?"

"To experiment and see how durable it is in a setting where no one would suspect what they were doing. They hope to use it eventually to locate downed pilots and lost soldiers. If it can survive life with Luke, it most likely could survive your average combat situation."

"I see. Are they also working on the warning from our future?"

"Let's just say they're leaving nothing to chance."

"Isn't this world crazy?"

"What do you mean? In what way?"

"August Pierce died so Great-Grandpa could live and we could be born. Captain Harding died so his device could be discovered and Luke could live. George and Brian died so I could live because I doubt Mom and you would've had me if the twins were healthy and normal. And to think—they're all buried or memorialized in the cemetery at the village green. The very cemetery that caused Miss Pickering to give me the assignment that led me to them."

"I guess you're right. I hadn't thought to look at it that way."

Figuring the situation was talked out and the time had come to change the subject, he casually asked, "What are your plans for tonight?"

"Mary and I were planning to go to the movies in Sag Harbor tonight. They're showing *West Side Story* and Mary wants to see it. I have mixed feelings. I want to go with her because tonight is her last night here. She has to go back to the city tomorrow. But after all the worry of today and being up the entire night last night, I don't know if I have it in me."

Reaching into his pocket to give me the keys to Sally Truck, he told me he had two words of advice for me: carpe diem!

I took Dad's advice and after a long nap that afternoon went to the movies with Mary. She watched the movie, but I watched her. I watched her giggle; I watched her cry; I watched her catch herself self-consciously in my gaze. And then we went to her friend's empty beach house to make a fire and watch the sun rise. I wouldn't have a chance to be alone with her again until Christmas.

eighteen

In the days that followed, our lives slowly got back to normal. Mom kept Luke busy and amused as she, Kelly and Grandma began to bake and decorate for Christmas. Dad decided we would drive upstate one weekend to cut down our own Christmas tree, so we did, staying overnight in the process.

Ellis Pond was beginning to freeze over as Christmas grew near. Luke beamed with the anticipation of ice skating on it, as Dad and he went out to the toolshed one day to clean and sharpen his skates. I, too, was looking forward to the pond freezing so that Dad and I could go iceboat racing on it.

We planned to get the boat ready right after the holidays. To cap things off, Santa Clause was scheduled to visit the firehouse on the Saturday before Christmas. He would let Luke and the other kids sit on his lap and tell him what they wanted for Christmas, and then his elves would give them a ride on a fire truck with sirens blaring and lights flashing. Luke could hardly contain himself as Mom helped him put his list together.

Yes, life was quietly returning to what it always had been, and the Carr homestead was once more beginning to feel like the safe haven, the refuge, it once was. That is—until word came that the man who kidnapped Luke had escaped from police custody by stealing a guard's pistol and killing the guard with it.

He was desperate to free himself from the abuse he was receiving at the hands of other prisoners for kidnapping a child. Considered armed and dangerous, he was last seen heading out east toward us.

Even more alarming was the graffiti found in his cell, doodling that read: DEATH TO CARR, REVENGE IS SWEET, and THAT LITTLE BASTARD'S FAMILY WILL PAY FOR THIS!

Dad decided not to take any chances, so he sent Grandma, Mom, Kelly, and Luke to stay with Mrs. Harding. He would've sent me as well, but I prevailed on him to let me stay with him and Linus. After they were gone, he took me to his gun rack in the attic and handed me a pistol. Kneeling, he showed me how to clean and load it, and then took me out to the barn to learn how to shoot it. Walking back to the house afterward, he gave me a dire warning.

"It's more common than you might think for people to be shot and even killed by their own weapon. The reason is they hesitate because they are afraid to use it to kill another human being. They often hope against hope that they can reason with an intruder and convince him to back down. The intruder usually takes advantage of the opportunity to overpower someone wielding a gun and kill him with his own weapon. This man has already overpowered and killed a trained police officer, so have no doubt that he will do the same to you if you give him the chance. Do you understand what I am telling you?"

"Yes, I do Dad. I promise you that I will not hesitate or be afraid to use this weapon. I know that I can pull the trigger if I have to."

"I hope you're right; it's not an easy thing to do. Oh, one more thing. Never point a loaded gun at someone unless you mean business."

"Okay," I said, as I got up to walk outside.

"Where are you going?"

"I'm going for a quick bike ride to clear my head. I'll be right back."

"I no sooner finish teaching you how to use a gun because a

dangerous man is gunning for us, and you want to go for a bike ride?"

"He's not looking for me. I doubt he knows I exist. I'm merely another kid on a bike. He's out for Luke and you guys."

"Make sure you're back before dark. And watch for lightning. Supposedly there's a big storm moving in."

"Okay."

I stepped outside, got on my bike, and rode down to the Pierce grave on the village green. I wanted to speak with Samuel Pierce and Ernest Pickering to get some guidance. When I got there, I began asking them the many questions swirling through my head.

· "Guys, I know that you had to be ready to kill your fellow Americans to preserve the Union and save the slaves from bondage. How did you prepare yourself to be ready to kill? When did you know you could do it? Or did you? Did it change you? I have so many questions, so many fears, but I can't leave Dad alone. What do I do? I know Mr. Werner would say it was my overactive imagination, but I felt like they were answering me and telling me not to worry, I would know when it was right."

After thanking them, I went over to speak with George and Brian Angel and asked them to please pray for me and Dad, and for Grandma, Mom, Kelly, and Luke. I wondered aloud with them if our family would ever be able to get back to the life we had known—a safe and happy life in a sleepy little place called Sagahawk—while this man was alive.

In time the sky began to darken and the rains came as predicted. When the thunder and lightning grew closer together, I knew it was time to go. Saying my good-byes, I jumped on the bike and pedaled into the teeming, windblown rain. It was coming down so hard and so fast that the roads already were beginning to flood on the edges, and puddles were forming. Riding the middle crown in the deserted road, I struggled against the wind as the tires kicked a steady stream of water up at me.

I barely could see in front of me and hoped nothing was coming the other way. The two miles or so felt more like four or five as my drenched clothing became heavy with water, and the cold wind chilled me to the bone. Finally, I turned into the driveway and dropped the bike to run into the house. Selma's branches were now bare but nevertheless creaked and crackled from being blown about by the storm's heavy winds. Dad was standing at the door with a towel, glad to see me, but angry I hadn't been better about heeding his warning.

"Go up and take a hot shower while I make you some soup," he ordered.

In no mood to object, I went willingly. The water felt great, and I lingered until he yelled up that the soup was ready. After drying myself and putting on a clean sweatshirt and jeans and then dry socks and shoes, I went down to the kitchen. While I slurped the soup, Dad took out a deck of cards, and when I was finished, we played to pass the time with our guns lying on the table beside us.

It was completely dark outside, except when the lightning momentarily lit everything up like the flash on a camera. We heard the rain pelting the roof and siding on the house and spilling out of the overworked gutters. Dad made a fire in the old kitchen fireplace, and we played on, occasionally arguing over a rule or two. We had settled into a nice conversation when suddenly all the lights went out.

"Must've lost power," Dad said. "The generator should be kicking in any minute unless I forgot to put gas in it."

When the welcome but annoying hum of the generator did not materialize, Dad got up to fetch a flashlight from the cupboard. It was missing, so Dad took out a candle instead and lit it. As the candle's flame flickered along with those in the roaring fireplace, Dad announced, "I'd better go check on that generator. This could be a long storm."

"That candle isn't going to do you any good outside. Want me to come with you?"

"No sense for the two of us to get wet. Why don't you call Mom at Mrs. Harding's house to see if their police protection came and they have power?"

"Why don't we have police protection?"

"I want to catch this guy once and for all. I don't need him getting scared off, only to come back another time when we aren't expecting him."

As Dad prepared to head outside, I picked up the phone, but it was dead!

"The phone is out too, Pop!"

"That's strange. I'll check the wire to the house when I'm out there."

Suddenly Linus sprang up from in front of the fireplace and became visibly agitated. Before I could say anything, he started to bark.

"What's the matter, boy?"

But he was barking too aggressively to pay any attention to me, and growling and baring his teeth in a way I'd never seen him do before.

"Somebody or something is out there," Dad said as he blew out the candle and reached for his weapon.

Already dressed for the outside, he instructed me to pick up my pistol and get under the kitchen table. I reluctantly did as he told me to do. Meanwhile, Linus was behaving like a mad dog, jumping at the front windows in the living room like he was trying to go right through them. Barking and growling, while foaming at the mouth in excitement, he repeatedly smashed into the window and fell back undeterred, only to charge into it again.

I yelled to Dad from under the table, "Stop him, Pop. He's going to kill himself!"

But the only response that came back in the darkness was, "Hush, son, and stay down."

Without warning, the glass on the front window shattered. I thought it was Linus finally smashing through it, but it wasn't. It was a rock—a big one that rolled and came to rest near me in the kitchen. This wasn't the storm; we were under attack!

At that moment, a bolt of lightning lit up the outside. The image I saw was instantly seared in my memory forever!

Dad had opened the front door and was stepping out, gun in hand. Linus was airborne on his way out the broken front window, baring his teeth and growling in a way that scared even me. Stepping out from behind Selma was the figure of a man about to throw a lit bottle or something like it through the window, his gun visible in his other hand. I recognized the figure from the picture in the news. It was the man who abducted Luke.

"Dad, watch out, there's a man behind Selma!" I yelled.

At the same time, Linus's rocketing body smashed into the man face-to-face, head-to-head, and both fell back away from the house and out of sight below the rail of the porch. The lit bottle fell from the man's hand and broke upon hitting the hard, drenched ground, bursting into flames and creating a scene that resembled lighter fluid being sprayed on the smoldering coals of a barbeque. As the man fell in a desperate struggle with Linus, his gun went off, and I saw Dad's body recoil as he was hit and fell to the porch.

Jumping up from under the table, I ran to the door. Dad was on his side and holding his shoulder. "I'm fine, son, stay down," he ordered.

But this time my instincts kicked in, and I sprang into action.

Linus had the man by the throat. His heavy outer coat was on fire, and Linus's fur was singed, but neither of them seemed to be aware as they were locked in a death struggle. The man was desperately trying to bring his gun hand around to shoot Linus when he noticed me out of the corner of his left eye. His reaction left nothing to doubt. Jerking his gun hand toward me, he fired. The bullet whizzed past my head, missing me, and lodged in the front wall of the house.

I jumped over Dad and down the front steps to get a better shot. I didn't want to accidently hit Linus, as he struggled with the fugitive. Determined to stop him before he could harm me or the dog, *I shot him dead without hesitation.*

I stood motionless in the dark, the rain pouring and with the pistol in my hand, now lowered and by my side. Without realizing it, I let it slip from my hand and fall to the ground. I felt no guilt, only relief, for I knew that until this man was dead, Luke would never be free from the threat he posed, and the happiness and tranquility that my family had come to enjoy in this sleepy little place we called home would not be *preserved.*

Sammy and Ernest had been right in what I believed they had told me. When you do the right thing, it'll feel right. And it did.

But with the threat removed and the tension of the moment dissipating, the effect of the adrenaline it had generated began to wear off with each passing minute. Doubts started to seep into my consciousness as the reality and finality of the fact that I'd killed another human being began to tug at my very core. I suspect I was in shock at what had taken place and didn't realize it. Nevertheless, I mustered all the willpower and strength within me to shutter these doubts, focus as best I could on the situation at hand, and assess what needed to be done.

Linus was sprawled on the wet lawn, exhausted from the fight and licking his wounds. Dad had been able to get up and come over to me. Holding his wounded left shoulder with his right hand, he smiled at me and said, "You may have to handle the main sail on the ice boat this year, son."

"I think I can," I replied, but I wasn't sure I could handle that night's events, let alone something that was still at least several weeks away. What he'd said was Dad's way of asking if I was all right without actually asking. And I wanted to assure him that I was, even if I wasn't so sure myself.

"I think so too," he answered with a wink.

I just wanted my innocence back. I wanted to be a little boy again and let my body tremble the way it was fighting me to do. I wanted to bury my head in Dad's chest and cry until I couldn't cry anymore. But I knew I had to be strong—Sagahawk strong—for him and my family and for my ghosts in the village green.

In the end I was. My innocence had been lost, and there was no going back. I'd been forced into manhood before my time.

The rain had begun to let up when I got Dad and Linus into Sally Truck and headed for the hospital. On the way we stopped at Mrs. Harding's house where Grandma, Mom, and Mrs. Harding made a fuss over us. The Southampton police officer who had been stationed there by the police chief to protect them called in to say that the fugitive was dead.

It was over.

nineteen

Dad had the front window fixed, the power and phone lines reconnected, and the house cleaned before he allowed Grandma, Mom, Kelly, and Luke to return. After an investigation, the authorities ruled my actions justified and in self-defense. The only evidence of what had taken place there was the scorched lawn out front, the sling on Dad's arm, the singed fur on Linus, and the bullet hole in the wall of the house. Dad insisted on leaving it, saying it was now part of the history of the place; he called it my badge of courage. Kelly and Luke hardly noticed, and Mom and Grandma gave no indication of being rattled by it. They were strong women. Nope, they went about decorating for Christmas as if nothing had happened.

I tried to do the same, but it wasn't as easy for me. I'd been there to see everything unfold; and I'd killed a man. I went to the cemetery a lot in the days that followed, even when the first dusting of snow had fallen and covered the ground. I needed my brothers and friends to help me get through it until Mary came back out. There is a harsh finality attached to the taking of another human life—even if justified—that a person of conscience must learn to live with, a struggle to not let it define or change who you are. At least, there was for me.

Christmas Eve fell on a Sunday in 1961. Mary and her family came out the day before, on Saturday, December 23. I helped Dr.

Hurd get the tree down from the rack on the station wagon and into the house. It was their family tradition to decorate the tree on Christmas Eve, and they invited our family and Mrs. Harding to come over and help. It was a lot of fun. A fire was roaring in the fireplace, the eggnog was flowing, and a Bing Crosby record was playing on the phonograph. I had a special Christmas ball made for Mary at Hildreth's that I gave her to hang on the tree. It was yellow and white and had "Pierre 1961" written on it. She asked me to explain its significance to her. I promised that I would—when we were alone. She agreed to wait.

After a lovely Christmas Eve dinner, Mary and I went for a walk. The sky was clear and the stars were shining.

"Tell me the significance of the ornament," she said.

"Well, first I picked yellow and white because I know that they're your favorite colors."

"How did you know that? I don't think I ever told you, did I?"

"No, you didn't, but your Dad did inadvertently."

"How?"

"When I was helping him to pack up your station wagon at the end of the summer, I commented on how much I liked the yellow and white color combination on it. He laughed and told me that in 1958 he had to order it from the factory and wait three weeks for it rather than take immediate delivery of a brown and tan one from the Ford dealer's showroom because you had seen the colors in the catalogue and made such a fuss over them. Is that true?"

"Yes, I loved everything in yellow and white back then. I did make a fuss."

"Are yellow and white still your favorite colors? I hope."

"Yes, but I'm not as rigid about it as I once was."

"I see."

"And what is the significance of the name Pierre?"

"First of all, I picked French over English because I thought it was more romantic. As I'm sure you know, Pierre means Peter in French."

"I do, but what is the significance of the name Peter?"

"When I was training to be a crucifer Dad impressed upon me that Peter is the name of the rock on which Christ built his church. Christianity in one form or another has lasted almost two thousand years. 1961 is the rock on which we are building our future together, so I picked Pierre 1961 with the hope that our relationship will be as strong."

Stopping to turn and give me a kiss, she said, "You are so romantic! That's one of the things I love about you."

Reaching into my pocket, I took out a box and gave it to her. "This is my Christmas gift to you," I said. "I want to give it to you now because we won't be together tomorrow morning when you are opening your gifts."

"What is it?" she asked as she took the box and opened it.

"It's a ring," I replied.

Somewhat surprised, she said, "You got me a ring?"

I reached over, took the ring out, and showed it to her. It had a flat, square top with a small diamond in the center and our initials, "J C" and "M H," engraved on the diagonal in each corner of the square. Inside the band was engraved "Pierre 1961."

"It's beautiful," she exclaimed.

Placing the ring on her finger, I said, "I am asking you to go steady and to build our future together. Will you?"

"Of course I will," she answered as she leaned over and kissed and hugged me.

We walked silently hand in hand, content to look at the stars and just be back in each other's company. It was a cold clear night and the chill in the air eventually drove us back inside to the warmth of the fire and the welcome of our families. Mary had to show everyone her gift, and Mom and Mrs. Harding made an appropriate fuss over it, never letting on that they'd helped me get it made.

And so it was that 1961—the year of the rock on which our future relationship was being built—came to a close.

1962

twenty

New Year's Day fell on a Monday in 1962. Mom hosted everyone for dinner at our house. After dinner, Mary and I took a walk on the beach before her family left for the city. It was sunny but cold and windy. We didn't care because we were so absorbed in our own world.

When everyone had left, Dad suggested we go to the toolshed and start working on the ice boat. I don't think he really wanted to do it, but he thought it would help busy my mind and get my thoughts off Mary.

It didn't work. Nothing would. I missed her, and I was going to continue to miss her until I saw her again. Only time could heal what I was feeling. However, we did get quite a bit done and had some fun doing it.

Dad had built the boat himself from quality woods and plywood he had picked up at Thayer's. Most ice boats in the area were built to hold only one person, but Dad built his to hold two so Mom could go along with him. She hated the sport and thought it was too dangerous, so Dad as usual got her goat by naming the boat *Fast Sally* after her. She didn't like the subtle implications of the name. But Dad only threw fuel on the fire by telling her, "Honey, if the shoe fits, wear it."

He loved to tease her, and sometimes when they got into their silly arguments and refused to talk to each other, they made me the go-between. I hated the "Tell your mom this" and "Tell your dad that" stuff. When I was little it scared me because I thought it was real. But later on I just shrugged it off, saying, "Tell him (or her) yourself!"

Dad did have one surprise up his sleeve for me. When I came back to the shed after having been sent to check on Luke, he had sanded off the name *Fast Sally* and had painted on a new name. The boat was now called the *Proud Mary*, and it belonged to me. Mom was glad to get the monkey off her back but was worried that I would get hurt racing the "darn contraption," as she called it. She made me promise that I would wear a helmet and goggles and gloves and spiked shoes, among other things that I can't even remember. I wore the helmet, the goggles, and the gloves.

Two weeks later, on Sunday, January 14, the *Proud Mary* was ready to go. Dad and I hauled her down to Ellis Pond in Sally Truck. The pond was what Dad referred to as *hard water*—a smooth, black, slippery ice, and there was a steady but not-too-cold breeze blowing. The conditions were perfect, and I could hardly wait to get underway. The course was laid out in a straight line up and downwind. Streaking over the ice and tacking back and forth with the chill of the air on my rosy red cheeks was exhilarating. I couldn't get enough.

With his arm still in the sling, Dad stood watching and beaming with pride at how well I was handling the *Proud Mary*.

It wasn't long before we were approached to race. A school buddy named Mike Johnson came up to me and challenged me then and there to a contest. I said yes, and we were off and racing. Pushing the boat to its limit, I was sailing *close haul*, within a forty-five degree angle of the wind, which was coming from the forward direction. Mike was trailing me but so close that any mistake on my part could cost me the lead. So I tacked to cover when he did. Then it happened: my halyard snapped and Mike went sailing by me. When I got back to Dad, I was disappointed, but it was early in the season, and breakage was to be expected. We hauled the *Proud Mary* home and made the repairs.

When we came in the house, Mom had hot chocolate waiting, and Dad and I sat by the fire to warm ourselves. My mind began to drift to Valentine's Day. In exactly one month, on Wednesday, February 14, I would be going into the city to see Mary for the day. Mom had a doctor's appointment that morning, and I would be driving in with her. She already had cleared it with my school and Mrs. Hurd. Mary also was going to be allowed to miss school.

The plan was that Mary and I were going to shop on Fifth Avenue while Mom was at the doctor's office. Then Mrs. Hurd would meet the three of us for lunch and the matinee showing of *A Man for all Seasons* on Broadway. Dad had gotten the tickets for us, but gave his ticket to Mrs. Hurd. With Grandma away again helping her sister, he preferred to stay home with Kelly and Luke and Linus. He planned to have a late dinner alone with Mom in Bridgehampton when we got back.

"What are you thinking about, Joe?"

"Valentine's Day," I replied.

"Reminds me—I'd better get out and shop for a card for your mother."

"And flowers and candy too," I added.

"Yeah, I know. What are you going to get Mary?"

"I don't know. I can't afford all that stuff."

"Why don't you give her a single red rose, some chocolate kisses, and a card? If nothing else, you should get her the card—the mushier the better. I'm warning you, they get upset if you don't give them a card."

"I'll get her a card, and I like the idea of the rose and chocolate kisses. I can handle that."

"Good. Now that we've resolved Valentine's Day, how are you doing?"

"Well, I really miss her."

"No, I meant regarding the kidnapping incident and the shooting of the man."

"Dad, I know this may sound strange, but I'm at peace with it now. I won't deny that it has been a struggle for me. I wonder sometimes if I could've merely wounded him. I was so panic-stricken and afraid after he shot at me. I was worried about hitting Linus. All I could think to do was to take the clear shot when I had it—and shoot to kill. I wish it hadn't happened, but it's best that it did. Our family never would've had a moment's rest while that man was alive. If I hadn't killed him and he came back to hurt Luke, I wouldn't be able to forgive myself."

"I think that's a healthy way to look at it. Even though the man was trying to shoot you, making your actions justified in self defense, and the authorities cleared you, I know it's not an easy thing to have to live with. I'm glad to see you dealing with it so well. I still live with the memory of my bombs exploding beneath the *Sweet Sally*, knowing that every burst of light brought with it death and destruction to countless lives. Even when they are the enemy and trying to kill you, too, that doesn't make it easy. Today the Germans and the Japanese are our friends, and they're good people—look at Max Werner. It's a crazy world we live in."

"What made you ask? Have I been doing something that gave you reason for concern?" I asked Dad.

"No, it's nothing like that. Mom has always objected to my taking you duck hunting with me because she doesn't like guns, and she didn't want me encouraging you to use them."

"Yeah, I know. Remember how she wouldn't buy me any toy guns until I started making them out of her hangers? Then she finally gave in and let me buy one."

"She meant well then, and she still means well. I had a talk with her the other day to say that considering what you've been through, it hardly makes sense to try and shield you from the use of guns. She has agreed to let you go hunting with me, providing

I teach you to kill only what you will eat. She doesn't want to see you just killing for sport, and I agree with her."

"I agree with that, too, Dad."

"Good, I expected that's how you'd feel. But I must ask you: Are you sure that handling a gun this soon after what happened isn't going to bring all the bad memories and emotions back to haunt you?"

"I don't think so, Dad. In a strange way, it might be good for me if that makes any sense."

"I think it does ... I think it does."

"When are you planning for us to go?"

"I thought we'd do it later this month before the season ends. That gives us time to get everything ready and Linus time to be fully healed. I want to take him with us to do the retrieving."

"Where will we go, and what will we be going for?"

"I'd like to go for scoters and long-tailed ducks on Peconic Bay. But we'll see."

"That sounds great."

At that point Mom came in to tell us that dinner was ready. Ironically, we were having roasted Long Island duckling with orange sauce, wild rice, and green beans. After Mrs. Davis died, Mom helped old man Davis out once a week with the bookkeeping on his duck farm in Mecox. Grateful for her assistance, he often sent her home with some duckling as a special treat for us. It was one of my favorites. Dad reciprocated by sending Mom there with potatoes, corn, and tomatoes from time to time.

During dinner Mom reminded me that I'd be graduating from the little white schoolhouse in June. It was time for us to be thinking about what high school I planned to attend. I was a little surprised because I'd always assumed that I would attend Bridgehampton High School.

"Why wouldn't I go to Bridgehampton?" I asked.

"You certainly can if that's what you want," she said.

"What other choice do I have?"

"Your father has a distant cousin, Dorothy, who works at the Iona Preparatory School in New Rochelle that is run by the Irish Christian Brothers. She told him that you can come live with her and attend that school if you like. Dad thinks it will do you some good to spend a little time outside of Sagahawk. The Wheatleys have a son coming back from the service who would like to learn how to farm. He may come work for Dad while you're gone. If for any reason you don't like it, you can come home at the end of the year."

"It sounds worth considering, but I wasn't expecting anything like this. I need some time to think about it a little more."

"Of course. You have plenty of time to decide. Keep in mind that Mary will be going to the Kent School in Connecticut next year, and you'll be a lot closer to her if you're in New Rochelle than if you're here. I wish we could afford to send you to a boarding school like Kent, but we can't. The only reason we can afford Iona is because the brothers gave us a break since Cousin Dorothy works there."

"How far apart are they?"

"I would say about an hour and twenty minutes."

"So I could go see Mary on a Saturday or Sunday?"

"Yes. Cousin Dorothy says there is a train that runs up that way, and she could take you back and forth to the station."

"What would I do if I wanted to come home?"

"You would have to take the train into the city and then catch another train to come out here. However, the football coach at Iona lives in East Islip and he said he would be willing to give you a ride back and forth to his house, and then we would have to make arrangements from there."

"I don't know, Mom. I have to think about it."

"I understand. Keep in mind Dad thinks you have a better chance of getting into a school like Boston College from Iona than from a school out here. You certainly would have a better shot at playing football in college if you went there."

"I know you and Dad are trying to do what is best for me. I think I just need some time to get used to the idea."

"You think about it," Mom said as she got up to start clearing the dishes. Luke and I helped her with the kitchen as Dad went back into the living room to read the Sunday paper. When we were done, I went in to speak with Dad.

"How do you feel about this, Pop?"

"I remained quiet at the table because I have mixed feelings about it, Joe. On the one hand, I think it will broaden your horizons and help your chances of getting into college. On the other hand, I don't know if I'm ready to see you leave home yet. More importantly, I don't think Luke is."

"Yeah, I think I'm having the same problems with it as you are. I wish I could go to school here for another year or two and then transfer when I'm old enough to have a senior driver's license."

"It would be tougher making friends and breaking into sports, but it isn't a bad compromise."

"Well, I guess I have a lot to think about," I said as I got up to go to my room.

It'd been a long day, and I was tired. After a hot shower, I got into bed with plans to read. I didn't get very far before I fell asleep with the light on and the book still in my hands. Mom had to come in and turn off the light and put the book on my nightstand. I never awoke until morning.

twenty-one

As the last weekend in January approached, Dad and I were putting the finishing touches on our preparations for duck hunting. The anticipation was building in me with each passing day. We put a fresh coat of camouflage paint on the low-profile boat that he'd modified years ago for hunting fowl. We oiled, fueled, then tested and camouflaged the small power motor before attaching it to the boat.

Next we installed a tentlike structure made of camouflaged canvas. We would stretch it out over the top of the boat and hide under it when we were hunting. Dad checked and cleaned our weapons and loaded them and the ammunition on board. Also, once the decoys were cleaned and painted, we put them under the seats.

When everything else was done, we hooked the boat and trailer to Sally Truck. Before leaving, Dad double checked the times and the range differences between high and low tide.

"Why is it important to check the tide cycles this way?" I asked him as we were putting on our gear.

"For two reasons," he answered.

Then taking a moment to puff on his pipe, he continued, "For one thing, it can influence the behavior of the birds, and knowing how they might react can give you an edge. Also, you don't want to get stuck in water that's too shallow because the tide has run out on you and the bottom is too mucky for you to wade ashore."

"Yeah, there's no way I want to get stuck out there in this cold weather."

"Neither do I. Now please go get Linus in the truck while I use the head."

"Okay."

As the big moment finally came and we were pulling out of the driveway, I asked, "Where are we going to hunt, Dad?"

"Originally, I thought we would go out by Theodore Roosevelt Park in Montauk, but I think in light of the tide cycle and weather conditions, we will go off Cedar Point in Sag Harbor."

Somewhat concerned, I hesitated for a few minutes and then asked, "What weather conditions?"

"There's an outside chance that a storm may blow in, according to the weather folks."

"Are you sure it's safe to go?"

Choosing not to answer me at first, Dad puffed on his pipe. He then took his time exhaling as he shifted Sally truck into a higher gear with the pipe in his hand. Smiling at me he finally replied, "I've been at this for years, trust me."

I didn't answer and we drove in silence for a while.

As we neared Cedar Point, Dad reached over, mussed my hair and demanded, "Well!"

I simply nodded and said okay.

When we got there, my worries changed to excitement as we launched the boat and climbed aboard with Linus. Dad started the motor and set out, but not too far from shore because of the possible storm. We next set about floating the decoys in the water on lines that we tied to the boat. Then the three of us sat and patiently waited.

Suddenly, there they were, silhouetted against the dawn sky as they flew in formation, honking and flapping their wings as they went. Dad confirmed with his binoculars that we could hunt them. Seeing the decoys as they approached, some of the ducks started to land, and then more followed suit. We aimed and fired. Pop's shot hit its mark, but mine missed. We then loaded and fired once more. Dad again scored, but I didn't. Wanting to give me another chance, Dad had us reload and shoot. Again Dad hit his, but I only wounded mine, and the poor bird fell to the water where it flapped around.

We stopped shooting and Linus was sent to fetch the birds. One by one he brought their limp carcasses back to the boat, holding them gently in his mouth. When they were on board, Pop attempted to shoot the wounded bird that was still struggling in the water. As he did, he told me it was important not to leave a wounded animal to suffer. The shots missed, and the poor creature escaped to the rocky shore and hid amongst them, unable to fly. Linus gingerly climbed onto the rocks, plucked the weakened creature from its refuge, and brought the wounded mallard to the boat, where Dad put it out of its misery.

By the time we were finished for the day, Dad had bagged two pintails, three mallards, and one black duck. I had the one mallard I'd wounded and that Dad finished off for me. I told myself that it wasn't bad for a first-time duck hunter. I was anxious to get better and wanted to hunt some more. However, the skies had begun to look threatening, and Pop insisted it was time to head for shore.

We loaded the boat on the trailer, packed up the gear, and beat the storm home. On the way, Dad asked me, "So how'd you like it?"

"I loved it," I told him. "I wish we could've stayed and hunted longer."

"There'll be plenty of time for more hunting."

"I guess you're right. Thanks again for taking me."

Once in the house, we sat in front of the fire and told Mom about everything that had happened to us. Then Dad went out to the shed to clean and freeze the ducks even though the storm was still raging. The rest of the day I spent reading homework assignments and anticipating my upcoming trip to New York City to visit Mary. Valentine's Day was only a little more than two weeks away. But they would be a hard two and a half weeks.

The next morning, Pop wanted to get started mending fences on the back five and wanted my help before I went to school. Up before the sun, we set out as the first light was appearing in the east. A heavy mist silently hugged the ground that severely limited visibility and made driving difficult until the morning sun would force it from its perch. A chilling wind was blowing, the kind that goes right through you. Dad nevertheless insisted on riding with his window open.

"Why can't you shut that window?"

"In a few minutes you're going to be working outside, so you might as well get used to it."

"Come on, Dad. Close the window before I freeze to death."

"You're wasting your breath. I want you wide awake when we get there."

"I will be. I promise."

"Interesting isn't it? When you're out there ice boating and duck hunting, I hear no complaints. When you're on your way to mend fencing, you're freezing to death. Stop the whining and toughen up."

"When you're moving around and excited, it's one thing, but when you just got out of a warm bed and are still half asleep, it's another."

"That was one hell of a storm last night: a combination of driving rain, treacherous sleet and blinding snow. It had to be brutal to be out in. I'm glad we got back before it hit. At least it didn't result in much accumulation."

"I wouldn't know; I slept through it all."

"And that is why I want the window open: to rid you of that sleepiness!"

"Yeah, yeah, yeah."

I wasn't really paying a whole lot of attention, but the last thing I thought I heard Dad say was, "This mist is a bear. I can't see a damn thing!" And then …

Bam! I got thrown forward as Sally Truck came to an abrupt halt. Still half asleep and with my hands in my coat pockets and my body slouched down on the seat, I was powerless to protect myself from smashing into the dash or windshield. Pop's oversized right hand grabbed my left coat shoulder the very last second and held me back.

As he did, I heard him exclaim in an audibly shocked tone, "Oh, my God!"

"What is it, Dad?" I asked in a dazed voice.

I looked through the morning mist, but I wasn't sure what I was observing. Debris was everywhere. Some pieces were stuck in the ground like a javelin as if they had been jammed in there by someone on purpose. There was an open suitcase with some clothing blown around and scattered about. Then I had to rub my eyes and take a second look to confirm for myself that what I was seeing through the thick, soupy stuff was the tail of an airplane sticking up in front of me! But how could it be?

"What is it, Dad?" I repeated.

"I think it's a small plane. Stay in the truck while I check it out. There may still be somebody alive in there, but I don't want to get any closer with the truck. I'm worried about fire. If anything happens, take the truck and head for home. Call Judy at the police station. She'll alert the fire department. Got it?"

I mustered a yeah in response.

With that, Dad got out of the truck, grabbed a crow bar from the back, and called Linus to come with him. They disappeared into the mist while I could do nothing except sit helplessly watching.

Time marches slowly, it seems, when you're worried and scared. It was marching very slowly for me that morning.

"Dad, you okay?" I yelled.

"I'm fine," came back the muffled voice from the murky haze.

Then I heard Linus barking the way he did the day before when he had located the wounded duck in the rocks. It was a beckoning bark with a tinge of excitement and immediacy to it. I told myself he'd found something. There must still be somebody alive.

A momentary silence followed only to be punctuated by more of Linus's barking. He was excitedly and impatiently calling out with anticipation in his voice, much as he had done as a pup when Mom was getting ready to feed him. It was a distinctive bark, and I would recognize it anywhere. It was accompanied by the creaking and screeching of bending metal. I told myself that Dad must have been prying open the fuselage.

"Dad, you okay?"

"I'm fine," came back the muffled voice from the mist once again.

It was hard to remain sitting there, but I told myself I had to be disciplined. As in football, everybody must play their assigned roles and stay in position. Otherwise, a broken play might lead to a touchdown. I would be their only hope of getting help if fire broke out. If I was out of position and with them when an explosive fire engulfed us, we might all perish. I had to stay back out of harm's way.

Then the barking and groaning of the bending metal stopped and was replaced by what sounded like the cries of a baby. The temptation was too much. I jumped from the truck and ran into the muck, stumbling over debris in the confusion. When I got to the scene, two bodies were lying on the ground. Dad must have pulled them from the wreckage. One was the nearly decapitated corpse of a man, and the other was the mangled body of a woman. Her clothing must have been partially ripped off by the force of the crash, exposing her bloodstained torso. Dad was standing next to her with a crying baby in his arms.

"Get some blankets from the back of the truck! Hurry!" he ordered.

"Okay," I replied. I ran to get them, too consumed by the event to worry any longer about the cold, or to be angry with Dad for not having told me about them when I was cold.

When I came back, Dad wrapped the baby in the cleanest blanket and had Linus lay next to it. He used the other blankets to cover the two bodies.

As he did, he turned to me and said, "I'm sorry you had to see this, son. You're too young to have to witness this sort of thing."

I tried to say that I would be okay but lost it and began to throw up all over the ground. I wanted to suppress it, but Dad told me I would feel better once I got it all out. He came over and patted me on the back with his right hand as I was bent over in convulsions. When I thought I was finished, I tried to stand up, but I was brought back down to my knees with more retching. Finally, I began to regain my composure.

Wiping my mouth with an extra blanket, I struggled to ask, "What do you think caused this to happen, Dad?"

"It looks to me like they were in trouble and trying to find East Hampton airport, but ran out of fuel and sky when the storm forced them down. The pilot appears to have lost his bearings and must've become disoriented at the end because they came down at a steep angle. The mother seems to have taken the baby out of its bassinet in the back seat and held it in her arms. I think her doing so may have saved its life. It appears that the baby was cushioned and protected by the mother's body from the full force of the impact."

With that he wiped his brow and picked up the baby from next to Linus. He started for the truck with the precious cargo snugly in his grasp. Linus and I followed him, and we all got in Sally Truck's cab. Dad told me to roll up that damn open window of his, and drive while he tried to warm the baby. I drove as quickly as I could without jostling the infant too much. The mist was now beginning to clear, and the visibility was noticeably better.

When we got to the house, Mom was up and must've become worried to hear us returning so soon. As we pulled up, she came running out of the front door and down the steps in her bathrobe and curlers. Seeing Dad covered in blood, sitting in the passenger seat, and holding what she thought was his stomach, she panicked and fumbled clumsily to rip open the front door, screaming all the while.

"Oh, my Lord, John, are you okay? Are you okay, honey? What happened?"

"I'm fine, Sally. I really am. Calm down, sweetheart."

Feeling his face and upper torso in much the same way that a blind person might, she seemed to have to prove to herself that he really was okay. Somewhat reassured and seeing the bundled blanket in his lap, she asked, "What do you have there, John?"

"It's a baby."

"It's a baby? A baby *what?*" she asked, apparently thinking we had found an animal in distress.

"No, honey, it's a real baby. I think it's a baby girl."

"A baby girl. Here give her to me," Mom said as she instinctively reached for the bloodstained bundle.

Dad was more than happy to give the infant to her.

As she took the baby, she again asked, "What happened? Where did you find her?"

"A small plane crashed on the back five. Unfortunately, I think her parents were killed in the accident, because I found the bodies of two adults, a man and a woman."

"Oh, my Lord, let me get her inside."

"Be careful, honey, I don't know if she has any internal injuries."

"I'll try to check her out, but you better call it in, and get an ambulance out here right away."

"I will," Dad said following Mom into the house.

As I watched him make the call to Judy at the police station, I noticed for the first time that the years were beginning to take their toll on Dad. He was slumped over a bit and visibly tired. Luke had still been sleeping but came down with his blanket and toy stuffed lamb in hand to see what was going on. He was consumed by the presence of the baby, and Mom had to keep him from the infant until she was sure there were no internal injuries. Kelly was in the shower and came down to help Mom when she was done. Grandma had gone down to the basement to find one of Luke's old bottles, and now was sterilizing it and warming some milk for the baby.

I went up to take a shower and change out of my messed-up clothing. When I came back down, both the fire rescue unit and volunteer ambulance corps had responded along with several fire trucks, a local Southampton patrol car, and a New York State Police trooper. Luke was on the front porch in his glory, watching all the blinking and revolving lights as they swirled about him with the radio chatter and sirens in the background. High above, the sound of helicopters could be heard. An officer was directing traffic in front of the house as folks came from all over to see what was happening. Then the coroner's black station wagon pulled up, deflating the mood of the crowd, which fell silent upon seeing it.

In the days that followed, Dad and I tried to stay out of the way of the investigators, who had cordoned off the crash site. It made our work more time-consuming and difficult to accomplish, but their job was not an easy one, and we didn't want to make it any more burdensome for them. Finally, they were done, and a large flatbed truck was brought in to haul the plane's remains away to a hangar at the airport, where the investigation would enter another phase. Slowly the facts began to emerge.

The *Sagahawk Chronicle* on January 31, 1962, reported:

Fatal Plane Crash Raises Ghosts from Sagahawk's Past

In the early morning hours of Monday, January 29, a tragic plane crash claimed the lives of a young

Maine couple and left a newborn baby orphaned. The crash occurred on the Carr farm on Sagg Main. Killed were the pilot, William Herbert Sanders, 28, and his wife of one year, Mildred Pierce Sanders, 27. Their three-month-old baby girl, Samantha Augustine Sanders, survived and was rescued by John Carr and his son, Joe, as they set out to work on the farm. The couple and their newborn were en route from Kennebunkport, Maine, to Exton, Pennsylvania, to reconnect with some distant relatives when the crash occurred in a blinding storm.

William Sanders was a new pilot who hadn't obtained his instrument rating. Speculation is that he was desperately trying to outrun the weather when he became trapped in it. The plane was a new Piper PA-28-150 Cherokee that the pilot had limited experience flying. One investigator said, "We think the young pilot became disoriented in the teeming rain and blinding snow, lost track of the horizon, and in his panicked state, failed to monitor his fuel consumption. Thus far, we've found nothing mechanically wrong with the plane other than it had run out of fuel before it crashed." According to a family friend who asked not to be identified, the baby was colicky. Further speculation is that the baby's crying may have presented an additional distraction for the pilot because the mother had removed the baby from her bassinet, and was holding her at the time of the crash. This may have saved the baby's life.

In a twist of fate, the farm on which the plane crashed was once owned by Mrs. Sanders's ancestor and namesake, Mildred Pierce, who sold the farm to John Carr's grandfather when she moved to Philadelphia in the early 1900s. Mrs. Pierce's son, August Pierce, had died of pneumonia after saving the life of John Carr's grandfather. The baby, Samantha Augustine, presumably is named for August and his brother Samuel Pierce. It wasn't lost on young Joe Carr that they wouldn't have been there to rescue Samantha if August Pierce hadn't rescued his great-grandfather a little more than ninety years earlier.

Mr. and Mrs. Sanders are said to have no close living relatives, causing authorities to be concerned that there may be no immediate family to care for the baby. John and Sally Carr have offered to take her in and raise her. The senior Carr said, "It's not often in this life that you get the chance to return a favor that's almost a century old, a favor done for your grandfather, and in the process also gain a beautiful daughter to whom you can give a very special gift—the gift of being raised in her ancestral home as part of a loving and grateful family." If that happens, she will be the first Pierce to reside in Sagahawk in almost sixty years.

And so it was in Sagahawk on a cold January day in 1962, only nine months away from our rendezvous with a warning of impending doom.

twenty-two

We were able to go into the city for Valentine's Day, because Sammy, as she quickly came to be called by everyone, wasn't scheduled to be released from the hospital before the sixteenth of the month. It was good to see Mary again, although I wasn't happy with her for insisting on calling me Jolting Joe. Her argument was that protecting Luke from his kidnapper and rescuing Sammy qualified me as a genuine superhero. Mom just smiled and gave me the same line Dad liked to use on her: "If the shoe fits, wear it." It was a small price to pay for being with Mary again, even if it was only for the day. And what a day it turned out to be.

After seeing Mom to her doctor's appointment on Park Avenue near Fifty-Seventh Street, I surprised Mary and took her to a place Mom told me she would like; a place I'd seen the year before in the movie *Breakfast at Tiffany's* with Audrey Hepburn. I took her to Tiffany's on Fifth Avenue to look at jewelry.

I was in shock to see the price tags. I'd no idea jewelry could be that expensive. The ring I had made for Mary at Christmas cost me fifty dollars engraved, and I thought that was a lot! Some of the things I was seeing cost over one thousand dollars.

Mary sensed my awkwardness and started to tease me that the dirt beneath my nails was going to have to be mine and not someone else's before I'd be in a position to shop there. I wasn't sure that even then I'd be able to afford it.

Nevertheless I wanted to put on my best face, so I said, "Someday, Mary, I am going to walk in here with you and tell the salesperson, 'Give her anything she wants!'"

"Oh, yeah!" She laughed, and asked, "Are you going to be wearing a mask and pointing a gun at him when you do?"

I don't know why, because I hadn't thought about it for a while now, but those words hit home with me. All the emotions of that dark, rainy night last fall came rushing back at me like an oncoming train. Mary could see the change in my expression, and wrapped her two arms around my right arm.

Burying her head in my shoulder, she whispered, "Joe, I don't need or care about fancy jewelry. All I want and will ever need is you and your love."

"I know that, Mary. That's not it."

I decided against telling her the real reasons for my sudden change in mood. Instead, I left it that I just wanted to be able to give her something special.

"You already have. I have you and I have the ring you gave me at Christmas—I feel very special, very blessed! You do understand that, don't you?"

As I said yes, there was a commotion behind me and I heard a lady scream. Turning, I saw a man grabbing the woman's shopping bag and purse and then making a run for the exit. He was practically out the door when I realized that I was the only one that had a chance to stop him. Leaping into action, I ran after him and was fast enough to catch and tackle him as he was going through the doorway. We both fell to the ground, rolling and tossing as he let go of the bag and the purse. Escaping my grip, he jumped up and ran out of the store. I got up, dusted myself off, picked up the lady's things and gave them back to her.

At this point, a crowd gathered around us, and the store manager came over, accompanied by a guard. The lady thanked me and asked me my name.

"Joe Carr, ma'am."

"Is that young lady there your friend?"

"Yes, ma'am. She's my girlfriend. We're going steady."

"Well, after such a good deed, it would be a shame to see you leave the store empty-handed, especially when you have someone so special with you."

Turning to the manager, she said, "Mr. Wingfield, please help this young man pick out something appropriate for his girlfriend and put it on my charge."

"Yes, ma'am, I'll be happy to do that," he replied.

She then turned and smiled at us, complimented me on my tackle, and thanked me once again. With that, she walked out the door and disappeared into the faceless crowd passing by on the busy Fifth Avenue sidewalk.

Mr. Wingfield turned to me and asked, "Do you know who that was?"

"No," I said.

"Her family owns the New York Giants."

"Really?"

"Really! So coming from her, a compliment on your tackling means something," he said as he started to laugh.

Once again feeling somewhat awkward, I just smiled and answered, "I guess so!"

Mr. Wingfield then helped Mary pick out a very pretty broach, which he proceeded to pin on her jacket for her. It wasn't very expensive by Tiffany's standards, but very generous of the lady and far more than I would be able to afford anytime soon, if at all. The beaming smile on Mary's face was priceless.

As we walked out of the store arm in arm, Mary looked at me and said, "Well, Jolting Joe, you certainly earned your nickname today. In fact, I'd say that you outdid yourself!"

"And I did it without a gun and a mask!" I exclaimed.

"Ouch, I guess I had that coming."

"Yes, you did!"

Stopping in the middle of the crowded Fifth Avenue sidewalk, oblivious to the annoyed crowds having to make their way around us, she leaned over and gave me a kiss before whispering sorry. Then she looked down at her broach and said, "Thanks, I'll always treasure this Valentine's Day gift and the special meaning it holds for me. I love you so much, Joe."

"I love you too, Mary."

At this point, some guy yelled, "Come on you two, let's move it. Whaddaya think you're doing?"

A cabby, observing everything from behind the wheel of his car while waiting for the light to change, yelled back at the guy: "Leave them alone, Mack! Don't be a moron. Can't ya see they're in love?"

Then the light changed, horns began to honk, and all moved on. The New York minute had passed, but not the memory of it for Mary and me.

When we met Mom and Mrs. Hurd for lunch, Mary had to tell them the whole story down to the last details. Of course she had to show off her new Tiffany broach. It was almost a relief for me when we took our seats in the theater and the play began. I was so embarrassed by all the unwanted attention.

While Mary enjoyed the play, I took pleasure in watching her, especially her facial expressions in the reflective glow of the stage lights. The play may have been *A Man for All Seasons*, but for me it was a face, her face, for all seasons, and it always would be. I knew it now more than ever.

When we were saying our good-byes, Mrs. Hurd winked at me and said, "We'll try to make it out east one weekend in March, maybe for the Saint Patrick's Day weekend."

I got excited at the prospect because Saint Patrick's Day would fall on a Saturday, which meant that I'd be able to take Mary to the corned beef dinner and dance that was scheduled to take place at the firehouse after the parade. All the way home in the car, I planned for it.

Samantha Augustine Sanders Carr was adopted, not just by Mom and Dad, but by the entire community of Sagahawk. Somewhat of a miniature celebrity, she received royal treatment in and out of the home. Her crib, changing table, nightstand, chest of drawers, and a Mickey Mouse lamp were donated by Hildreth's. Her baby formula and diapers were a gift from Nickel's Pharmacy, and several of her outfits were contributed by Christine Broughm's Baby Wear of Bridgehampton. It seemed everyone in town who had recently had a baby girl also brought over clothes and toys.

When they came out for the Saint Patrick's Day weekend, Mrs. Hurd dusted off and brought over Mary's old baby carriage that was languishing in the basement of their house on Hedges Lane. Billy at the local spirits shop always snuck an extra bottle of wine or bourbon into the bag when Mom went in to buy liquor, and Thayer's dropped off a little mechanical swing. Mom's doctors and the hospital refused to bill her for their services. Many of the ladies in town brought us an endless supply of casseroles, roasts, trays of macaroni, and pies and cookies, several of which were made from prized family recipes. Dad's farmer friends gave us chickens, turkeys, and various types of produce, and old man Davis saw to it that we always had a duck or two in the freezer for Sunday dinners. And so it went.

Dad liked to say that the Pierce family had been one of the founding families of Sagahawk, and that it was as if the young princess had returned to assume her rightful place on the throne. He may have been kidding, but it really wasn't very far from the truth. The village elders voted to allow the late Mr. and Mrs. Sanders to be buried in the Pierce grave at the village green.

While this in and of itself was remarkable, what made it

especially noteworthy was that they made an exception and permitted the two of them to be buried there even though there was only one remaining spot. They reasoned that since the grave was so old, it wouldn't be a problem. However, they required the volunteers to painstakingly dig the grave by hand and under the supervision of the coroner so as not to disturb any of the other remains. Mom kidded that it looked more like an archeological dig than a grave digging. But they eventually completed the labor of love, and the young parents were buried together. Father Thompson gave the graveside blessing, and Dad said the eulogy. He finished by paraphrasing in English the words of the sailor aboard Tristan's ship in Wagner's opera *Tristan und Isolde*:

Fresh blows the wind to the homeland;

My [children], where are you waiting?

"In heaven with Mildred, the other Pierces, and Pickering, I'm sure," he added.

When he was finished there wasn't a dry eye in the crowd.

The culminating event for me came on the Saturday of Saint Patrick's Day. It happened when Jimmy O'Donoghue, a local police officer, who was directing traffic by the Candy Kitchen on the Montauk Highway, stopped traffic in all directions to let Mom cross with Sammy in the Hurds' baby carriage. With traffic backed up as far as the eye could see, he stopped to bend down and admire Sammy, tickling her on the chin before tipping his hat to Mom. All of this took place while city folks in their fancy cars sat cooling their heels.

The princess owned the town, and her subjects were set on reminding the weekend visitors that they were merely passing interlopers. To their credit, not a horn was heard! Even they seemed to understand, or at least acquiesce. After all, they were in the presence of royalty!

Mom was worried about how Kelly and Luke would react to Sammy and all the attention she would be garnering. Kelly seemed to relish the idea of having a sister—an ally in what she viewed as a household dominated by a male brotherhood of me and Luke. Now the odds were even at three apiece. Mom, she, and Sammy would be able to hold their own against Dad, me, and Luke. I didn't see things in such an exaggerated fashion, but I was happy to oblige her and cede to my sister the responsibility for helping Mom with Sammy. Changing diapers, even royal ones, weren't part of my superhero job description. Mary capitalized on my squeamishness and never missed an opportunity to tease me, reminding me constantly that I'd have to learn how to do it when we were married. I told myself that some things are best left to the future.

In a moment of weakness, I did feel sorry for Kelly in early April. She had a beautiful singing voice. Unbeknownst to Mom and Dad, she'd been asked by three high school boys from the north side of Route 27 to sing with their band at a Bridgehampton High School dance. Their regular girl singer got herself in trouble and had to drop out the last minute. A local disc jockey was present at the dance and heard them. He found the band an agent and a recording studio, and they recorded a version of "Angel Baby," a song made famous by Rosie and the Originals a year or so earlier, with Kelly singing the lead.

When Mom found out, she went ballistic, not so much because the boys were from the other side of town, but because Kelly was only thirteen years old and too young in her opinion to be hanging around with them. The guys found another girl singer, and Kelly settled back into her routine—that is, until the disc jockey started playing the record on his Long Island radio station.

The song was a local sensation, and was heard by a weekender who was a booking agent for *The Ed Sullivan Show.* He wanted to have the band appear on the show, and contacted them. They came over and asked Kelly to appear with them, worried that the booking agent wouldn't be interested if the lead singer was not the singer on the recording. Mom dug her heels in and refused. Kelly was understandably devastated, and I found myself feeling bad for her. The band gave up and decided to go with their new lead singer, who would lip-sync the song. It wasn't ideal, but it was the best they could do under the circumstances.

When Kelly and I found out that because of a teacher's meeting, there was no school on the Monday after the show, we concocted a scheme. On the Sunday night of the performance, she would tell Mom she had a sleepover at her friend's house. I would come and get her and bring her to the train. Mary would meet her in the city and bring her to the Ed Sullivan Theater. After the show, Kelly would stay with the Hurds, and Mary would put her on a train in the morning. I would meet her at the station in Bridgehampton. We borrowed the money for the train ticket from Luke's piggy bank with every intention of putting it back.

As crazy a scheme as it was, at first it seemed to work just fine. Kelly went to her sleepover, and I went and picked her up and put her on the train. I spoke with the conductor, who promised to keep an eye on Kelly until Mary met her. Then I went home as if nothing had happened. The show ran from eight to nine that Sunday night. Dad and Mom only occasionally watched it because our reception wasn't good.

As luck would have it, that night they decided to watch, and the reception wasn't half bad. Mom turned white as a ghost when she saw Kelly being introduced with the band and singing "Angel Baby." They were a huge hit, and the audience gave them a great ovation.

When it was over, Mom went to call Mrs. Robson, in whose house her sleepover was supposed to be. She told Mom that I'd picked Kelly up earlier in the day. I knew I was in trouble. The only question was: How much trouble?

Mom came back into the living room with tears in her eyes and asked me, "You helped her disobey me didn't you?"

"I'm sorry, Mom, I did."

"How could you hurt me like this?"

It was killing me to see her cry, and I realized for the first time, that it may not have been as harmless an idea as I at first thought it was.

With my head down, I mustered the strength to say, "I didn't mean to hurt you, Mom. I just felt so bad for Kelly. How often would an opportunity like this come along for her?"

"After I've lost two sons, and almost lost a third to a kidnapper, you take this kind of reckless chance with your sister. I've always thought you were so responsible. How could you do this? What if something happens to her? She has no experience with handling herself in these types of circumstances. Do you really think it's worth risking her life like this? I'm shocked and hurt that you'd do this."

I thought of telling her that I'd taken reasonable precautions, such as speaking to the conductor and arranging for Mary to pick her up and return her to the train, but I knew in my heart that they fell short of what concerned Mom. I just never thought of Luke's kidnapping, how raw its memory still was, the loss of the twins, and the scars my mother's heart would be carrying because of them.

For the first time, I saw how stupid a stunt I'd pulled. If anything ever happened to Kelly because of it, I would never forgive myself. I wished I could go back in time and undo what I'd done, but I couldn't. It was done, and I was left to hope that it turned out all right. Seeing Mom so stressed out and disappointed in me was ripping the heart right out of me.

It was an almost welcome relief when Dad stood up and said, "Let's go, son."

He didn't have to say anything else. It was understood. We were on our way to the shed. It was one of the hardest lickings he'd ever given me. I felt his seething anger with every sting of the strap. I didn't think I would be able to sit for a week. But the sting of that old, black leather belt was nothing compared to the sting of seeing Mom so upset and hurt by me. I never wanted to be responsible for causing her that kind of pain again.

After he was done with me, he put his belt back on and told me to go to my room. I told him I'd arranged for Kelly to stay with the Hurds. He just nodded his head and grunted. When we got back to the house, he told Mom to call Mrs. Hurd and tell her that he'd be coming for Kelly and expected to get there around eleven to eleven-thirty that night. He then kissed Mom good-bye, got into Sally Truck, and drove to the city.

Dr. and Mrs. Hurd were surprised to learn from Mom that she and Dad knew nothing of what was going on. My scheme even managed to get Mary in trouble with her parents. Fortunately, Dad had calmed down by the time he got to the city and left Kelly to be punished by Mom. I was worried he was going to give her a beating as well.

The Bridgetones, as the band called themselves, went on to national success. They recorded several records and appeared on shows such as *American Bandstand*. Their biggest hit remained the version of "Angel Baby" with Kelly singing the lead. They didn't forget Kelly and gave her a share of their earnings from the record. Mom and Dad put that money into a bank account to help with her college education—after paying back Luke's piggy bank, of course.

Some good came from the bad. Kelly and I became much closer than we'd ever been before. Our doing so brought a smile to Mom's face long after the ordeal that prompted it had faded into the past.

As April gave way to May and spring began to manifest itself, the many buds that had been quietly emerging burst open in a majestic show of beauty. Their blooming flowers revealed a rainbow of colors and a burst of fragrances to delight the senses. Birds chirped and darted about, chasing each other with reckless abandon. Young fancies everywhere were turning to love, and mine was no exception. I started to think of Memorial Day. The summer was almost here, and with it, Mary's return.

As part of my punishment, I was not allowed to see or speak with Mary for a month, so having her arrive for the weekend was especially exciting for me.

Mary and her family came out for the Memorial Day weekend, not to stay for the summer, but to get the house opened and ready for when they could. Mary still had the school year to finish back in the city. Nevertheless, even the three days or so together felt wonderful. We attended the parade in the morning. However, this year our family was invited to ride in the amphibious naval vehicle with the mayor because Sammy was the guest of honor and parade queen—the youngest ever—by popular demand. I chose to watch from the sidelines with Mary and Dr. and Mrs. Hurd. It was a sight to see.

Later the picnic lived up to all its expectations, even without Mom having entered any pies in the contest for the first time in years. Grandma was away again helping her sister, who had taken a turn for the worst, and the new baby was monopolizing Mom's time leaving her exhausted. Old man Foster took back the title by winning the tractor pull with his Ford. Dad had neither the time nor the energy to get the old John Deere into shape for the contest, and it showed. Nobody cared. Sammy was worth it all and more.

Mary and I stole some quiet walks alone on the windy beach, bicycled about the back roads in the brisk spring air, and caught a movie up at the drive-in. All in all it was a great time, and it wasn't so hard to see Mary leave because I knew she'd be back shortly.

I'd decided to attend Iona Prep in the fall and live with Cousin Dorothy. So when I walked out of the little white schoolhouse a few days later for the last time as a student, it meant leaving behind the only world I'd ever known. Miss Pickering was there at the door to wish me well. On the way home, I stopped to say hello to August and Samuel, the Pickering fellow, and to George and Brian Angel. Hopping the fence, I walked over to them. Deep in the recesses of my mind, it was still worrying me that I wouldn't be here in Sagahawk in October. As much as I wanted to believe Mr. Werner, there was a part of me that said he was wrong. We'd been given a warning, and we were ignoring it at our peril.

All that would change suddenly, much sooner than I anticipated.

twenty-three

Saturday, July 7, 1962, dawned an ordinary summer day. The fourth of July fell on a Wednesday, so many of the summer people had taken the week off and were out and about. The Hurds were no exception. Dr. Hurd was working in his garden when Mrs. Hurd came out to say that she was taking the family station wagon. He still had some plants he'd bought at Whitmore's earlier sitting on the open tailgate of the Ford, and got up to remove them.

Wiping his brow, he asked, "Where're you off to, honey?"

"I'm taking Beth up to the nursery in town to buy some flowers, and then we're going to have a little lunch together before we go to the village green to plant them. Today is the eleventh anniversary to the day of her husband's disappearance. He vanished on Saturday, July 7, 1951."

"That sounds very nice, sweetie. It's hard to believe that Tom has been gone eleven years. Take your time and have fun. I have plenty to keep me busy here."

At that point, Mrs. Harding came walking into the front yard from her house next door. She seemed in good spirits and was dressed in yellow shorts and a white blouse. Once Dr. Hurd removed his things and shut the tailgate, the women drove off in the wagon. As they did, Mary and I came out of the house and got on our bikes to head for a day at the beach. We said good-bye to her father as we pedaled away.

Yes, it was an ordinary summer Saturday, a typical July weekend day in Sagahawk. Or was it?

At about a quarter to seven that night, Mrs. Harding was preparing herself some supper in her kitchen. The Hurds had invited her for dinner, along with me and Mom and Dad, but she'd said that she preferred to spend it alone. The anniversary of her husband's disappearance was understandably a sad time for her.

I was already at the Hurds. Grandma was away helping her sister. Kelly had agreed to babysit for Luke and Sammy, and Mom and Dad were giving her some final instructions. The last thing they told me as I was leaving was that they were expecting to join us momentarily. Dr. Hurd was preparing vodka tonics for the adults, and I was helping him by cutting up the limes for the drinks. Mary had gone over to Mrs. Harding's house to borrow a bottle of tonic water. And then everything changed.

Mary was coming up the stairs from Mrs. Harding's basement with the bottle of tonic, and Mrs. Harding was putting the final touches on her dinner when they heard the front door open. Mary at first thought it might be me, but it wasn't.

"Honey, I'm home, and you won't believe what happened to me," came the voice from the tall, handsome man, wearing nothing but a bathing suit, as he walked into the kitchen at a quarter to seven on that Saturday night, July 7, 1962.

Mrs. Harding turned quickly to look in disbelief that she could be hearing that voice. When she saw him, she fainted and fell to the floor.

Alarmed, the man ran to help her, asking Mary to assist him. But Mary was in shock. Dropping the bottle of tonic, she ran out of the house and back to her own. When she came through the door she was hysterical and could barely talk. She looked like she'd seen a ghost! She thought she had.

By this time, Mom and Dad had arrived and were sitting with me and the Hurds on the back patio, awaiting the tonic water that would make their drinks complete. We all jumped up and ran to Mary, who collapsed on the living room floor.

"What's the matter, sweetie?" Dr. Hurd asked as he ran over and reached down to lift Mary up.

"Captain Harding ..."

"What about Captain Harding?" Dad asked as he helped Dr. Hurd get Mary to the couch.

"He's ... he's back."

"What are you talking about?" Mrs. Hurd asked as she dipped her napkin in a glass of ice water and started to wipe Mary's forehead.

"You don't understand," she exclaimed in a panic-stricken voice. "He's back!"

"Back where, what are you talking about?"

"He's back in Mrs. Harding's kitchen!"

Dad looked at Dr. Hurd as they both stood up. Dad said, "This must be someone playing a sick prank on that poor widow."

"We'd better go over and check the situation out," Dr. Hurd said, and Dad agreed.

I was about to join them when we all stopped dead in our tracks. Standing in the doorway was Captain Harding, still wearing nothing but his bathing suit.

"Can you come look at my wife, doc? She passed out on the kitchen floor."

"Tom, where have you been?" Dad asked.

"You wouldn't believe me, if I told you."

"You can tell us after I tend to Beth," Dr. Hurd said as he went into the closet to get his black bag.

They all went over to check on Mrs. Harding while I stayed back with Mary, who was still shaken.

"It can't be Captain Harding, can it?" she asked.

"I don't know. Dad has known him for a long time, and he seemed to accept that he was."

"It can't be. Where was he all this time?"

"I wish I knew. Now try to get some rest. I'm going to stay right here and protect you."

"I don't know, this may be more than even you can handle, Mr. Superhero—Jolting Joe."

"Well, I'm glad to see that you haven't lost your sense of humor anyway."

"I'm afraid it's just nervous energy. I'm so frightened by all of this!"

I picked up the wet napkin that her mother had been using and started to wipe Mary's forehead. She was so scared that she was trembling. The last time I'd felt this helpless was the night I'd concocted the scheme to get Kelly on *The Ed Sullivan Show* and was powerless to undo the pain and disappointment I'd caused my mother.

I asked myself why I wasn't scared, but deep down I knew the answer: I was right! It had been a warning all along. Captain Harding's disappearance was only the latest chapter in a story that had started in 1947, a year after I'd been born. I was convinced that his disappearance was tied into the work he'd been doing in his study. I told myself that maybe now Mr. Werner and our government would take Mary and me seriously and heed the warning.

At the Harding house, Dad and Mary's father helped get Mrs. Harding up to her bedroom, and Mom and Mary's mother helped her get into her nightshirt and into bed. Dr. Hurd had given her a sedative, and she was only partially aware of the goings-on. After Mrs. Harding was fast asleep, Mom and Mrs. Hurd, and Dad and Dr. Hurd, took a few minutes to gather their thoughts and plan their next steps. Captain Harding sat quietly in the living room.

Dad spoke first and asked Dr. Hurd, "Paul, what is your assessment of the situation?"

"I think Tom is displaying signs of being in shock, John," replied Dr. Hurd.

"Such as?" asked Dad

"His car and belongings are missing and he has made no effort to call the police to report them stolen. He is sitting downstairs in nothing but a bathing suit, and he hasn't tried to change into other clothing. He hasn't noticed that we have aged and things are different in the house. These are just a few of the signs I am seeing," replied Dr. Hurd.

Before Dad could say anything, Mrs. Hurd chimed in to say, "It's a good thing he hasn't tried to change into something more comfortable, because there is no clothing of his in the closet. I would think he'd find that upsetting in his current state."

Mom then spoke up to agree with Mrs. Hurd, "Nancy is right, when we went into the closet to get Beth's nightshirt, there was nothing of his there. It's all her stuff. I'm sure she packed up or disposed of his things years ago."

"All the more reason, we must handle him gingerly, John," said Dr. Hurd

"I agree," said Dad

"What should we do?" Mom asked.

"You and Nancy stay up here with Beth, while Paul and I go down and question Tom," answered Dad.

Mom and Mrs. Hurd nodded okay.

Next Dr. Hurd jumped in to say, "John, I think at some point it would be wise for Nancy and I and Sally to find an excuse to leave, so you can be alone with Tom. You know him best, and he is more likely to speak openly with you."

"Agreed," Dad answered, asking, "Should we be giving him a sedative at this point?"

"Not right now, he will probably get agitated and resist," replied Dr. Hurd. Reaching into his black bag and taking out some pills, he said, "Here take these and give them to him later when you think the time is right. For now, I would try to liquor him up, if you can. This will dull his senses and hopefully mellow him somewhat."

"Okay," said Dad.

With that Pop and Dr. Hurd went downstairs to question Captain Harding and try and make sense of what had transpired. Mom and Mary's mother stayed with Mrs. Harding.

"Tom, please tell us what happened," Dad asked as nonchalantly as he could.

"How's Beth?" Captain Harding asked in return.

"Sally and Nancy are with her. Paul gave her a sedative and she is sleeping comfortably," replied Dad.

"Great! Do you mind if I make myself a drink first?" Captain Harding asked as he walked over to his liquor cabinet.

Dad and Mary's father looked at each other, and nodded. The normal and ordinary way in which Captain Harding was behaving was confirming that he still was in shock. You would have thought he'd just gotten back from a dip in the ocean, not from being missing for more than a decade. Wanting to keep the sense of casual normalcy going, and worried that the liquor cabinet would be depleted and very different from how he remembered it, Dr. Hurd jumped up and said, "Tom, let me get it for you!"

"Sure, I'll take a scotch on the rocks."

Getting some ice from the kitchen, pouring the drink, and handing it to him, Mary's father repeated Dad's question: "So, Tom—Tell us what happened?"

"I was working in my study this afternoon when I decided to go down for a swim in the ocean before dinner. Beth was busy in the kitchen preparing the food and said it would be fine, provided I get back by seven. I returned by a quarter to seven, the way she asked me to, and when I walked into the kitchen, she passed out on me."

Dad interrupted. "Tom, you are talking about today?"

"Yeah, John, what else would I be talking about?"

"Go on, Tom," Dr. Hurd said in a soft voice.

"I drove down to Sagg Main Beach, parked my car, and walked onto the sand. After I put my stuff down and was about to go in the ocean, I saw one of those lights over the water. You know what I'm talking about, John? It was similar to the ones we'd see from the cockpit of the *Sweet Sally* when we were flying over Germany. Only this baby was much bigger and brighter and just above the water."

"Then what happened?" Dad asked.

"I didn't know if it was an optical illusion, but I felt it was coming closer in to shore—coming toward me. I decided to swim out to where it was. As I did, I leaped over a breaking wave. I must have banged my head on something hard on the bottom when the wave knocked me over. I felt woozy and was fumbling around."

"Then what?"

"I guess I managed to get myself back to shore because the next thing I remember is lying on my back and looking up at this blinding bright light over me."

"Yeah, go on ..."

"I must have passed out because I then had the craziest dream. I think it had something to do with the stuff I've been working on in my study. You wouldn't believe it!"

"Try me," Dad said.

Taking a sip of his scotch, Captain Harding continued.

"I'm in this bright, clean, circular room, and standing over me are people that look like the figures in the pictures from Roswell. They are small, with clean, grayish-white skin, and they have big heads and eyes and larger than normal ears and hands."

"Did they say anything to you?"

"This is where it starts to get strange."

"Go on!"

"They tell me that they are from our future and that they have come to warn us that World War III is going to break out in October of 1962 when Cuba fires Soviet missiles at us and we retaliate against them and the Soviets. They seem to be all excited that it is going to happen in a few months instead of eleven years from now. But I finally managed to calm them down by promising to listen carefully to everything they had to tell me."

"Did they actually speak to you, and was it in English as we speak it?"

"No, I spoke to them in English, but they simply communicated with me telepathically. It's hard to explain, but somehow we understood each other."

"And what did they tell you?"

"They told me that Russia and Cuba are wiped out and that we lose our two coasts, but the Midwest heartland survives. China also survives and grows to become our biggest threat. A nuclear winter envelops the earth when the fallout cloud blocks out the sun, causing mass deaths from starvation and radioactive poisoning. The discontent in the US becomes so great that our president is assassinated a year later in November of 1963."

"Who is the president that gets assassinated?" Mary's father asked, as a way of testing Captain Harding.

"You're going to get a kick out of this one, doc. It's supposedly that rich kid from Massachusetts—you know—the one whose father made all his money from this stuff," he said as he held up his glass of scotch and took a gulp. "I think his name is Kennedy."

Dr. Hurd and Dad couldn't help themselves and looked at each other with raised brows. But Captain Harding didn't notice because he was busy taking another swallow of scotch.

"Then what happened, Tom?" Dad asked.

"They kept pounding the same point over and over again until I promised not to forget to tell this President Kennedy what they were telling me."

"And what were they telling you to tell him?" Dad asked,

while trying to remain nonchalant and matter of fact about the situation.

"They wanted me to advise this President Kennedy that at the height of this so-called missile crisis with Cuba in October of 1962, the Soviets have more than 150 operational tactical nuclear warheads in Cuba, in addition to the nonoperational strategic ballistic weapons the US knew about. They don't want us to make the same mistake again, and end up in a nuclear war because of faulty intelligence."

"What faulty intelligence, Tom?"

"They weren't aware that these tactical nuclear weapons were there and were operational."

"The US apparently decided to invade or attack Cuba, I'm not sure which, not knowing that the tactical nuclear warheads were operational, and the locals fired them at our troops and the East Coast in retaliation. And the US responded by launching ballistic missiles against them and the Soviets, thereby setting off World War III."

"I see," said Dad, as Dr. Hurd sat silently in disbelief but trying his best not to show it.

"Heavy stuff, don't you think, John?"

"Yeah, it is, Tom. You said earlier that you thought this dream was tied into what you were working on in your study. In what way does it tie in?"

Appearing to be ignoring the question, Captain Harding held up his glass and said, "I think I need another drink first."

"Tom, I'll get it for you," Dad said. Meanwhile, Mary's father excused himself to use the bathroom.

While Dr. Hurd was out of the room, Captain Harding turned to Dad and said, "I don't know how much of this I should be talking about in front of the good doctor."

"It's okay, Tom, I wouldn't worry about it."

But the situation took care of itself. When Dr. Hurd returned, he announced, "I'm going to go upstairs and check on Beth, Tom. If she's still sleeping comfortably, I think Nancy and I are going to head home and have our dinner. It's getting late."

"Paul, please take Sally with you, and I'll follow shortly. Don't wait dinner on my account. I want to talk a little more with Tom."

"Okay," said Dr. Hurd. "But don't worry, John. We'll most likely be having a drink first. Speaking of that, Tom, do you mind if I help myself to a bottle of tonic water?"

"Not at all, doc, you know where we keep it?"

"Yes, and by the way, if you're hungry, Tom, feel free to come on over. We have plenty of food."

"I think I'll pass, thanks."

When Dr. and Mrs. Hurd had left with Mom, Dad got back into the conversation with Captain Harding.

"Returning to our earlier conversation, in what way did your dream tie in to what you've been working on in your study?"

"The encrypted documents from Roswell referenced the number 1062, as well as a map of what appears to be present-day Cuba with an *X* through it. I had begun to think that 1062 was not one number, but two numbers, namely, 10 and 62. I also had been trying to analyze the liquid we had retrieved under my microscope, when I accidently splashed some on my lips and face. Now I'm wondering if it made me woozy or caused me to hallucinate."

"Well, did you ever figure out what that liquid was?"

"No, I'm still not really sure what it is. As I said, I looked at it under my microscope and tested it chemically, but all I could come up with was that its composition matched that of distilled water. But in my dream, the visitors told me that it had something to do with their being able to make contact with me."

"In this dream, did they communicate with you about anything else?"

"Yes, they got into a detailed explanation about their time

travel, but I'm too tired to get into all that right now. I've had a rough day."

"Tom, I understand. We can talk about it tomorrow if you like."

"It's that I can't imagine why someone would want to take all my things."

"What do you mean?"

"When I woke up or came to, whichever it is, someone had taken all my stuff, including my new 1950 Ford convertible. Then when I ran home, there was some strange girl in the kitchen with my wife, taking some soda from our basement, who ran screaming out of the house after Beth fainted."

Reaching up with his left hand to momentarily cover his mouth, Captain Harding exclaimed, "Oh, shit! I just realized, I don't think I called the police yet, to report my things stolen."

"Listen, Tom, I need to talk to you about that. Sit down and let me get you another scotch."

"Thanks, I could use it."

As Dad handed Captain Harding the glass of scotch, he said: "Tom … today is not Saturday, July 7, 1951, anymore. It is eleven years later. Today is Saturday, July 7, but it is the year 1962."

Putting his hand on Captain Harding's knee, Dad asked, "Do you understand what I'm telling you?"

"No, what you're saying makes no sense."

"Tom, nobody took your things or your car. You disappeared eleven years ago without a trace and were presumed to have drowned. That's why Beth passed out this evening when she saw you. She thought she was seeing a ghost. The strange girl in the kitchen with her was Mary Hurd. She's fifteen now, about to be sixteen soon."

"That can't be, John."

"Tom, take a close look at me. Don't I look older to you?"

Squinting the way someone who has had too much to drink

does, when they're trying to focus and concentrate, Captain Harding eventually replied, "Now that you mention it, yes you do."

"Here, let me turn on the TV and show you."

With that Dad got up and turned on the television. When the news announcer stated that it was July 7, 1962, Captain Harding began to lose it and ran out on the patio where he proceeded to get sick. Dad leaned over him in much the same way as he had leaned over me the day we discovered the plane crash. He spoke softly to Captain Harding.

"I know this is a terrible shock for you, and the best thing that you can do right now is to get some rest. Paul gave me these pills for you to take. They should help you relax enough to be able to fall asleep."

Dad then helped Captain Harding get into bed and take the medicine, before coming back to the Hurds for a quick dinner. It was a much more somber and quiet dinner than I'd anticipated. But who could have possibly predicted such an event happening?

After dinner, Dad told Mom to take the car and drive home, and he returned to the Hardings' house to sleep on the couch. He wanted to be there for his copilot should he need him. Dad brought Captain Harding and the rest of the crew on the *Sweet Sally* home safely from more than thirty-eight missions over the heart of Germany, and now he wanted to get him home safely from wherever it was he'd been. It's a good thing he was there.

At about 3 a.m., Captain Harding awoke. Still groggy and disoriented from too much liquor and the medicine, he went to the bedroom closet to get his bathrobe, and it wasn't there. None of his things were there. He went into the master bathroom, and none of his things were there, either. He began to take notice that walls were painted different colors than they should've been, and that pictures and decorations had changed along with some of the furniture.

He came downstairs and into the kitchen. The calendar on the fridge said 1962. He went up to his office, but it wasn't his office anymore; it was an empty shell of itself. The only recognizable object was the picture of the *Sweet Sally*. It was back hanging on the wall behind his desk. However, the room was now full of sewing materials and rolls of fabric. It was all too much for him to handle.

He stormed upstairs and began to violently wake Mrs. Harding, shaking her as he demanded, "What the hell have you done with my things? Is this some kind of game to make me think I'm insane? Is there another man? Are you looking for a divorce or something? What the hell is going on?" He shook her with increasing force as he repeated his questions in rapid-fire fashion.

Mrs. Harding, still very much in shock herself and confused by the medicine and the day's events, began to scream! In her state she may have not even recognized her husband and may have thought it was an intruder.

Hearing the commotion, Dad ran up the stairs, burst into the bedroom, and pulled Captain Harding from Mrs. Harding. As he did, Captain Harding swung around to punch Dad in the face.

He shouted, "What are you doing here? Oh, I get it! So it's you. You're having an affair with Beth? My best friend and my wife. Classic, man, classic! What bullshit!"

Dad stumbled backwards from the unexpected punch, and before he even had a chance to recover, while Mrs. Harding was still hopelessly trying to make sense out of the fog of confusion and shock she was in, Captain Harding stormed out of the room in a rage.

"You can have the bitch. The two of you deserve each other!"

Dad let Captain Harding leave, and went to help Mrs. Harding back into bed. As he was assisting her, she began to regain some cognizance of her surroundings. Now semi-aware that she was in her nightshirt, she made a feeble attempt at modesty as she clutched the top of her shirt with her left hand, instinctively bunching it up in her grasp to shield from his view any jostling of her unsupported breasts beneath the loose-fitting garment. As she did, she looked up at him with a concerned inquisitiveness and asked, "John, what are you doing here? It must be the middle of the night? Is it my imagination, or did that man sound and look like Tom?"

As he reassured her and settled her down, Dad said, "It's okay, Beth, get some rest. You'll feel better in the morning. It will all make sense to you then, I promise."

Soon the medicine kicked in again, and she fell fast asleep.

Meantime, Captain Harding, forgetting his car was gone, went into the garage to get it. He wanted to head off to the refuge of his apartment on Prune Island. But when he entered the garage, expecting to see his car, he found instead, his wife's new white 1961 Ford convertible. Agitated and disoriented, he wandered into the night still dressed in his bathing suit.

Dad called Mary's father for help. Mrs. Hurd came over to stay with Mrs. Harding, and Dad and Dr. Hurd set out in the Hurds' station wagon to look for the missing Captain. He hadn't gotten far on Hedges Lane, about one hundred yards away. They found him wandering barefoot on the side of the road.

When they finally got Captain Harding back to the house, Dr. Hurd went home to get some of his cloths for Captain Harding to wear. On his return, he gave them to Captain Harding to change into. He also gave him another sedative. The three men then sat down in the living room and Dad began to re-explain to him that he'd been missing for eleven years. So as not to agitate him, they speculated that he may have gotten amnesia from banging his head, and may have been in an institution for all this time. This was more acceptable to Captain Harding, and he began to calm down.

Dad also assured Captain Harding that he wasn't having an affair with Mrs. Harding but had stayed on the living room couch just in case his help was needed. Mrs. Harding had disposed of most of his things, and Mr. Werner had come to clean out the study because he was presumed to be dead. Slowly it seemed to begin to sink in, and Captain Harding began to speak more matter-of-factly about his disappearance. Dad seized upon the opportunity to learn more about the so-called dream Captain Harding had.

"Tom, it might help us all to figure out this riddle of where you've been these eleven years if you tell us more about this dream you had. Do you feel up to it?"

"I think so, but first I want to say I'm sorry for punching you."

"It's not a problem, I understand. I think you were going to tell us about our visitors from the future and their claimed method of time travel."

"Yes, I'll do my best, John. But I must warn you that it's complicated and far-fetched. I'm not sure how much I still remember."

"It's okay, Tom. Just do your best. It may help us figure out what happened to you, that's all."

A more relaxed Captain Harding began to speak.

"They told me that at first they developed the ability to live below ground, even in the ground underneath the ocean, as a way of escaping the radiation and nuclear winter, which is what they kept calling the effect from the fallout cloud blocking out the sun. Then they began to think that if they could travel forward in time, they could fast-forward to a time when the cloud was gone and things had returned to normal."

Dad interrupted to ask, "Why didn't they try to travel *back* in time, the way they did at Roswell in 1947 and with you in 1951?"

"That's just it, John. They didn't travel *back* in time. They travelled *forward*."

"Wait a minute … That makes no sense! What are you saying? That they travelled forward to travel back?"

"I know it sounds crazy, but yes, that is what I'm saying. You see, John, they tried to travel back in time, but they couldn't. Well, they could, but they could go back only to the point where they'd invented the technology to do it. They couldn't get past that point without man and machine vanishing into thin air, so to speak. They didn't exist anymore after that point."

"What happened to the machine and its occupants?"

"They found themselves back at the starting point as if they'd never left. Consequently, they abandoned the idea in favor of trying to travel forward."

"I see. And then what happened?"

"They were able to go forward in time, but not far enough."

"What do you mean? What stopped them?"

"What they found is that man and machine continued to age, maybe not at exactly the same rate, but at enough of a rate to become a limiting factor. Simply put, the crew eventually aged and died off, and the machine eventually succumbed to its functional and structural limitations."

"Let me see if I understand what you're saying. The machine and the occupants moved rapidly forward into the future, telescoping the time it would normally take them to get there, but in the process they became the same age as they would have been when they got there in normal time?"

"Yes. Let's say they went forward in time ten years, and did it in a matter of five minutes. At the end of those five minutes, man and machine had aged ten years, not five minutes."

"I got it. So then what did they do?"

"They think that our universe is the result of a huge explosion of matter; something akin to the big bang theory that we've been theorizing about. From this they concluded that time is moving only forward, because earth and the other particles from this explosion are still moving outward. It's like the ripples from a rock thrown in the water or the fragments from a grenade exploding."

"It makes some sense to me, but what happens to earth and the universe when they stop moving forward—when the force of the explosion dissipates? Using your example, ripples eventually vanish and grenade fragments ultimately fall to the ground."

"Look, I told you it was convoluted. But there is more. Unlike the ripples in the water or the grenade fragments, they claim everything in our universe eventually reverses itself and comes back to the source of the big explosion, like a boomerang or a yo-yo. And when it does, time also reverses itself, and runs in the opposite direction. At least, that is how I understood what they were trying to tell me."

"Did they explain what causes that to happen?"

"Yes, they've concluded there is a dense mass with a tremendous gravitational pull out in space. It's what they term a *black hole*, where gravity is so strong that it sucks everything in, including light, the way a huge whirlpool would. When it gets too dense, it explodes, but as the force of that explosion begins to wane, the strength of the gravitational pull brings everything back in to the mass."

"I think I understand. Are they saying that when the force of the explosion finally dissipates, the gravitational pull of this dense mass pulls everything back in?"

"Yes, that is my understanding of it. Furthermore, they theorize that this process repeats itself in cycles. You have an explosion outward, a point of reversal, and a pullback to the point of origin; then another explosion, reversal, and pullback, and so on and so on."

"Do they know how many cycles we've been through?"

"No, they don't know yet if we're living through the first and only cycle or if this is the one hundredth cycle. That is why they can only theorize that the cycle repeats itself."

"I see. Let's say this is the first and only cycle and we're still moving forward or outward. How do they know that it will reverse and be pulled back into this dense mass that they think exists?"

"They discovered what they call a *time bridge* or *tunnel* that allowed them to enter and exit the pullback phase of the cycle. That is how they got here in 1947 and presumably in 1951."

"I don't follow what you are saying. What is a time bridge or tunnel?"

"Any explanation I give you will be an oversimplification, but imagine a highway with a divider. The highway runs from point A to point B, but along the way there are breaks in the divider that allow you to turn around and go back toward point A without having gone all the way to point B. These time bridges or tunnels are like the breaks in the highway divider. Do you follow what I'm saying?"

"I think so. But how is that different than going back in time?"

"Staying with my highway analogy, going back in time is like riding against the traffic on the outbound side as opposed to crossing the break in the divider and riding with the traffic on the inbound side."

"Let me see if I have this straight. The year is 2038 and they are moving with 2038 outbound traffic when they cross the divider and head back with 2038 inbound traffic to inbound 1947, and then they cross the divider again to arrive in outbound 1947—our 1947—using two different time bridges or breaks in the divider. Is that right?"

"Exactly!"

"And how do they get back to 2038?"

"That's where the liquid that I accidently splashed on me factors in. But before I get into that, I have a question for you, John. How did you know that in 1947 they came from 2038? How did you know that there's a ninety-one-year gap between the time bridges or tunnels? I haven't told you that yet!"

Dad didn't want to tell him that I'd already deciphered that information with the help of the model flying disc, so he fibbed and replied, "The year 2038 was just a hypothetical—a random pick or lucky guess, you might say."

"Well, that is amazing, because up until now they've only been able to use this method of time travel to go back ninety-one years.

Sticking with my highway analogy, it is as if there are only two breaks in the highway divider, one in their present year and the other exactly ninety-one years prior. So if we are now in 1962, they must be in 2053. And this bridge or tunnel is available at only one time every year, on or about July 7, but they don't know why."

"That is very interesting," Dad said. "But I still don't understand why occupant and machine don't vanish once they enter the outbound side, since the machine wouldn't have been invented yet. Put another way, at that point, why don't they have the same problem they did when they tried to go back in time to before the machine was invented?"

"Again, the answer lies in the liquid that I accidently splashed on me. That liquid that I concluded was merely distilled water had properties that I couldn't ascertain. When the time machine was dipped in it and coated with it, something strange became possible."

"What do you mean?"

"It caused the atmosphere of the return cycle, or the inbound highway in my example, to envelop and stick to the machine so that when the machine crossed the time bridge or tunnel to the outbound side, the machine stretched that inbound atmosphere with it and remained in it while the machine was on the outbound side.

"Let me try to explain it another way. When we work on dangerous or infectious diseases, we often use a glass partition with holes in it that have plastic gloves attached to them. The disease pathogens are on one side of the glass while we're on the other. We stick our hands in the gloves and work on the pathogens on their side of the glass partition while we and the atmosphere inside the gloves remain on our side of the partition. Do you follow me?"

"Yes I do."

"If the machine remained in the cocoon of the inbound atmosphere, it didn't vanish when it was on the outbound side, even though it hadn't yet been invented in that outbound year. It had already been invented in the inbound year whose atmosphere it still was in."

"I see. But how were they able to interact with you without piercing the cocoon and thereby causing themselves to vanish?"

"When I splashed the liquid on me that July 7 Saturday afternoon, it was enough to envelop me in the 1951 inbound atmosphere, although I didn't realize it, because it felt no different from the 1951 outbound atmosphere. However, it enabled them to contact me without having to pierce the cocoon. What happened to the missing eleven years or how I got back here, I don't know because, as I've told you, this all is a crazy dream, or so I thought."

By this time the sun was beginning to come up. Dad and Dr. Hurd thought it best to stop and let their time traveler get some sleep. After Captain Harding was back in bed and sedated, they left. As they walked down the front path of the house, the birds were already out and about, chirping and chasing one another. In the distance, the mist was beginning to lift on the potato fields when the two men stopped to talk.

"I tell you, John, I have to pinch myself from time to time to be sure this saga isn't just a bad dream."

"I know. But what's even scarier for me is that my son and your daughter figured this out a while back, and we ignored their pleas to heed the warning. I really believed Max Werner when he explained all this away as a Soviet hoax."

"Do you think Max truly buys into what he told you, or do you think he was just trying to obfuscate the situation?"

"I don't know, but I'm beginning to think that maybe he is hiding something. And then I ask myself, why he would want to do that when he's the one who came to me and asked for my help."

"You're right, something doesn't add up here. I would try and talk with him if I were you."

"I think I'll reach out to him later today once I grab a little sleep."

Watching a flock of geese fly by on their way to Ellis Pond, Dad said to Dr. Hurd, "It's hard to stand here on this beautiful summer morning, having just spent a week celebrating this country's birth, and think that in some prior iteration—perhaps even now—World War III could be looming."

"Like I said, John, I have to pinch myself to be sure this isn't a bad dream. I'd like to think that there's some simple explanation for Tom's disappearance such as amnesia and a long hospital stay somewhere, but there is too much coincidence between what he's saying and what our kids came up with from the encrypted documents for that to be the case."

"You're right, Paul. I have to speak with Max, and probably the sooner the better."

"Let me know how you make out."

"I will. Now go in the house and get some sleep. You still have to drive back to the city later today."

"How are you going to get home? Would you like me to give you a lift?"

"No, I think I'll walk it. I need the time to sort things out in my head."

"All right, see you later."

"You got it."

With that the two men parted company. One went into his house and locked the door behind him, the other disappeared like a ghost into the morning mist, as he walked down Hedges Lane, lost in his thoughts. It'd been a long night for both.

twenty-four

Mom planned to allow Dad to sleep until we got home from church that following Sunday morning, July 8, because she knew what time he had finally crawled into bed. She was just getting up when he came in. However, when we walked in the door from church, Dad was up and on the phone with Mr. Werner.

"Hello, Max?" asked Dad.

The voice on the other end answered, "Yes, who is this?"

· "John Carr."

"Yes, John, what can I do for you?" answered Mr. Werner.

"I need to see you right away. How soon can you get here?"

"Well, as you must know if you reached me here, I've been on vacation this week in Martha's Vineyard with my family. We're just packing the car now to head back to New York. However, I plan to be on Prune Island on Tuesday and can swing by to see you in the afternoon if that works?"

"No, I need to see you today!"

"Today! What could possibly be so important you need to see me today?"

"I'd prefer not to discuss it over the phone. The captain returned from his 1951 expedition yesterday, and I think you'll be interested in hearing what he has to say about his experience."

There was a long pause on the other end of the phone, before Mr. Werner finally asked, "Are you serious?"

"Dead serious, Max, and you'll want to hear what he has to say."

"I most certainly will! Is he available immediately?"

"Yes."

"Let me see if I can book the ferry, and we'll come across from New London to the North Fork. If you can meet us in Riverhead, I'll let my wife drive on to New York with the family, and I'll come with you, okay?"

"That sounds great. I'll pick you up in Riverhead, and you can stay the night with us. We have the room."

"Great, I'll call you when we get to Orient Point."

"Sounds like a plan," Dad responded before hanging up.

Seeing me, he said, "I need to speak with you. Let me get out of these PJs and throw on some clothes, and I'll meet you on the front porch."

Just then Mom came into the room with a hot cup of coffee and some donuts she'd picked up in town to bring to Dad.

"Please put them on the porch, Sally, I'll be right back down." As he headed up the stairs, he stopped momentarily to say, "Thanks, honey." And then he was gone out of sight.

Mom followed me out to the porch with the goodies, placed them down, and stopped to admire Selma and the blue sky that was the tree's backdrop before going back in. I waited and nibbled on a donut until Dad came out and sat down next to me.

"You and Mary were right all along. What you decoded was a warning and not a Soviet hoax. Furthermore, your deciphering job was pretty damn good. I spent half the night interrogating Tom, and he told basically the same story: a Cuban missile crisis ends in World War III and a nuclear winter, etc., etc."

"Do you think they'll listen to us now?"

"They damn well better! If knowing we have only three months to live doesn't do it, I don't know what will. Max is on his way here now, and I'd like you to sit in, when we meet with Tom.

I would've liked Mary's father to sit in, too, because his observations as a doctor would be helpful. But he may need to leave for the city beforehand."

"I'd be glad to sit in. I have a baseball game at two this afternoon on the field by the firehouse, but I don't think I can focus on it. I'm too excited."

"I want to keep things as normal as possible around here, so please go. I'm sure you'll be fine once the game gets under way. I doubt we'll meet with Tom before four or five in the afternoon. I have to drive to Riverhead to get Max."

"Do you think Mr. Werner will be comfortable with me sitting in?"

"I plan to insist upon it, so I wouldn't worry about it."

"Okay," I said as I got up to go put on my uniform.

Mary came to the game with me, and when I brought her home, I took the opportunity to say good-bye to her parents. This time the yellow and white Ford wagon was already packed and her father was checking the house and locking up when Dad called to say he was back with Mr. Werner. Since I was next door, he asked me if I would pick up Captain Harding and give him a ride over. Dad didn't want him driving himself, and he didn't want to make Mrs. Harding drive him either.

As I turned into the driveway with Captain Harding, Mr. Werner and Dad were already on the front porch. We got out of Sally Truck and went up to greet them. In short order, we were deep in discussion. Dad summarized what he'd learned thus far, and Captain Harding was called upon from time to time, either by Dad or Mr. Werner, to confirm what was being said. I was asked to compare what Captain Harding had learned with what I'd extrapolated from the documents. Surprisingly for me, there were very few differences.

As the meeting on the porch progressed, it became clear to me that Mr. Werner had convinced himself that Roswell was nothing more than a Soviet hoax and wasn't simply trying to deceive Mary and me. However, it also became apparent that our government, notwithstanding Mr. Werner's views, wasn't leaving a stone unturned in trying to see if there was any truth to the warning scenario. They'd been busy at the secret base in the Nevada desert reverse engineering the technological treasures the crashed flying disc had provided us. Mr. Werner's questions told me so.

"Tom, up until now I've been convinced that the Roswell incident was nothing more than the Soviets trying to test our defensive systems in 1947 and disguising their effort as an alien encounter of some kind. Your account of what happened to you in combination with what John's son Joe and his girlfriend Mary have postulated is making me rethink my position.

"I understand the theory of an overly dense mass exploding and sending matter out into space that then is pulled back by the intense gravitational pull of that same dense mass. It isn't unlike the operation of a yo-yo or bungee cord. I also can appreciate the limitations they described to you with trying to go back or forward in time and how the two-way divided highway explains their concept of going forward to go back using time bridges or tunnels to accomplish it. Even the idea of an elastic cocoon to envelop their craft in a time where it is in existence so that it can travel into a time where it hasn't yet been invented without vanishing makes some sense to me, believe it or not. But I still need answers to several more questions before I can be entirely convinced."

"I'll try to answer them if I can," Captain Harding replied.

"Our autopsies of the dead occupants showed them to have damaged vocal cords and to be severely retarded. How could they communicate with you?"

"Their brains had mutated. What you interpreted as retardation was in fact a mutation. Furthermore, they communicated telepathically and no longer had a need for vocal cords."

"I need to understand what they were trying to accomplish at

Roswell in 1947 and what went wrong. In your dream, did these people give you any explanations about this?"

"Yes, Max, they did. They'd developed technology that allowed them to send unmanned probes that were flown by remote control and computers. They had sent several of these probes across the time bridge to the inbound cycle, searching for a time bridge to re-enter the outbound cycle at an earlier point in time. These probes eventually found the time bridge at the end of the ninety-one-year gap. Presumably, these are the lights that we saw over Germany in the *Sweet Sally*. After those successes, they decided to attempt a manned mission in 2038; the 1947 Roswell crash was that ill-fated manned mission."

"Why did they choose to send thirteen-year-old boys on a manned mission instead of experienced pilots?" Mr. Werner asked.

"Max, they weren't thirteen years old. They were 104 years old. That is how old they were when they crossed the time bridge in 2038, and started down the inbound side. Remember, as they headed inbound, time was reversed and went backwards, and they decreased in age. They were thirteen when they crossed the time bridge again at the end of the ninety-one-year gap in 1947. Life expectancy had increased to 125 years by 2038, and a 104-year-old was a prime candidate for such travel."

"Did they tell you this, Tom?"

"They did, but they didn't really have to because I already suspected it."

"You did? Why?"

"Max, when you cleaned out my study, did you take a jar with a hand in it?"

"Yes."

"Well, if you examine that hand, you will find that the bone structure resembles that found on a thirteen-year-old boy, but that the age of the bone itself is closer to that found on a one-hundred-year-old man. I was working on this theory at the time of my disappearance, and they confirmed it for me in my dream or encounter. They were thirteen-year-olds. But they were inbound thirteen-year-olds travelling forward in time on the reverse leg of their boomerang ride back to the dense mass, not outbound thirteen-year-olds."

"I see. Tell me, why did the flying disc and its occupants not vanish and return to their starting point according to your theory? They must've pierced the cocoon when they crashed?"

"You're correct, they did pierce the cocoon when they crashed. The occupants were all thirteen years old in 1947 and in existence. Consequently, their history was re-written. They were four thirteen-year-olds that died in 1947 or thereabouts. Unfortunately, anything that may have happened to them in the prior iteration after that point, such as marriage and children, was wiped out with the rewriting of their history. They all were casualties of time travel."

"And why didn't the craft vanish and return to its 2038 starting point?"

"Great pains were taken to make it out of materials that were known to exist in 1947. So without its own propulsion system, it was just another piece of debris. It wasn't much different than an old merry-go-round when it wasn't functional. It's true that the technology of radar-absorbing surfaces and designs was not fully understood at that time, but the ingredients were there to be found, and we were left to discover them for ourselves."

"Speaking of that, Max, hopefully you found the sample of shiny silver material in my office and are in the process of studying it."

Mr. Werner was visibly taken aback by that last comment, and struggled to regain his composure and not telegraph his surprise. But his efforts failed him, and all concerned, including Captain Harding, could see that a nerve had been struck.

The Lockheed Skunk Works in the Nevada desert indeed

were working feverishly on developing radar-absorbent materials and designs to reduce radar detection in connection with project OXCART, and Mr. Werner had given them the sample of shiny silver material.

Anxious to move the conversation along, Mr. Werner asked, "If the craft didn't have its own propulsion system, how did it get here?"

"It was transported here in a mother ship and was launched much like a shell is fired from a canon. Then it parachuted to earth attached to a weather balloon of a type contemporary to 1947."

"And how did they steer or control this balloon?"

"There was a device that looked like a model flying disc that, when attached to a docking station on the craft, allowed the craft to be remotely controlled from the mother ship."

"And what made it crash?"

"It collided with what was at that time a top secret experimental high-altitude surveillance balloon that was monitoring Soviet nuclear testing as part of a program named Mogul, and the two crashed to earth."

"I see. If the documents were designed to warn us, why were they encrypted, and how were we expected to decipher them?"

"The documents were encrypted to protect them from falling into the wrong hands. Our future expected the occupants on the craft to help us decipher these documents using the device that was in my office that looked like a model flying saucer."

At that point, I jumped in and told Captain Harding that I'd deciphered a portion of the encrypted materials using the device, but that it had since been destroyed. He asked me how I came to know to use the device in this manner, and I told him it was purely by accident. He said that was impossible, and I asked why.

"Because the device could only be activated remotely from the mother ship if it was still within the cocoon of the inbound atmosphere. Once that cocoon had been pierced by the crash, the mother ship had no way of activating it and it became a useless toy."

"Captain Harding, there must be another way of activating it because I deciphered it in my room last year without any help from any mother ship."

"You must have splashed some of the liquid that was in the bottle in my study on yourself and enveloped yourself and the device in the cocoon where the mother ship would be able to activate the device. Did you get any of that liquid on you?"

"In fact, I did get some of the liquid on me by accident. It happened one night while Mary and I were going through the stuff in your study, but I scrubbed it off afterward in your powder room."

"I thought so. You can't scrub it off. It stays with you and spreads or distributes itself all over you and to things you handle, such as the device."

"What do we do now that the device has been destroyed? It no longer works. I've tried it."

"If you saved the pieces, I think I can put it together again and get it to function. It operates basically like a transistor radio."

Mr. Werner interjected to say that he still had the parts I'd given to him last year in his office on Prune Island. He said he would bring them to Captain Harding in the next day or so.

Dad stood up and asked to be heard. After taking a puff on his pipe, he waited a few seconds to exhale and to let our anticipation build and set the stage for what he wanted to say.

"I hate to be the pragmatist in the group, but I would like to remind all of you of something William James once said. He said he didn't believe in God, but he went to church for one hour on Sundays to hedge his bets just in case he was wrong. He called himself a pragmatist for doing it. We have the rest of our lives to speculate on whether we've been visited by our future and how they may have done it—whether by going forward or backward, or through time tunnels or bridges and the like.

"If we want to hedge our bets and take their warning seriously, we have only a few months to act. I say we forget about whether we've been visited, how the visitors got here, or where Tom has been for the last eleven years, and focus on the message."

Everyone spoke or nodded in agreement. So Dad continued to speak.

"Tom, did they tell you why they chose you to be their messenger, and how they wanted you to deliver this message to the president?"

"It's funny you should ask that question, John. They told me that they didn't choose me but that I selected myself for the task."

"Did they say how you did that?" Dad asked as Mr. Werner chimed in to second him.

"Yes. They said that they were like a spider in its web waiting for a bug to fly in and get stuck."

"I'm not following you, Tom."

"They had to wait in their cocoon for someone to enter the cocoon the way that I did, by getting the liquid in the bottle on me. When I got that liquid on me on Saturday, July 7, 1951, they were ready and waiting for me."

"I see. And then what?" Dad asked, and Mr. Werner again seconded, but with a heightened interest.

"I had this irresistible urge to cleanse myself. At first I thought about jumping in the shower, but then I decided that since I already had my bathing suit on, I'd go for a swim in the ocean. I figured that the salt water would remove most anything, and then I'd come home and shower anyway. And that is when I disappeared for eleven years."

"Did they tell you anything else during your dream, like how they wanted you to get this message to the president?"

"They told me that a young boy had selected himself who would be a great asset to me in getting the warning out."

"Did they tell you anything about that young boy, or who he was?"

"They didn't tell me who he was, but they told me a lot about him."

"What did they tell you?" Dad asked, as my ears perked up with interest.

"They told me that he was a time traveler in spirit. He'd had a unique experience becoming acquainted with the man who was indirectly responsible for his existence—a man who'd saved the life of his ancestor. They also told me that he'd selected himself because he became interested in my life and had gotten the liquid from the bottle in my study on him the way that I had. At the time I had no idea who they were talking about, but now I'm wondering if it was you, Joe."

"Captain Harding, I had to do a project for my teacher, Miss Pickering. I was late for a Latin exam last year and ran across the cemetery in the village green. She saw me and considered what I did to be disrespectful, so she gave me a summer assignment to investigate the lives of three people buried there and prepare a report on each of them. I did a report on a man named August Pierce, who saved my great-grandfather's life. I wouldn't be here if he hadn't saved him.

"Then I did a report on you, because they have a tombstone there for you. While I was doing the report on you, Mrs. Harding let me into your study at Mary's request, and that's when I spilled the liquid on me. I must be the person they were talking to you about."

"I would agree, Joe, except there are still two critical pieces missing."

"What are they?" I asked, as Dad and Mr. Werner sat up in their chairs to listen more attentively.

"The boy in question visited with them the way that I did. But his visit was a brief one and duplicated a prior experience he'd had.

This boy was troubled with feelings of guilt because he'd learned that not long before he was born as a healthy infant, he'd had twin brothers who were born with problems and died immediately or shortly after birth. In his mind, he wouldn't have been conceived if they'd been healthy and lived. The visit was to assure him that his life had special purpose and that he had an appointment with destiny that would save millions and millions of lives."

Pausing for a moment to observe my reaction, Captain Harding asked, "Nothing like that has happened to you, has it Joe?"

"The part about the twin brothers is true. The third report I did for Miss Pickering last summer led me to find out that I had twin brothers named George and Brian Angel who died from trisomy 13 at or shortly after birth. But I never visited any time machine—at least not that I'm aware of."

"Wow, there sure are a lot of coincidences here. Now that you mention it, I think I remember when your mother gave birth to the twins. Did you ever have an experience that seemed to be a complete repeat of a prior experience?"

"No, not that I can think of right now."

"They told me that's how I'd know the boy."

Dad interrupted again to ask, "Why all the riddles, Tom? Why couldn't they just tell you the boy's name and be done with it?"

"Even though we've both connected with them through the cocoon because of us both having come in contact with the water in the bottle, we have to connect with each other in our own 1962 time. According to them, it's a must if we're to accomplish our goal of avoiding World War III in October."

"But Tom, who could it be other than Joe? Who else came in contact with that water?"

"I agree, John. But Joe hasn't had the requisite experience. Have you Joe? Think hard. Maybe you don't remember the visit to the time machine, but did you have an eerily similar duplicate experience?"

"Not that I can think of. Sorry," I said apologetically.

"Let me tell you about my experience, Joe, and maybe it will help you remember something similar."

"All right," I replied without much hope that it would.

"The week before I disappeared, I was working in my study. I'd started at 3:06 in the afternoon. When I got the urge to go for a swim in the ocean, the clock in my office said 6:03 p.m. I was already in my bathing suit and shirt, so I went downstairs. My wife was preparing dinner. She told me to be back by a quarter to seven. I went out, got into my car, and drove to the beach. On my way I passed a little boy on a red bike. He was wearing a blue bathing suit and a white T-shirt.

"My experience on the next Saturday, the day I disappeared, was the same experience, except I had to run home because my car was gone. The time was the same on the clock when I left my office, and Mrs. Harding greeted me the same way as I left for the beach. I was wearing the same bathing suit and top, driving the same car, and I saw the same boy in the same outfit on the same bike at the same point in the trip. And when I came home the other day, it was a quarter to seven, and I was still wearing the same bathing suit, only it was eleven years later. Did you ever experience anything like that?"

"Yes, now that you mention it, I did! Sort of.

"The day I got into trouble with Miss Pickering, I'd fallen asleep at my desk studying for my Latin exam. The last thing I remembered was looking at the clock on my desk. It read 3:08 a.m. The next thing I remembered was waking up and seeing it read 8:03 a.m. I jumped up and grabbed my books and my clothes that were still lying where I'd left them on my neat and untouched bed. Putting on the clothes, I ran into the hall bathroom to splash some water on my face and brush my teeth before descending the stairs to the kitchen, where I reached for an apple on my way out the door.

"Finding my bike had a flat tire, I ran toward the schoolhouse about two miles down the road. Ten minutes had elapsed leaving me with seventeen minutes to make it through the schoolhouse door before Miss Pickering closed it at exactly 8:30 a.m. As Dad knows, she was a stickler for punctuality. Once shut, the door would not be reopened and I would automatically fail Latin. As I rounded the bend in the road, I saw Miss Pickering at the door. She had her back to me and was talking to Reverend Thompson, who was facing my way."

Here I asked Dad and Mr. Werner if I could stop to go inside and get a drink of water. They agreed, and I did. After returning from the kitchen, I continued.

"The old cemetery with its split rail fence stood between me and the open door to the schoolhouse. If I ran around the cemetery fence, I wouldn't make it in time. But if Miss Pickering saw me jump the fence and run through the cemetery, I'd be in trouble with her for being disrespectful to the people buried there. I had no choice but to risk her wrath, and so I jumped the fence.

"After tripping over a gravestone and gathering myself, I prepared to leap the fence at the other side of the cemetery. Just as I was airborne over the fence, she turned to see me as I dashed toward her and the open door. It was 8:30 a.m., and I could see her excusing herself and preparing to shut the door when Father Thompson stopped her to ask her something. I think he sensed my predicament and was trying to be of help.

"I seized upon the opportunity to dash through the open door and take my seat. When she had shut the door, Miss Pickering came over to me and said that she would let me take the test, but that I should stay to see her after the exam. It was then that she gave me the assignment to write the reports that I was telling you about earlier."

"And when did the duplicate event take place?" Captain Harding asked.

"That first event took place on Wednesday, May 24, 1961. The duplicate event occurred a little more than a month later, in July of that year.

"After dinner that night, Mom and Dad were going out and asked me to watch Luke. I was already up in my room, working at my desk, so I said fine. Luke came in with his flying saucer in hand, and I took out the encrypted document and began to pore over it in much the same way I imagined you had, Captain Harding.

"Before long, Luke was sound asleep. I picked up the flying saucer and placed it on top of my desk, and then carried Luke and tucked him into his bed. When I came back, I had the shock of my life."

"What happened?"

"For no particular reason, I began to run the toy flying saucer slowly over the encryptions, and soon I realized that it was high-lighting some portions and ignoring others. I had to concentrate to read the highlighted portions and put them together to obtain a coherent message. A slight movement of the device moved letters out of focus or completely out of sight. But I had all night. I didn't have to meet with Miss Pickering until 8:30 the next morning to present her with my second report—the one on you, Captain Harding.

"As soon as my report for Miss Pickering was finished, I turned to the document and started to painstakingly read it. The process was tedious and tiring. I had to adjust the saucer, read, stop to write down what I had seen, readjust the disk, read some more, stop and write that down, and so on and so on—until I was bleary-eyed."

"Yes, go on."

"The last thing I remember was looking at the clock on my desk. It read 3:08 a.m. I must've fallen asleep studying the document because the next thing that I remember was the feeling of sheer panic when I looked up and saw that same clock showed the time to be 8:03 a.m.

"I jumped up, grabbed my things, ran into the hall bathroom

to splash some water on my face and brush my teeth, before I ran
out the door. Again finding my bike with a flat tire, I ran toward
the schoolhouse. The same ten minutes had elapsed, leaving me
once again with seventeen minutes to get there. As I rounded the
bend in the road, I could see Miss Pickering at the door. She had
her back to me and was talking to Reverend Thompson, who was
facing my way."

"Reverend Thompson was there again?" Dad interrupted,
asking in a surprised voice.

"Yes, he was."

"That really is a coincidence. And then what happened?"

"The old cemetery stood between me and the open door to the
schoolhouse. I faced the same choice. If I ran around the cemetery
fence, I wouldn't make it in time. But if Miss Pickering saw me
jump the fence and run through the cemetery, I would be inviting
another round of punishment. I had no choice. I had to risk it, so
I jumped the fence.

"Tripping on the Pierce grave, the same one as before, and
gathering myself, I prepared to leap the fence at the other side of
the cemetery. But just as I was airborne over the fence, she again
turned to see me as I dashed toward her and the open door. It was
8:30 a.m., and I could see her excusing herself and preparing to
shut the door, when Father Thompson—as he had done before—
stopped her to ask her something. I think he once again sensed my
predicament, and was trying to help me.

"I once more seized upon the opportunity to dash through the
open door, but this time Miss Pickering reached out her arm and
grabbed me as I did.

"Winking at me and smiling, she said, 'I saw what you did.
It was very nice of you to take time from your harried schedule
to stop and say hello to Sam and August Pierce and the Pickering
fellow. I know it must've meant a great deal to them. They don't

get many visitors these days.' Relieved, I simply nodded to her, as Reverend Thompson smiled at me."

"Did you find that strange?" asked Captain Harding.

"Yes, I even said to myself that Yogi Berra knew what he was talking about when he said, 'It's déjà vu all over again.'"

"No, I mean that Miss Pickering didn't get mad at you for running across the cemetery."

"Yes, now that you mention it, I did find that a little strange."

"Well, maybe it's because things didn't happen the way you think they did."

"What do you mean?" I asked, echoed by Dad and Mr. Werner.

"Are you sure that you already had undressed that night when your brother came into your room to stay with you? Is it possible you had planned to do it, thought that you had, but had not actually done it when he came to stay with you?"

"Why do you ask?"

"Because you said that in the morning you grabbed your things, but you didn't say you put them on. Isn't it possible the reason is you already had them on, unlike at the time of the first incident, on May 24 of last year, when you did mention putting them on?"

"I'm trying to remember."

"Let me help you. Were you wearing the same clothing when you got to the school that day as you had been wearing the day before?"

"Yes I was, now that you mention it. In fact, I was wearing the very same clothing I'd been wearing on May 24, at the time of the first incident."

"I knew you had, because I also had been wearing the same bathing suit on both occasions. Do you remember me telling you that earlier?"

"Yes."

"Now, let me ask you if you were wearing the same clothing the night you got the liquid on you in my study?"

"Yes I was, now that I think about it."

"When I got the liquid on me on Saturday, July 7, 1951, I was already dressed in my bathing suit and shirt—the same bathing suit and shirt I'd been wearing the prior Saturday."

"But Tom," Mr. Werner asked, "what difference does it make whether he was in his pajamas or underwear, or was in his clothing, or if he was wearing the same clothing on those three occasions? How does that place him in the cocoon and on the time machine or whatever the hell it is?"

Ignoring Mr. Werner for the moment, Captain Harding turned to me and asked, "Are you sure, Joe, that after you carried Luke to his bed that night, you didn't come out here on this porch and walk down those steps to get a breath of fresh air and look up at the sky?"

"I don't think so, but now I'm not sure of very much anymore."

"Let me try and help you once again. Is it possible that when you were standing down there by the elm tree and looking up you saw an unusual bright light in the sky that seemed to you as if it was over the village green and the cemetery?"

"You know, now that you mention it, I think you may be right. Maybe I did come outside and see an unusual bright light. I'm just not sure."

Dad interrupted to caution me, "Joe, don't let Tom's suggestions put ideas in your head that weren't there in the first place."

Turning to Captain Harding he said, "Why are you trying to convince him that he did all this crazy stuff, when he told you he fell asleep at his desk?"

"Because he didn't go back to his room, and he didn't find that the toy helped him read the encrypted document. Rather, he came out here, saw the light, and followed it down the street toward the cemetery. Then something happened that led to his encounter with our visitors from the future. He learned what he did about the encrypted document from our visitors, who left him with the memory that he'd learned what they told him from running the device over the encrypted document on his desk."

"And how do you know that, Tom?"

"The reason Miss Pickering wasn't mad at him is because she saw him in the cemetery while he was still sleeping or passed out in front of the Pierce grave after returning from his encounter. She thought he'd come early and was paying his respects before his appointment with her. From then on, his experience was real and as he remembered it. But from the time he put Luke in his bed until that moment, it was a rerun of his experience on May 24 of 1961. Think about it, John. It's at least as likely a scenario as the one where everything happened in exactly the same way as the time before, which he has described."

"But he wouldn't have his report on him to give her, if he did what you say."

"He finished the report and put it in his back pocket before he moved Luke to his bed."

"Where was your report, Joe?" Dad asked.

"It was folded and in my back pocket as Captain Harding said, Dad."

"I see," Dad conceded, but I wasn't sure he was fully convinced.

"I can't believe that I would wander off and leave Luke alone like that. It just isn't like me to be that irresponsible."

"You didn't plan to do it. You thought you were investigating an unusual light that caught your attention. You may have gone only a few steps into the street when you had your encounter."

"I think I understand what you're saying, Captain Harding. But how can you be so sure that the device didn't decipher the document for me?"

"They told me that I'd know the young person who selected himself because he would think the device had helped him decipher the encrypted document. They informed me that the sole function of the device was to remotely control the craft that crashed, and it functioned only in that role when it was in its docking station on the craft. Its function as a deciphering device was a mere smoke screen. You couldn't have learned what you did the way that you say you did."

"Then you must have known that I was the person you were looking for when I first mentioned to you that I'd deciphered the information using the device. Why did you go along with what I was saying and not stop me and tell me then?"

"Keep in mind that up until a few hours ago, I thought I was still living in 1951 and was just having a bad dream. I not only had to test my own memory, I owed it to you to be sure that you are the right person they'd told me to find. Now I'm certain that you are."

"All right," Dad said, "let's assume that Joe is the person that you were told to find—then what? Didn't they give you any instructions on how to go about getting your warning heard by the president?"

"No, they said they couldn't help me because in their history or reality there hadn't been such a warning given, and the president got them into the war as the result of poor intelligence."

"So basically they told you we're on our own in this regard, is that correct, Tom?"

"Yes, I'm afraid so."

"Well, I assume they at least showed you how to decipher the encrypted documents, didn't they?"

"Yes. There is only one genuine document. The others are decoys."

"And what is the translation of that document?"

"What Joe has already told you is basically correct. However, the full translation provides much more detail. It translates as follows:

On October 15, 1962, a confrontation begins, with the Soviets and Cuba on one side and the US and its allies on the other side, when the US discovers that the Soviets are setting up nuclear ballistic missile sites in Cuba. The confrontation escalates and explodes into all-out war on October 27, 1962. The US is enforcing a blockade on Cuba, which it calls a quarantine, demanding that the ballistic missiles be removed. What US intelligence agencies don't know is that in addition to the ballistic missiles that are being set up, also deployed in Cuba by the Soviets are 100 to 150 tactical nuclear missiles that already are fully operational and can be launched by the local (Cuba-based) Soviet commander without authorization from the Kremlin.

At approximately noon on that day, a US U-2 plane is shot down by a SAM missile while on a reconnaissance mission over Cuba. Unknown to the US, the decision to shoot it down was made by a local Soviet commander acting on his own, not by Moscow. The Kennedy administration had already decided that if such a flight were to be shot down, they would order a strike on the missile sites. Their reason was that the Cubans didn't have the capability to shoot down a U-2, and the decision by the Soviets to do it signaled a desire by the Kremlin to escalate the situation.

On the same day, the USS Beale tracked and dropped signaling depth charges on a Soviet Foxtrot submarine, B-59, which, unknown to them, was armed with a nuclear torpedo. Surrounded by US warships and needing desperately to surface because it was running out of air, the Soviet submarine fired its nuclear torpedo at the Beale. The torpedo

malfunctioned, but added to the Kennedy administration's view that they were being provoked by an
escalation on the part of the Soviets. Having already
planned to invade Cuba if the confrontation entered
a third week, the decision was made to bomb the
missile sites and move up the invasion. The Soviet
commander in Cuba retaliated against the invasion
and bombings by firing the tactical nuclear missiles
at the invasion force and the southeast coast of the
United States. The US retaliated against the Soviet
Union and Cuba, and the Soviets attacked in response. When it was over, the Soviet Union and
Cuba had for all intents and purposes been wiped
out, and the East and West Coasts of the US had
been devastated. The midsection of the country
survived, but almost 100 million Americans had
been killed, and more than 100 million Soviets and
Cubans had died.

The US decision to invade Cuba was made on the
assurance of the Joint Chiefs of Staff that all the
Soviet missile sites in Cuba could be destroyed
by the bombing, and all known sites were. It was
the tactical nuclear missiles that weren't known to
them that triggered World War III. Please advise
President Kennedy of the existence of these tactical
missiles. Also please advise the president that the
two escalating factors—the SAM missile and nuclear torpedo firings—were decisions made by local
commanders, and not Moscow.

China is an indirect beneficiary of the confrontation, and becomes a rising threat to the United
States. Use your discretion in advising the president

that the nuclear winter that befalls the planet creates much hardship, suffering, and death, including his own at the hands of an assassin in November of the following year. The assassin will be a former US Marine with top-level security clearances from having worked at a U-2 base in Japan.

"And that, my friends, is the translation of the warning!" Captain Harding said, ending with a bit of a flare.

"Very interesting," Dad commented. "Did you memorize that?"

"Memorize, you ask! You forget that they had eleven years to drill that into my head, over, and over, and over again. It is imprinted on my brain. If you like, I can do it in Latin for you."

"That won't be necessary, I get the picture. What is the code for deciphering the document?"

"They hid it in plain sight, John!" Captain Harding was quick to answer as he spelled it out. "The document is written in Latin. Every first letter is one letter back from the intended letter, so a *B* would be an *A*. Every second letter is what it is, so a *C* would be a *C*. Every third letter is six letters forward, so an *A* would be a *G*. And every fourth letter is two letters forward, so a *D* would be an *F*. In other words, the code is 1-0-6-2. Numbers are done in Roman numerals."

"I see," Dad said. He turned to Mr. Werner and spoke. "Max, you've been very quiet. What do you make of all this?"

"I'm a German engineer, used to dealing in facts and not suppositions. If we're going to convince President Kennedy and his advisors not to take the actions that got us into World War III, we must uncover for them the fact that there are operational Soviet tactical nuclear weapons in Cuba at the time they are making their critical decisions. If we try to go to them with a story that has no factual underpinning but is based upon what is from their perspective the dreams of a man who has been missing and presumed dead for eleven years, and on the warnings of a sixteen-year-old boy who either had a graveyard encounter or used a toy to decipher encrypted documents the government has yet to be able to decipher, I don't think we'll get very far."

"I agree with you, Max, but how are we going to be in a position to uncover such facts if our government isn't able to?" Dad asked.

"If we believe in our warning, we don't necessarily have to uncover the facts. We must convince our government that *they* have uncovered them. Let me explain:

"First, we remove Tom from the equation because his background is too sketchy. We find some benign way to explain away his disappearance, and we allow him to melt back into a quiet life with his wife in Sagahawk.

"Second, I'll devise a way to run a contest challenging the best and brightest young minds in the country to decipher the document recovered from the crash site in Roswell in 1947. Young Joe Carr here will enter the contest and decipher the document, based upon the formula Tom has just outlined.

"Third, I'll go to our government before announcing a winner and show them what Joe has produced. They'll verify with their computers the formula he's used and the results he's uncovered. They will ask me to announce that no one has won, and Joe will most likely be invited to the White House for a private meeting where he's asked to remain silent about what he's uncovered and is rewarded in some other way for his efforts.

"And from there, we should be off to the races!"

"Hold your horses there, Max. What if the US doesn't send up the U-2 flight on October 27 because they know it will be shot down? And what if the Soviet nuclear torpedo doesn't malfunction this time around for some reason and blows up the Beale and some of the other US warships? I guess I'm asking you how far we can go in rewriting history without jeopardizing the desired outcome?"

"It's a good question, John. We should try to minimize the extent we alter the past. We are working on better radar-absorbing materials and paints. I'll see if we can apply them to the U-2 to give us more confidence that it won't be shot down. However, even if it is, the president will most likely be more inclined to give the Soviets a pass if he knows it was a local decision rather than one generated in Moscow.

"As for the nuclear torpedo, it would be better if it weren't fired this time around. I'm an ex-submariner, and I'm acquainted with Vasili Arkhipov, who I believe serves on the B-59 or a Foxtrot like it. I'll find a way to let it slip out to him that US warships have been instructed not to fire on a Soviet sub that must surface for air during the usual cat and mouse games both sides play with each other. Hopefully, he'll remember that tidbit, and it will factor into the decision that's made on October 27.

"The important thing is to be sure that President Kennedy refuses to order an invasion of Cuba unless the Joint Chiefs of Staff can guarantee the destruction of all the Soviet missile sites in Cuba through air strikes. We now know they can't make that guarantee because they don't know where the tactical nuclear missile sites are, and so there will be no invasion to trigger World War III."

"What do you think, Tom? It sounds pretty good to me," Dad asked his old co-pilot.

"I hate to have to sit this one out, but I agree with Max. I have too much baggage."

Then they all turned to me and, with a look that told me that this would probably be a life-changing event for me, asked, "Are you up for this, kid?"

I stood silently for a moment as the gravity of it all began to sink in for me. The leaves on Selma began to rustle as a gentle breeze came up from the south from the direction of the village green. I knew it was August and Samuel Pierce and Ernest Pickering along with my twin brothers, George and Brian Angel, telling me this was my destiny, my rendezvous with history. It was the reason they had died so that I could live. They would be with me every step of the way.

So I answered, "God willing, yes."

twenty-five

The rest of July of 1962 came and went without a whimper. It was the quiet before the storm. Dad asked me to be as ordinary and inconspicuous as I could. It's amazing how *extra*ordinarily hard that can be when you have to work at it. My days were spent with him in the fields or with Mary biking to the beach or to town. Even Luke and Kelly took little note of me, my comings and goings were so routine.

The labor on the farm was always hard and physical, but that July was especially bad, made so by a relentless sun. The day in and day out of clear, unseasonably hot, sunny weather was wonderful for the summer folks sunbathing at the beach, but an inferno of sorts for us. Often the exposed metal on the equipment would get so hot that we had to wear gloves to protect ourselves. The plowed land was especially dusty, and it didn't take much of a breeze to stir it up. Water was too scarce a commodity that summer to waste it trying to keep dust from blowing around.

The equipment had dust everywhere, even in places you normally would think were protected. As much as we battled to keep them clean, the best we could do was slow things down. Eventually we had to take precious time away from the fields to change filters, clean parts, and in some cases overhaul them.

The dust wasn't any easier on us than it was on the machines. It didn't take long for your mouth to fill with the fine dirt unless you wore a bandana around your neck that you could pull up to cover your mouth. Some days we even wore goggles and a hat—not fun in the blazing sun.

In a strange way it *was* fun. Maybe knowing what lay ahead in October if we failed in our warning made us appreciate even this miserable hard work more. It was made that way by the fact that it was so magnificently ordinary and routine. There was a comfort to be had from taking refuge in the normally grudging daily grind that I can't explain, but that I could tell Dad felt as well. Much of the work, such as laying irrigation, required our total concentration because any carelessness or inattention could result in injury or serious harm. The focus that was required left little room to think about anything else, even the end of the world in a few months.

Where the work was more relaxed, Dad and I took the opportunity to talk as we toiled away, talk that was pensive and deep, even philosophical sometimes, the kind of talk that knowing a sunset to life might be coming generates. I learned things about Dad I'd never known: childhood experiences, war time escapades, secret fears—you name it.

One childhood incident he recounted stuck with me because it touched so closely on my experience investigating the Pierce and Harding cases as a part of Miss Pickering's assignment. It seems that not long after Dad had learned how to swim in earnest, but before he'd had much of a chance to go in the ocean alone, he took an early-morning jaunt in the sea. It was summertime, and a storm that had blown through the night before cleared out the humidity, leaving behind a clear, dry day that already was promising to be a record-breaking hot one. The waves were rougher than usual because of the weather the preceding night, but the water gave no clue of the dangerous rip current that lurked beneath the surface.

Dad went out farther than usual and swam numerous laps back and forth parallel to the beach before heading for the shore. Tired but refreshed as he swam in, he noticed that he wasn't making any headway regardless of how hard he swam. His arms and legs were beginning to feel rubbery, and he was concerned about getting a cramp.

He could see the beach only yards in front of him, yet he felt as though it was slowly slipping away from him. His refreshing tiredness was changing to terrified exhaustion, when a peaceful resignation began to come over him. He started to reflect on his young, but full life. Remembering one thing and then another, he smiled to himself and said a short prayer when a ball suddenly splashed in the water in front of him and caught his attention. Looking up from his self-absorbed state of resignation, he saw a black Labrador retriever running down the beach toward him and the ball. With all the strength he had left in him, he strove to reach for the ball before the current took it away from him.

The big Lab came charging in at him, splashing as it swam to him. Giving the dog the ball, but grabbing onto its collar, he let the muscular animal tow him in until he could stand. As Dad stumbled onto the beach and collapsed in exhaustion, the Lab came over to him and dropped the ball from its mouth in front of him.

At that moment, Dad heard a voice shout, "Come on, Linus! Get the ball and let's go!" It was a familiar voice, but not one he completely recognized.

"Help," he yelled as best he could, hoping he'd be heard. Dad's legs were cramping up, and the pain was excruciating. When he looked up, standing over him was the face that went with the voice—a welcome sight indeed.

"What's the matter?" the voice with a face asked.

"I was out for a swim and couldn't get back in, and now I'm cramping up."

The person whose face went with the voice bent down and began to massage Dad's legs with his hands. "Is that helping any?"

"Yes, thanks. You look familiar, but I'm not sure why."

"The name's Matt Kerr, and my family has a summer place on Parsonage."

"I'm John Carr, and we live on Sagg Main."

"Carr? Is your dad also named John Carr?"

"Yes."

"I think he watched our house for us while it was being built several years back."

"That's where I met you. We tossed a football back and forth once or twice when my father came out to check on things, and I came with him."

"Could be. Well I've got to go. You going to be okay now?"

"I think so. That's a great dog you've got there. He saved me."

"Linus is a former rescue dog, so it's all in a day's work for him."

"How did he get that name?"

"He's named after the *Peanuts* cartoon strip character in the paper."

"I won't forget him anytime soon."

"Next time remember to swim on the diagonal when you hit a current like that. Don't ever try to fight it head on."

"Thanks for the advice. Hope to see you around."

"Me too."

So of course I asked Dad if that's how we came to have a black Lab named Linus. He nodded yes.

I also wanted to know what happened to Matt Kerr and his dog. Dad told me that over the coming summers he would see Matt from time to time when Matt was working on the Dean family farm down the road from us. However, once Matt went off to the Kent School and then Yale, he saw less and less of him. He knew that Matt joined the marines with the outbreak of World War II, when he enlisted in the army air corps, but after that he lost track of him completely.

He never saw the black Lab again after that fateful day, nor did he ever ask Matt what happened to him. He preferred to picture the handsome animal as he remembered him—a welcome sight, muscular and sleek, charging and splashing toward him. The answer to a prayer.

Dad never spoke to me about the war until that July. But one story he told me made a lasting impression on me.

It was late afternoon on a clear and sunny day. The squadron was over the English Channel, returning from a particularly difficult bombing mission deep in the heart of Germany. Dad was squadron leader and had previously ordered all the planes to slow down to allow a badly damaged B-17 to keep up with them. The stricken plane, ironically named *Lucky Lady*, had its nose partially blown off, was operating on little more than forty percent power, and had a huge gash in its tail section from a collision with a German fighter. Dad observed the tail weaving back and forth precariously in the wind and knew immediately it must be attached by the thinnest of means.

Almost out of fuel and with its damaged tanks continuing to leak, their options were to have the crew bail out safely and crash the plane over the channel or else risk making it back to base. Dad was radioing ahead to see if there were any ships nearby that could rescue the crew when the captain of the *Lucky Lady* called to say that they weren't going to bail out. They wanted to chance making it back. The captain explained that the ball turret gunner was trapped and couldn't get out, and the tail gunner was severely wounded, and had used his parachute to help keep the plane intact. The crew had been with each other for twenty-five missions and decided they would either all make it or perish together. But they weren't going to bail on their buddies and leave anyone behind.

Dad knew it was his job as squadron leader to save as many of the men as he could and to think of the safety of the people on the ground, but he couldn't bring himself to deny them their noble gesture. He felt they had earned the right to try, and if they had to crash, they would do everything possible to avoid hurting anyone on the ground.

Dad ordered the rest of the planes to fly on ahead at normal speed while he stayed back with the wounded craft. Concerned about the drag on the plane's already diminished speed that lowering the landing gear would have, they waited as long as possible before lowering the wheels. When they did, the gear wouldn't budge and had to be cranked down manually, a laborious and time-consuming task made worse by the fragile state of the plane. The pilot and co-pilot had all they could to do to keep the plane from stalling as the crew feverishly worked at cranking down the landing gear.

Finally, the wheels were down as the runway came into view, but the engines began to sputter from lack of fuel. Dad watched helplessly as *Lucky Lady* struggled to make the runway in much the same way he'd struggled to make the shore that fateful day Linus had saved him. My father told himself that by all rights the crippled B-17 shouldn't still be airborne. He hoped its luck would hold out just a little longer. It was a testament to the distressed craft's young pilots and its designers and manufacturers at Boeing that it still was flying.

Running on fumes with engines sputtering, *Lucky Lady* touched down in one piece and eventually rolled to a halt. All were safe and on the ground as Dad started his approach to land the *Sweet Sally.* It moved me to think that the men who could have safely bailed out chose instead to risk dying with their wounded and trapped comrades in an effort to save them. That inspired me more than ever to try to do my part to save the world from its prophesized date with nuclear destruction in a few months.

It wasn't very different with Mary on the rare occasions that I could get time off to spend biking, swimming, or just being lazy with her. Dad was good about that. As much as there was to do on the farm, and as desperate as he was for my help, he always made sure I had my time with Mary. In a weak moment, he shared with me that Mom told him about the troubling conversation she'd overheard Mary and me having at the top of the stairs the day last year when we thought we were alone and Mary was contemplating taking our relationship to a more intimate level. Her worries weren't so much about morality or whether Mary was a "nice" girl. (She knew she was.) The concern was more about what could've prompted such uncharacteristic behavior on Mary's part.

At the time, Mom didn't know about the encryptions we'd been trying to decipher or the ominous message they seemed to be sending us. But now she did—and that changed things for her. She and Dad wanted us to have our time together because we needed each other more than ever considering what might lie ahead. But they hoped that we would have the sense to stay grounded in our values in the hope that all worked out for the best.

Dad fumbled around trying to explain to me about indiscretions or hasty marriages he'd seen during the war that resulted in divorces and other problems when it was over. Finally, he came clean with me for having broken his self-imposed silence on the war by telling me the story of the *Lucky Lady*. He hoped that, like the plane's crew, Mary and I would stay true to our values even in the face of dire circumstances. If only he knew there was nothing for him and Mom to fear! Mary and I had our heads screwed on right.

Yes, Mary and I engaged in the same soul searching talks that Dad and I were having, and we had similar fears and worries about what might happen. But we didn't need an excuse to take things to another level. We knew we could if we wanted to. The opportunities were always there, and knowing that was enough for us. We were only sixteen, and we had a lifetime ahead of us—this we were determined to see come to pass. And we were content to focus our energies accordingly. If we did our job, there would be plenty of time for the rest when we were the right age for it.

And so it was in July of 1962.

With the arrival of August, Mr. Werner's plan was put into action. He fabricated an explanation for Captain Harding's disappearance with the help of his friend, John Sullivan at the Central Intelligence Agency, and then cleverly allowed it to be leaked to the press, who ran with it. The story went that Captain Harding had been in the service of the agency, flying clandestine missions in Southeast Asia and Latin America during the eleven years in question. Of course the CIA disavowed any knowledge of the explanation, which only heightened interest in the matter. As the press was busy looking down that rabbit hole, Mr. Werner cleverly started laying the groundwork for the contest that I was to win.

Captain Harding played his role well, insisting that he must have banged his head that day in 1951 and developed a case of amnesia. As hard as the press questioned him, he stuck to his story that he had no idea where he'd been and that he was helpless to be of any value to them. The news frenzy reached a new level in early August when a reporter from the *Sagahawk Chronicle* uncovered the fact that Mrs. Harding had taken several trips to Southeast Asia and Latin America during the time that Captain Harding had been missing. The trips had been with her book club and garden club and had been booked by a local travel agent in town. But it didn't matter. The press drew the conclusion that these trips were a cover for a secret rendezvous with her husband.

Mrs. Harding struggled with the attention she was receiving, and Captain Harding begged the reporters to respect their privacy. In a press conference, he pleaded with them to give him and his wife a chance to catch up with each other after eleven long years of separation. When that failed, he announced that they were putting their house up for rent and would be chartering a sailboat for a long and lazy cruise around the South Pacific. Mr. Werner rented their home, and not long thereafter, they were gone.

On August 13 the contest was announced with little to no

publicity, and a sign for it was posted in the Sagahawk Post Office, as it was in most other post offices. When I went in to get our mail that day, Miss Pickering was there speaking with Ray, our postmaster, and they showed me the sign and encouraged me to enter. Adults were welcome, but the clear focus of the announcement was directed at the nation's teenage population. The winner would receive a full scholarship to pay for college. I took a copy of the application form, said I would think about it, and left. Later that day, I came back to mail in my completed application. *The game was on.*

The August 18 mail brought a copy of the encrypted document and the rules of participation. I was sad to see that applicants were required to work on it alone and sign a pledge to keep their findings confidential. I had wanted Mary to work on it with me. When I asked Mr. Werner about it, he explained to me that there would be intense government scrutiny and demands for secrecy once the authorities became aware of the message. He said it would be best to limit those who knew about it to me, Dad, and him, and leave Dr. Hurd and Mary out of it, even though they were involved with the original decoding. He and Dad had security clearances, and I would be obligated by the confidentiality agreement I'd be required to sign. I labored over it at the library, dutifully asking Mrs. Curtin for reference books here and there, and using the opportunity to tell her that I had entered the contest. I also sought out Miss Pickering's help on Latin questions from time to time. By the arrival of the September 3 deadline for submitting my finished product, pretty much the entire town knew what I'd been doing. Many of them had watched me struggle, and now were rooting for me. But none had seen the final result. *The game was on--- really on.*

On September 16, it was officially announced that no one had been able to successfully decipher the encrypted document. Moments before that announcement, I'd received a call at home from the contest committee to tell me that my submission had been disqualified because of my prior acquaintance and involvement with Mr. Werner, the organizer of the contest. The concern voiced to me was the appearance of impropriety even though none had actually been found. When I asked if my submission would have won if it hadn't been disqualified, the caller said that they didn't speculate or comment on hypothetical situations.

However, on September 30, Mr. Werner called expectantly to invite me to meet "someone special" at the Waldorf-Astoria Hotel. He told me to be ready in an hour. Too hurried to be nervous, I rushed around as Mom pressed my only suit. On the ride to the city I got increasingly anxious, but Mr. Werner wouldn't tell me anything more. When we got there, we parked, entered through a side entrance, and rode a private elevator to our floor. Once at the door of the Presidential Suite, we stopped and Mr. Werner told me to go in by myself. Nervously I knocked as a tall man with dark glasses opened the door. Inside, sitting alone, was the president of the United States.

"Son, you did a fine job of deciphering this document, and I thought you had a right to hear it from me."

"Thank you, Mr. President."

"Of course, you must realize the chaos this message would cause if knowledge of it were to get beyond this room."

"I think I do, Mr. President."

"You think, or you know?"

"Sorry, Mr. President. I *know.*"

"Since you entered the contest and translated this document, you haven't told anyone what you learned, have you?"

"No, sir. I'm obligated by my confidentiality agreement not to."

"Joe, I don't know how you managed to decipher this document, but your nation will always be grateful to you for what you've accomplished. I promise you that I will keep this warning in mind if such a Cuban missile crisis should develop next month. You have my solemn word that I will resist the calls of the Joint Chiefs of Staff to invade Cuba with the upmost vigor, and such an invasion will not take place unless they can give me a guarantee that air strikes on Cuba can destroy all of the Soviet missile sites that are there, including any tactical missile sites."

"Thank you, Mr. President."

"Finally, I want you to be firmly resolved not to breathe a word of this to anyone."

"You have my solemn word, Mr. President."

At this point, the president stood up, and with his left hand in his jacket pocket shook my hand with his right. As I turned to walk out of the room, he called to me to say, "I understand you hope to attend Boston College in a few years. When you're ready for college, we will see that you get the scholarship you've earned."

I turned to look back at him as I walked through the open door to the suite and replied, "Thank you, sir! That will mean a great deal to me."

As the tall man with dark glasses was shutting the door behind me, I heard the president say, "You're welcome, son."

On October 15, 1962, the thirteen-day confrontation that became known as the Cuban Missile Crisis broke onto the international stage as predicted. On the morning of Saturday, October 27, 1962, Major Rudolf Anderson Jr. of the United States Air Force took off from McCoy Air Force Base in Orlando, Florida, in a U-2 aircraft, Air Force Serial Number 56-6676, repainted with overall gray radar-absorbent materials and air force insignia, for a reconnaissance flight over Cuba.

At approximately noon, he was shot down and killed by a SAM missile launched from the Caribbean island. The decision to fire at Major Anderson's U-2 was made by a Soviet commander in Cuba acting on his own. Even though he'd said earlier that he would order a strike on the missile sites if a U-2 were fired upon and shot down, President Kennedy chose to stay his hand and give Moscow the benefit of the doubt, at least until another attack was launched.

On the same day, the USS Beale tracked and dropped signaling depth charges on a Soviet Foxtrot submarine, B-59, which unknown to them was armed with a nuclear torpedo. Surrounded by US warships and needing desperately to surface because his submarine was running out of air, the submarine's captain, Valentin Savitsky, ordered the torpedo to be made ready for firing. However, Vasili Arkhipov, the deputy brigade commander captain second rank, persuaded him to change his mind, and the Soviet submarine surfaced without incident.

When the Joint Chiefs of Staff admitted that they couldn't guarantee the destruction of all the Soviet missiles in Cuba through air strikes, President Kennedy, true to his word, did all he could to avoid an invasion of the Caribbean island.

The next day, Sunday, October 28, 1962, saw the thirteen-day confrontation come to an end when President Kennedy and Premier Nikita Khrushchev brought the world back from the brink of nuclear disaster by agreeing to a mutually acceptable solution that called for the removal of Soviet missiles from Cuba in an exchange for an American promise not to invade the Caribbean island, and an undisclosed understanding that US Jupiter missiles would be removed from Italy and Turkey.

Instead of almost 100 million Americans and more than 100 million Soviets and Cubans dying in a nuclear-charged World War III, one American died so they could live—Major Rudolf Anderson Jr., who was posthumously awarded the first Air Force Cross by his president. While other service personnel and aircraft were lost in accidents related to the incident, Major Anderson was the sole combat casualty of the tense confrontation, and his U-2 aircraft was its only loss.

While I was grateful that 100 million Americans had been saved, including me, my family, and Mary, the loss of even one

American, Major Rudolf Anderson Jr., was one too many in my view. But Dad explained to me that history is a delicate creature and may sometimes be more easily preserved than changed.

At least this time Yogi Berra was wrong: It *wasn't* déjà vu all over again. In large part, it was so because a Russian submariner named Vasili Arkhipov convinced Foxtrot B-59 to come up for air, and in so doing helped spare the world.

twenty-six

As a result of Mr. Werner's contest and the crisis in October, I didn't go to live with Cousin Dorothy and attend Iona Prep until January of the following year. Mary left in late August for Kent, and Dad let me ride with Mr. and Mrs. Hurd when they took her up to school in the Ford wagon. I missed her terribly, especially during the crisis and the time leading up to it.

It was hard to concentrate on my schoolwork or get into a decent routine at Bridgehampton High School. Until October 27 came and went without a US retaliatory air raid on the Soviet missile sites in Cuba or an invasion of that Caribbean island, I found myself much more absorbed and concerned with the crisis than any of my classmates. I experienced a great deal of difficulty with not being able to share what I knew with them.

The climax came on Saturday, October 27, when a bunch of us were watching the news coverage of the standoff on a TV in our football locker room. We had come in from a bruising game when the picture on the screen switched to the image of a Soviet submarine sailing on the surface of the water, surrounded by US warships, and the announcer proclaimed with a burst of pride that the Americans had forced it to surface. The cheers from my teammates exceeded the ones we'd shared moments before, when we finally won our hard-fought game.

One guy yelled, "Way to go, Navy, you show those Russki

assholes who's boss!" And the place erupted in a cacophony of pride and joy, punctuated with an ample quantity of profanities and bluster.

In contrast, I just sat quietly on the bench in front of my locker, unnoticed by the others, and thanked God, my president, the Soviet premier, and two guys I never met but would not forget— one named Anderson and the other Arkhipov. For the first time since I discovered the warning the year before, I finally could truly relax. It was over.

Thanksgiving of 1962 was my seventeenth thanksgiving. It felt like my first; it was the first time I understood the true spirit of the holiday. My feelings of gratitude and thanks for being alive and well, in a world at peace, with my family and Mary in Sagahawk, meant more to me than all the great food and fun.

It was my first true thanksgiving!

Mary was home from Kent, and the Hurd family came out to be in Sagahawk for the holiday. Mr. and Mrs. Harding were back from their cruise and insisted on having everyone come to their home for the feast. Mrs. Harding told Mom she wanted to host the dinner because this one had special significance for her. It would be the first Thanksgiving in eleven years that her husband would be there to celebrate it with her, and she wanted all of us to be a part of their joyous thanksgiving reunion.

I had a football game that morning against our archrivals, but afterward we all planned to gather at the cemetery in the village green as they replaced the Harding gravestone that had been the subject of my second report for Miss Pickering. It was a labor of love on the part of Digger O'Dell, as our local mortician was fondly known. The new stone had only the Harding name and the picture of the angel on it in memory of little Mary Bernadette. It would have to wait for its other occupants to finish their newfound life with one another, a future together that they were most thankful to have.

I made it a point to also visit with August and Samuel and the Pickering fellow as well as with my brothers George and Brian Angel. No longer having a third case because of Miss Pickering's assignment, I gave myself one and remembered Major Rudolf Anderson Jr., whose family I knew would be having a difficult Thanksgiving. I would remember him every Memorial Day as well.

After the ceremony at the village green, we all went to the Harding home for a feast. We had turkey with bread and chestnut stuffing, brown gravy, and cranberry sauce. We had mashed sweet potatoes with marshmallows melted on top, green beans with almonds in them, and mushrooms stuffed with the ingredients of an old secret family recipe. And when we thought we couldn't eat another thing, Mom and Grandma brought out their bevy of homemade pies for dessert. Afterward, Mary and I went for a long and wonderfully uneventful walk on the beach. It was chilly but we didn't care. It was the first chance we had to be alone with one another in what felt like a lifetime.

And so it was in the fall of 1962—President John F. Kennedy's finest hour.

1963

twenty-seven

New Year's Day 1963 was a day of new beginnings for me. Dad recently had bought a new truck and gave me Sally Truck to take with me to Cousin Dorothy's house in New Rochelle. I had only a junior license, but Dad put some farm produce in the back for her and told me that if I was stopped after dark, to tell the police officer I was making a delivery of produce. As I loaded my things in the back with the produce, I hoped I wouldn't have to use that excuse.

I turned and said my good-byes, starting with Grandma, who recently returned from caring for her sister, and then Sammy, Luke, Kelly, and Linus. I paused to look at Mom prior to hugging and kissing her. Dad just gave me a nod. Before I knew it, I was alone in the truck and in the world, or so it felt, driving down Sagg Main. Leaving the only life I'd ever known, I was heading for the Montauk Highway and then my future at Iona Prep in a place called New Rochelle.

I fought hard over the last two years to save this future, and now I was determined to make the most of it. The ghosts in my past—Samuel and August, the Pickering fellow, my twin brothers, and now Major Anderson—had died so I could have this future. I couldn't let them down. I had to make the most of it for them, as well as for myself.

As the passing blur of the Bridgehampton Bank building caught my peripheral vision on the way out of town, I found myself deep in thought. I was thinking of how ironic it was that I knew more about Banes, Cuba, where the Soviet missile that shot down Major Anderson's U-2 was fired, than I did about New Rochelle, New York. For that matter, I probably knew more about August Pierce than I did about Cousin Dorothy. I'd seen a picture of her, but I didn't know how recently it was taken. And I'd never met her in person.

After many wrong turns, I finally found Winnebago Road and turned in to see her small Cape Cod style home covered with snow. It was beginning to get dark, and I was glad to have the trip behind me. It had gone without incident, so I didn't need to test Dad's flimsy farm delivery excuse. She must've been anxiously expecting me, because I no sooner turned into the short driveway, and she came out to greet me.

She looked prettier and younger in person than in the picture. Giving me a big hug and then standing back to take her measure of me, she announced, "You're a chip off the old block all right!" Then she smacked me on the back.

"Thanks," I said, not sure what to make of it all.

"Come on, let's get you inside. I have a roaring fire going, and the Orange Bowl game is on the TV. It's an exciting game. Alabama is thumping Oklahoma, and President Kennedy is at the game. He made an Alabama cheerleader cry when he invited her up to the presidential box and shook her hand. She probably won't wash it for a week!" she said as she laughed.

Just then I heard some barking and whining, and Cousin Dorothy told me that it was her cocker spaniel, Cookie.

"Her real name is Chocolate Chip Cookie because she looks so much like one. But I've taken to calling her Cookie. Listen, I'd better let her out to meet you since she tends to piddle when she meets someone new."

"Sure," I replied.

With that Cousin Dorothy opened the door, and out came this

cute wiggly little thing of a dog that danced around me and piddled by my feet in excitement.

"I told you she'd piddle!"

"Can I pick her up?"

"Sure, now that she's been out, she's fine."

I picked her up and began to pet her when Cousin Dorothy said, "Let's get inside."

Putting Cookie down, I grabbed my stuff and the produce from the back of the truck and followed her in. As we went through the front door, she said, "It's eighty degrees down there. Can you believe it?"

I thought to myself, *If you only knew Cousin Dorothy. In another iteration it would have been a nuclear winter in a bygone place.* But those were thoughts best kept to myself.

Soon we were having leg of lamb with mint jelly and wild rice and a hot apple turnover with vanilla ice cream for dessert. My room was upstairs and across from hers. We shared a hall bath. I told myself it couldn't be any worse than sharing one with Kelly, and it wasn't. Cookie slept at the foot of my bed that night.

Wednesday, January 2, 1963, was my first day of school at Iona Prep. I was up early and dressed and out of the bathroom before Cousin Dorothy needed it. When she was ready, we said good-bye to Cookie, got in the car, and drove to the school. It was located on North Avenue at the back of the college campus in a three-story red brick building with a staircase leading to a big white set of doors at the center of the building. You could have fit my little white schoolhouse inside ten times over. Cousin Dorothy had the privileges of faculty and staff, so we parked in the back and walked in the back door. She accompanied me to my home room, room 308, and then went on to her office.

Having to wear a jacket and tie was hard. I'd worn them only a handful of times before and found them confining. At Cousin Dorothy's suggestion, Mom had gotten me a madras jacket at the

St. Ann's thrift shop along with a white shirt and a black tie. The pants were new and something they called chinos. My shoes were penny loafers I'd gotten at Christmas. They weren't broken in yet, but the thick white socks helped. Everything fit, but I felt like a mannequin. It wasn't long before I loosened the tie and undid the button on my shirt collar. Everyone seemed to wear them that way.

I met a lot of new people that day, many of whom would go on to become good friends of mine. There was Paul White, or "Whitey" as his buddy Pete Huggins liked to call him. There also was Nick Long, quarterback of the football team. And then I met a George B. Angelson. I couldn't believe my ears, and had to ask him to repeat his name.

"Did you say George B. Angelson?" I asked.

"Yes."

"What does the *B* stand for?"

"Brian," he said, and I almost dropped dead.

"I had twin brothers named George and Brian Angel, who are no longer living."

"No kidding? That's a coincidence!"

"Yeah!"

"What happened to them?"

"It's a long story, but they had something called trisomy 13. They had an extra thirteenth chromosome, which impacted their central nervous system and caused them to stop breathing from time to time, and one time they simply went too long to start again."

"Well, I'm sorry to hear about your loss."

"Thanks."

This had to be a special connection. The karma was there. So we went to have a soda together at the diner across from the school on North Avenue. Cousin Dorothy had to work until 4:30 p.m., so I had time to kill. George took a bus that stopped across the street on North Avenue, so he was flexible about which one he'd catch for home. The time went quickly since we had so much to talk about while getting better acquainted. But then it was four thirty, and I knew Cousin Dorothy's car would be appearing at the front gate to the school shortly. She struck me as punctual and would be anxious to get home to walk Cookie.

"I'd better be going," I said. "My ride will be here any moment."

George looked at his watch, and seeing the time, said, "I'd better be catching the next bus home, or my mother is going to start to worry about me."

We paid our bills and started to walk out when George bumped into a kid from New Rochelle High whom George introduced to me as Chris Carter. Chris was coming in with his girlfriend, Michelle, who didn't seem to be all that fond of George. I found it strange that they both called him madras instead of George. When I tried to ask George about it, he just laughed and told me it was a long story.

My friendship with George grew stronger as the school semester progressed. He knew as little about Sagahawk as I did about his hometown of Yonkers. From time to time his family would have me over for Sunday dinner, and I gradually got to know them and the town better. We ran indoor track together, along with Paul White and Chris Carter, the kid from New Rochelle High, so I got to know them better, too. I was getting more comfortable in my new surroundings, as was Cookie, who had taken to regularly sleeping on my bed with me.

When Valentine's Day came, it was a Thursday, but Cousin Dorothy said she would cover for me at school and drove me to the train. I travelled up to Kent to see Mary for the day. It was a short but sweet visit that only made me miss her more. St. Patrick's Day was a repeat of Valentine's Day as I made another short visit to see her that Sunday, which again only made me miss her even more.

When Easter rolled around, I drove home in Sally Truck, fortunate once more not to have to make the acquaintance of any police officers along the way. It was good to see Mom and Dad again, as well as Grandma, Kelly, Luke, and Sammy. Linus was starting to show his age and had a little trouble getting up and down the stairs. But he wouldn't be denied—at least not yet. The night before I had to leave, Luke and Linus came in and slept in my room with me. Mom told me my absence had been especially hard on Luke. It was a nice visit that only made me miss them more. My life was changing, albeit slowly. Some of it was welcome; some of it was scary.

That spring Paul White invited me to play golf at his country club with him, Pete Huggins, and Nick Long. I wasn't much of a golfer, but they were. Making matters worse, we played the course where the Westchester Classic was scheduled to be played. It was far more difficult than anything I'd ever seen in Sagahawk, but they were good sports about it, and we ended up having a great time.

Soon it was summer and time to head for home. I was enjoying school and my new friends. Furthermore, Cousin Dorothy and Cookie couldn't be more loving. However, I told myself that with a return to Sagahawk would come the old normalcy that I was craving in my life. As I drove east on the Montauk Highway, every mile brought with it an increased anticipation of seeing Selma and that welcoming front porch. They were the signposts for the family that would be waiting for me inside. Even Dad's pipe smoke seemed to have acquired a nostalgic aroma for me, and I found myself almost smelling it as the tires systematically clumped over the tar dividers of the seemingly endless concrete road.

But it wasn't Dad's pipe smoke I smelled. It was Sally Truck overheating. I pulled over to allow the old girl to cool down and then took a can of water from the back to add to the radiator. Soon we were once again on our way, but I stopped periodically to add more water. A small leak had developed in the radiator, but the strategic placement of my partially chewed gum was doing the job now that I had left the radiator cap off. Slowly I nursed her home, and she got me there in time for dinner. When I made the right turn from the Montauk Highway onto Sagg Main, we both breathed a sigh of relief. Well, I breathed a sigh of relief, and Sally truck blew out the gum and enlarged the hole it had been plugging in her radiator. It didn't matter; we were home!

I was so very much looking forward to this summer. Soon Mary and her family would be out, and we would be free to see each other for more than a few stolen hours here and there. My daydreams were filled with thoughts of long days at the beach followed by bonfires at night as the two of us sat alone under the stars. There would be meandering bike rides to explore all that had happened since we'd left, with stops for sodas, burgers, and ice cream cones at the Candy Kitchen along the way. The Fourth of July would bring the beach picnic and barbeques, the fireworks and parade, and all that I missed about my small-town life. I yearned for it to be like old times, so much so that I even welcomed the idea of helping Dad again on the farm—to get the dirt beneath my nails and the taste of the dust in my mouth.

The summer turned out to be everything I'd hoped for and more. Mary and I were free to be ourselves—carefree teenagers. There were no ominous warnings from the future to deal with, no contests to enter, and no black cloud on the horizon for the upcoming fall to worry us. They truly seemed to be the lazy, hazy, crazy days of summer.

Then again, not everything is always what it seems, and the summer of 1963 was no exception. Unbeknownst to me and Mary and most Americans, there were sinister forces at work that threatened to take the life of the president, even after he and Mr. Khrushchev had brought the world back from the brink of nuclear disaster only a few months earlier.

I first came to learn of the concerns of a possible assassination plot on Thursday night, August 1, 1963. The radiator on Sally Truck had been fixed. I was out on a date with Mary in the truck when Jimmy O'Donoghue of the Southampton Police Department pulled me over—the same Jimmy O'Donoghue who had stopped traffic on the Montauk Highway to admire Sammy in her baby carriage on a busy Saint Patrick's Day holiday weekend the prior year. He was an old friend, so I wasn't too concerned.

As Jimmy got out of his cruiser and walked over, I leaned out of the truck window and asked, "What are you doing, Jimmy? You know I don't have a license to drive at night?"

"I know, you're delivering produce. I'm sure there's an old rotten potato rolling around back there somewhere, as he momentarily gazed at the truck's bed, but thought better of looking too diligently. That's not the reason I stopped you. My mother is working dispatch, and she called me to track you down. She got a call from your dad, who needs you home as soon as possible."

"My father called the police to track me down when he knows I'm out driving at night with only a junior license? Is this some kind of joke?"

"No, I'm serious. He really does need to see you immediately."

"Is everything okay at the house?"

"I think so, he told Mom to have me tell you it's nothing to be worried about."

"All right, but ask your mother to please call and tell him I'm dropping Mary off and will be home in five minutes."

"You got it. By the way, you have a burned out taillight."

Mary leaned over from the passenger side and said, "Jimmy, rumor has it you're trying to get a date with that girl Gail from Valley Stream who works at the Dairy Queen. Is that true?"

"Yeah, do you know her?"

"I do, and I'll make sure to put in a good word for you."

"You will? Thanks!" And with that he waved good-bye and walked back to his cruiser, completely forgetting about the taillight that Sally truck didn't even have. Dad had knocked it off years ago. However, there definitely was a new bounce in Jimmy's step.

As I drove away, I asked Mary, "Do you really know this girl, Gail?"

"Yes, she's Gloria's niece. You remember?"

"You mean Gloria, who works at the firehouse?"

"Yes."

"Oh, yeah; now I think I do. Doesn't Gail have curly hair and a sister named Karen?"

"That's the one. She's sort of serious and quiet; the opposite of her sister, Karen, who is always laughing and talking your ear off. Have you forgotten what you had to say about Karen?"

"I think I said she'd better marry a quiet Joe, because the poor guy will never get a word in edgewise."

"That's right. That's the phrase you used: Quiet Joe. I couldn't remember exactly."

We both enjoyed a good laugh at Karen's expense.

With that we reached Mary's house. I helped her out of the truck, walked to the front door with her, and stole a quick kiss good night before returning to the familiar sound of the idling engine and the faint smell of oil from the exhaust. During the short ride home, I tried to think of what could be so important. The answer would become apparent immediately upon my arrival.

When I pulled into the driveway, Dad, Mr. Werner, and Captain Harding were sitting on the front porch. You could cut the pipe and cigarette smoke with a knife as it swirled up into the night sky, caught momentarily in the twin beams of Sally Truck's front lights. All three were deep in what seemed to be a serious discussion.

As I came up and joined them, I asked, "What's the matter? Did something happen?"

"We've kept you out of it until now, but on July 7, Captain Harding had another visit from our future."

I interrupted to ask, "But you haven't been missing or anything like that. Where and how did this happen?"

"It was more like your encounter, Joe. I was out for a late-night run and passing by the cemetery in the village green when I saw the light again, bigger and brighter than ever, and knew exactly what it was."

"What did they tell you?"

"Well, it was short and to the point, and there seemed to be a sense of urgency and panic in their communication. They kept emphasizing it was their last chance to warn us and to please pay careful attention."

"But what did they tell you?"

"They repeated their original warning, only this time they were more specific. They said the assassination would take place in Chicago at the beginning of November."

"It's still supposed to be carried out by an ex-marine who previously was stationed at a U-2 base in Japan?"

"Exactly!"

"Then what's the problem? What's it you need me to do?"

Dad stood up to empty his pipe over the railing and into the bushes below. When he finished, he turned to me and said, "We've kind of been hoisted by our own petards."

"What do you mean?"

"We've been trapped by our lies. We told the president that the warning for the Cuban Missile Crisis came from your translation of the 1947 encrypted Roswell document. We made no mention of Tom's eleven-year ordeal or of your experience with the toy saucer. How do we now tell him about this most recent encounter Tom had at the cemetery without revealing all that old baggage and compromising our credibility with him?"

"Gosh Dad, don't you have all the credibility you need now that the Cuban Missile Crisis went so well?"

"No. You and I know what happened in the first go-around. The president knows only how it came out this time. There is a tendency to think after the fact that the success would have happened in any event, and that the warning was overblown or a case of crying wolf, if you know what I mean."

"I think I do. Mary's uncle is a lawyer who jokes that it's tough being one because if you win, clients don't want to pay you because they were right in the first place, and if you lose, they don't want to pay you because you lost the case. I guess what you're saying is that the president will tend to think that his skills would have gotten him through it anyway, with or without the warning."

"That's the general idea, Joe."

"What are you going to do?"

"Max is going to claim to have pored over your translation of the document and conclude that there is a possibility that the assassination attempt is not inextricably tied to the nuclear winter scenario and may survive as an independent prediction or warning. From that he will advise the president that extra precautions should be taken in planning his schedule of events next November."

"Does that mean that you aren't going to mention Chicago and the beginning of November to the president?"

"Not at first because it can't be directly tied to the 1947 Roswell document. But we hope to have the situation evolve into a scenario that includes that much specificity. That is where you come in."

"The president is making several unpublicized trips to New York in the upcoming weeks and months and will be staying in the presidential suite at the Carlyle Hotel. He's asked to meet with you again, to reiterate his gratitude to you for your work on the deciphering of the contest document. Max suggested to him that it would be a fine gesture, and the president agreed.

"We think this would be an excellent opportunity for you to mention to the president that the document does not explicitly tie the November assassination plot to the discontent caused by the nuclear winter and could be interpreted as applying to a broader, more general discontent. You can tell him that you're very concerned for him and want to be sure that he was aware of this ambiguity so that his Secret Service detail could take special precautions in November, especially early November."

"I don't say anything about the location being Chicago?"

"We don't see how you can. You would have no way of knowing that fact from the contest document. We just have to hope that he takes your caution seriously and that the Secret Service does its job."

"It's a little scary, Dad. I'm uncomfortable with not saying anything. What if something happens? I would never be able to forgive myself."

"It's called sitting on the horns of a dilemma. If we come clean, we run the risk of looking like a bunch of kooks that just happened to get it right last time, and we may lose all credibility. If we confine ourselves as we're proposing, we run the risk that your caution will not be taken as seriously as it should. The essential point is that it's still better than doing nothing."

"I guess you're right, Dad. When do I meet with the president?"

"Max will set it up and let us know."

"Okay. I think I'm going to go inside and watch some TV now if that's all right."

"Sure, Joe. It will do you good to relax a little. You look like the weight of the world is on your shoulders."

I got up to leave, said good night to both men and Dad, then I headed inside. I did indeed feel like the weight of the world was once again on my shoulders, and I didn't want it there. I'd been enjoying being a kid again. But then my ghosts whispered to me as the breeze once again began to rustle Selma's leaves, reminding me that they'd died so that I might live, and now it was my turn to make sure their sacrifices weren't in vain. It was an awesome responsibility. When I was a little kid, I dreamed of being a superhero. Now I yearned to be just a little kid again.

As I stepped through the doorway to the house, Dad and Mr. Werner called out to remind me of my pledge to the president and told me I couldn't say anything to Mary, or anyone else for that matter. If the president asked me, I had to be able to assure him that I'd been true to my word. I nodded okay.

Before all this happened, I'd never kept anything from Mary, so it was hard. It was a great deal of responsibility, and I would've preferred it hadn't fallen on me to shoulder. But I knew in the end it was my destiny and resigned myself to my fate and honored my pledge.

It wasn't long thereafter that I was in a car with Mr. Werner, being whisked into the Carlyle Hotel for my meeting with the president. He was as gracious and friendly as I'd remembered him from our last meeting. As I walked into the room, he was speaking with a young intern, and when their business was finished, she left. He shut the door and came over to me.

"Hi, Joe, it's good to see you again. How've you been?"

"Fine, Mr. President."

"I wanted to take this opportunity to thank you again for all your hard work. It really helped me navigate through the crisis last fall."

"You're welcome, sir." And then I decided to go for it and said, "I hope you don't mind, Mr. President, but I wanted to ask you a favor."

"Sure, what is it?"

"It's been haunting me that in the document I translated, the warning about your being assassinated this coming November isn't directly tied to the Cuban Missile Crisis having gone bad and the resulting nuclear winter. For some reason, the unrest doesn't seem to be directly tied into the death and misery arising from that disaster. It could be viewed as still applying, even with a favorable outcome, like the one you achieved. I just want to ask you to please be extra careful this November with your travels, especially to big cities like this one or Chicago, or even places like Miami or Dallas or around Washington, DC."

"You have nothing to be concerned about. The Secret Service worries about me too much as it is. But I'll ask them to take special care, just as you ask. And I thought you were going to ask me to get you tickets to the Army/Navy game."

"You can do that?"

"I just happen to have four here," he said as he reached into his pocket and pulled them out. Then he kiddingly pulled them back and said, "Maybe I should first ask who you'll be rooting for."

"Dad was in the army's eighth air force, but now the air force is separate, so I guess I can be neutral. I know all about you and PT-109."

He handed me the tickets, saying, "You have a future in politics, Joe. That was a perfect answer!"

We shook hands, and I left. I was so excited that I couldn't wait to tell Dad. He was a big fan of the navy quarterback, Roger Staubach. I planned to invite Dad, Mom, and Mary to join me.

The four of us did go to that game. It was played in Municipal Stadium in Philadelphia on December 7, 1963, and Navy won 21-15, but the president I expected to see there wasn't there. He was in the ground in Arlington National Cemetery. He was destined to become one of my ghosts.

twenty-eight

The carnival came to Sagahawk in August of 1963. Mary and I were at the top of the Ferris wheel when it stopped unexpectedly. There was a beautiful moon that night, and the stars were twinkling in their places in the heavens. All seemed so well with the world. My fears for the president's well-being had faded into a distant memory now that he'd reassured me that the Secret Service already worried about him too much and I needn't be concerned.

I decided to seize upon the moment and leaned over to kiss Mary. My urge to share with her the full measure of the inner peace I was experiencing refused to be denied. It was a long, quiet kiss, the kind that allowed all my feelings and emotions to flow from me to her in a perfect communion of silence. When I finished, I said nothing. Nothing needed to be said. The kiss expressed all that I wished to convey—I could see it in her eyes.

She smiled as the Ferris wheel once again began to move and whispered, "You're getting much better at the kissing game, Jolting Joe."

It felt so good to just be a kid again.

The rest of the summer was spent stealing such moments together in the dunes at the beach or behind the Candy Kitchen or the library in town, or at an impromptu picnic during a bike ride. But as with all good things, eventually the summer had to come to an end, and with that end came the need to go back to school.

I felt better about returning to Cousin Dorothy's house and the Prep this time around, but I still didn't really want to leave. I knew I'd be fine once I was into my routine there and with my friends. But my roots had begun to take once again in Sagahawk, and it was painful to pull them up and set out for that place called New Rochelle. What made it especially hard was leaving early for football camp, well before Mary and her family had to head back. She was at my house when I finished packing up Sally Truck, including the produce Dad had given me for Cousin Dorothy. The entire family was outside to see me off, including Linus, who had to be helped down the stairs.

Mary decided to ride with me as far as the Candy Kitchen in Bridgehampton. It would give us a little more time together and a chance at a more private good-bye. As hard as I found it to leave her behind, I knew the time had come. Stealing one last kiss through the open window before putting Sally Truck in gear, I drove west out of town into the waning summer of 1963.

Cousin Dorothy was glad to see me. And of course Cookie saw fit to baptize my shoes with a welcome piddle. Football camp started the next day and was hard, but nothing I couldn't handle after working alongside Dad in the fields. I was happy to make the team and see my friends again. Paul White, Pete Huggins, Nick Long, and George Angelson were on the team with me.

Some of our football games were played on Sundays at Memorial Field in a place called Mount Vernon, so Mary promised to come down and see as many of them as she could. Dr. and Mrs. Hurd came on occasion, and we would have a tailgate picnic afterward. The old 1958 Ford wagon gave way to a new 1963 Ford Country Squire wagon that season, but the tailgates remained the same— fun and chock-full of goodies. They were a little bit of home for me, I think.

Dad surprised me and came to a game. He had Linus and

Luke with him. Mom stayed home because Grandma and Sammy weren't feeling well and Kelly was away with the Girl Scouts.

As November approached, I found myself paying more attention to the news. My concern about an assassination plot had begun to rear its ugly head again. When November 1 came, I turned into a news junkie, reading everything I could find. So you can imagine how relieved I was when Dad called me at Cousin Dorothy's house on Saturday night, November 2, to tell me that President Kennedy had cancelled his trip to Chicago. An ex-marine named Thomas Arthur Vallee, who had served at a marine base in Japan that housed the U-2 aircraft, was arrested at around 9:00 a.m. Chicago time, apparently for traffic infractions.

I said to Dad, "Do you believe it? We dodged the second bullet after all. We are two for two. We saved the world in 1962 and we saved the president in 1963."

But Dad would have none of it, and sternly admonished me: "We did our part in a very complex situation and helped attain a result everyone should be grateful for. But we didn't save anything on our own. We had a lot of help and more than our share of luck. Fate was good to us."

"Sorry, Dad, I know how you feel about tempting fate and all that. I was very excited. It's been weighing on me, and it feels so good to have it finally be over. But you're right, it was arrogant and presumptuous of me to say it that way, to have us take all the credit. But I have to be honest with you: Mary is down visiting, and we're going to party tonight! Tomorrow I promise to get back to the grindstone."

"I told you once before, Joe: You make sure you take care of that girl! She's a good girl, and she will probably be your wife and the mother of your children someday. Don't go doing anything foolish. You're not too old to be taken out to the shed. Do right by her and let your future together develop in due course. There's no need to rush things. Do you hear me?"

"Yes, Dad. I do. You have nothing to worry about, I promise!"

"All right then, go out and have fun. But before you do, your mother wants to say hello to you." With that, he handed the phone to Mom, and we chatted briefly.

When I quietly hung up the phone that night, I realized how special Mom and Dad were to me. They were two God-fearing, loving, humble people. The dirt beneath Dad's nails and the stained apron around Mom's waist bore witness to that fact. One could have been a noted Columbia University Professor in Latin or a high-ranking officer in the United States Air Force who had brought his plane and crew home safely from thirty-eight missions over Germany. The other was a gifted writer who could've been a renowned author or publisher. Instead, they'd chosen to keep a promise made by my great-grandfather to Mildred Pierce to farm the land on which Selma stood and raise a family that now included one of her own, for Sammy had made the circle complete.

Oh, what a Saturday night that was! Mary and I danced and partied late into the night. But as difficult as it was, I stayed true to those Sagahawk values, and believe me when I tell you it was hard! The future had been preserved, both ours and the nation's—or so I thought.

On Friday afternoon, November 22, 1963, we had come back from lunch and were getting ready to start our Latin class at Iona Prep when the principal's voice came over the loud speaker to announce that the president had been shot in Dallas, Texas, and had been pronounced dead at Parkland Hospital. I fell silent in my seat, shocked in disbelief. I told myself it had to be a mistake, but in my heart I knew it wasn't. School was dismissed, and I rode home with Cousin Dorothy. At one point she was crying so hard we had to switch and I dove. Her eyes were so bleary that she couldn't see.

When we got back to the house on Winnebago Road, we turned on the TV and spent the day watching the details of the assassination unfold, the swearing in of the new president with the grieving widow in her bloodied pink suit at his side, and the arrest of an alleged assassin. I was devastated when I learned details about the suspect, who'd been apprehended in a movie theater after shooting a police officer. The man was described as a disgruntled ex-marine named Lee Harvey Oswald, who had served on an air base in Japan that housed the U-2 aircraft.

I was distraught. How could it be? How could there have been two possible suspects with such similar backgrounds?

I called Dad. When he answered, I tearfully asked, "How could it be?"

He responded, "It was meant to be! Look, son, as far as I know, in our world Thomas Arthur Vallee has never been accused of anything more than traffic infractions, and the president has been assassinated in Dallas. But if you believe the version of reality told to us by our future, it was meant to be. They killed him after the nuclear war; they killed him a second time in Chicago after the peaceful resolution of the crisis that avoided that nuclear war; and when he once again wouldn't stay dead, they killed him a third time in Dallas. History is a delicate creature, more easily preserved than changed. And until our future can find a way to go back more than ninety-one years, I'm afraid this verdict will have to stand."

Humbled, I hung up the phone. I guess I'd finally learned the lesson Miss Pickering had been trying to teach me: Respect the dead. They may well have died so that you could live. For me it was true of Samuel and August and the Pickering fellow. It was true of my twin brothers George and Brian Angel. It was true of Major Anderson. And now it was true of our fallen president.

And so it was on a beautiful but sad Friday afternoon, November 22, 1963—the day Mom says the final curtain came down on *Camelot*.

twenty-nine

On Saturday, November 23, 1963, the weather outside and the weather in my heart were gray and gloomy as I watched the television coverage with Cousin Dorothy and Cookie of our fallen president lying in state. Glued to the TV, still in shock and disbelief at what had happened the day before, we were in a trance as we looked *past* the picture on the set as much as *at* it. How could the most powerful man in the world have been so easily and abruptly felled by this Lee Harvey Oswald guy?

We were watching with a secret hope we dared not admit or mention that a news flash would come on to say it had all been a cruel hoax. But in our hearts we knew it wasn't. The childhood nursery rhyme my mother read to me was prophetic—all the king's men couldn't put Humpty Dumpty back together again. And all the president's mourners couldn't put his life back together again. Even the life of the most powerful man in the world was as fragile as an egg. It was this that our nation was struggling to come to terms with as it watched that day.

Saturday night I insisted to Cousin Dorothy that we get out of the house and grab a bite to eat at Pete's tavern in nearby Bronxville. We met George Angelson and his family there for a burger. The mood was subdued, but it felt good to get away from the television.

As if the prior two days had not been enough, on Sunday,

November 24, 1963, we watched on television in shock as the president's suspected assassin, Lee Harvey Oswald, was shot by Jack Ruby while in police custody.

"What's going on?" I asked Cousin Dorothy.

"This is scary! First, the Secret Service can't protect the president, and now the Dallas police can't protect his suspected assassin," replied Cousin Dorothy.

"I don't know what to make of it," I said.

"I think it's an inside job. I think Lady Bird is behind it. She wanted to see her husband be president!"

"I don't think so, Cousin Dorothy."

"Well then, who do you think did it, the Soviets? Or maybe the Cubans? Perhaps you think the mafia or our own government was involved?"

I knew I couldn't say anything about the warnings our future had given us, so I tried to end it by saying, "I don't know. Maybe this guy Oswald really did do it all by himself."

"Nonsense! It's not that easy to shoot the president of the United States. We'll all be dead by the time the truth finally comes out. You'll see."

I had to laugh to myself at the way Cousin Dorothy chose to phrase her comment, but I knew what she meant and let it ride. More importantly, I knew what she was feeling. On the one hand, she was terrified to think that this might have been a well-organized conspiracy. On the other hand, she found it hard to fathom that the most powerful man in the world could be killed so easily by a lone gunman.

The future had warned us that he would be shot by an ex-marine, but in their iteration it had taken place at the beginning of November in Chicago, not at the end of the month in Dallas. The fact that there were two ex-marines in two separate places at different times, told me that Dad was right when he spoke in terms of "they," but who the "they" were I didn't know, and

I didn't think Dad did either. Maybe Cousin Dorothy was right: Only time would tell.

Thanksgiving, more so than Christmas, was subdued that year as the result of the tragic loss of the young president. For many of us, that day in November would become the defining day in our lives, the day on which everyone remembers where they were and what they were doing when they learned the news. I suspected it was much like Pearl Harbor must've been for Dad and Mom's generation.

Dad once told me exactly where he was and what he was doing when he learned that Pearl Harbor had been attacked. He was on his way to visit a college classmate and was waiting to be picked up at the Crestwood Railroad Station of the New York Central Railroad when he heard the shocking announcement on that fateful Sunday afternoon. It remained as vivid to him then as it did the day it happened. I knew that my memory of November 22, 1963, would remain just as vividly with me for the rest of my life.

And so it was in 1963.

1964 to 1966

thirty

Life goes on. It must if there is to be a future. The year 1964 was a new year, and spring was upon us, a time of new beginnings. As the birds started to make their presence known and the flowers provided them with a background showcase of beautiful colors and sweet scents, lives began to return to normal.

My friend George now had a new girlfriend named Kelly, who lived in Bronxville and went to Marymount. When Mary would come down from Kent to visit, we would often go on a double date to the movies and the Nielson's ice cream parlor in her town. I was older than George and could drive due to the fact I was held back as a youngster. It was because of the schooling I missed when Dad ran into problems and almost lost the farm.

When I drove George to get his driver's license, he and I learned to our surprise that we shared the same birthday: June 2. It was just another in a series of so many coincidences in our lives.

The summer of 1964 was uneventful. I spent it back at Sagahawk helping Dad on the farm. Mary and her family came out as usual, and the Hardings were getting back into their routine. Bicycle rides, lazy days at the beach, and ice cream sodas in town were par for the course. It was a wonderful summer.

On September 24, 1964, the Warren Commission issued its report, concluding that Lee Harvey Oswald had acted alone in assassinating the president. It made no mention of Thomas Arthur

Vallee and the Chicago incident. I was surprised that it didn't, so I took a trip up to Kent to discuss it with Mary. She was one of the few people with whom I could talk about it, and the one I felt most comfortable with expressing my disappointment.

As I got off the train in Kent, Mary was there waiting for me. After hugging and kissing her, I suggested that we go down the street to get something to eat. On the way, we began to talk.

I asked her, "What do you think about the fact that the Warren Commission makes no mention of Thomas Arthur Vallee and Chicago?"

"Well, why would they?" she answered.

"How can you investigate what happened in Dallas without figuring out what was in the works for Chicago earlier that month?"

"Joe, you know the significance of Chicago because you've been told that the president was assassinated in Chicago by a disgruntled ex-marine in a different version of our future. They don't know that. In their world, Thomas Arthur Vallee was a guy taken into custody for traffic violations and let go when the president's trip to Chicago was cancelled. Who knows how many times people are taken in and questioned in connection with trips planned by the president and nothing ever comes of it?"

"The FBI warned the Secret Service in advance about the possible plot in Chicago," I retorted. "Why wouldn't that alone be enough for the Warren Commission to at least check it out as part of their investigation? It goes to the heart of the notion of whether Dallas was an isolated incident perpetrated by a lone assassin."

"Like I said, who knows how much of this stuff happens before every presidential trip?"

"But we're talking here about two ex-marines with strong views on Cuba who both served on top secret U-2 bases in Japan under CIA control and who both conveniently got jobs along the president's planned motorcade route. Oswald got his job at the

Texas School Book Depository, and Vallee got his at a warehouse on West Jackson Boulevard. A little bit of a coincidence, don't you think?"

"Joe, honey, you've got to let it go now!"

"Let it go! I can't. It's more than two years of my life, and furthermore, I owe it to my ghosts."

"Listen to what your father had to say. It was meant to be. And until our future can find a way to go back more than ninety-one years, this result will have to stand. Like he told you, history is a delicate creature, more easily preserved than changed."

"But it's almost as if they don't want to know!"

"My Latin teacher at Kent likes to quote an ancient Roman saying that he attributes to Petronius: *Mundus vult decipi, ergo decipiatur.*"

"Oh, I know that saying. Miss Pickering liked to use it, too. I just didn't know where it came from. I guess you're right. If the world wants to be deceived, let it be deceived!"

"Let it go, honey, it's time to move on. You aren't going to change anything. Your Jolting Joe days are over."

And so it was in 1964, the year I left the future behind and returned to the present—returned to being plain old Joe Carr. A year that would best be remembered, not for my transformation or the issuance of The Warren Commission Report, but as the year the British invaded America for the second time and with much more success.

My sister got Mary and me tickets to *The Ed Sullivan Show* to see the Beatles. When they opened with "All My Loving," Mary, along with every other girl in the place, went into a frenzy and stayed that way until they finished with "I Want to Hold Your Hand." I leaned over to tell her she had all my loving and that I wanted to hold her hand. But it was no use. She'd been swept up and away from me by the moment and was in another world.

thirty-one

During the first three months of 1965, I drove home on the weekends. I wasn't playing any winter sports at Iona, and I wanted to spend the time with the family. Dad and I decided to race the *Proud Mary* in earnest, and we took back the Sagahawk Cup from Mike Johnson, but not without a fight. It was a photo finish, which took the judges several minutes of caucusing before they could rule in my favor. Mike was a good sport about his disappointing loss and vowed to win it back next year.

Dad and I also went duck hunting whenever the opportunity presented itself. We had some deep and serious talks while doing it. My father was growing increasingly worried about what he saw developing in Vietnam, long before most of us realized the significance of what was happening. His concern stemmed from having learned that on March 8, two marine battalions had been sent by President Johnson to Vietnam to guard the US airfield at Danang. They were the first combat troops to be committed to Vietnam. Dad knew they wouldn't be the last. As he put it to me, we had mounted the tiger before giving sufficient thought to how we were going to dismount without being eaten.

After what he'd seen take place in Korea once China entered the war, he was concerned that I might be drafted to fight a limited war, a war we would fight not to lose, rather than to win. He didn't want to see me placed in harm's way unless we had a clearly defined purpose that was critical to our survival as a nation, the way World War II had been.

With the arrival of spring, I started spending more time at Cousin Dorothy's place and at school. I did go home one weekend to take Luke on a Boy Scout trip to Montauk. It really was nice to have the time alone with Luke and see how nicely he was progressing. We set up our own tent, started a fire without matches, cooked soup and melted marshmallows, and told scary stories around the fire.

The summer of 1965 was a remarkably ordinary one. I labored on the farm with Dad, saw Mary every chance I got, and worked out for football. The coming season would be my final one as I would be a senior. I had a good shot at a starting position, and I didn't want to blow it. Luke and Linus would often come to keep me company when I ran at the Bridgehampton High School track. Linus was too old and stiff to run anymore, but he would wait for me at the spot where he knew I would finish. Luke would start out with me and last about a lap before he became bored with the idea of running in circles.

At the end of August, I reported early for football camp. It was good to see Paul White, Nick Long, Pete Huggins, George Angelson, and the rest of the team again. But the two-a-days in the hot summer sun weren't much fun. Coach Lamb saw to that. We were a determined bunch and played courageously against daunting odds. After disappointing losses to Chaminade and Mount St. Michael's, we beat Cardinal Spellman and our rival, Stepinac. We lost to Holy Cross but beat Cardinal Hayes before tying St. Francis in a controversial game. Finally, we lost to New Rochelle on Thanksgiving Day. Chris Carter came over afterward to talk to George and me. It would be the last time we would play against each other. Mom and Dad, together with Kelly, Sammy, Luke, and Grandma came to spend Thanksgiving with Cousin Dorothy and see my final game. Although we didn't win any titles, I was proud of the way we had played.

After the game, when Dad and I were walking alone, I told him I owed him an apology.

"An apology, what for?" he asked.

"Last winter when you were so worried about Vietnam, I thought you were getting carried away and your concerns were overblown, but now I am beginning to appreciate what you were saying."

"What happened to change your mind?"

"On November 15, Army Second Lieutenant John Lance Geoghegan, Iona Prep class of 1959, was killed fighting with his men in the successful defense of a strategic position in the Ia Drang Valley near Plei Me, South Vietnam. Coach Lamb told us about it during practice, and it brought Vietnam home for me and many of my friends on the team."

"I'm sorry to hear about that loss, son. Your mom and I will keep Lieutenant Geoghegan and his family in our prayers."

"Thanks. My senior class has decided to dedicate our yearbook to him."

Pulling out a piece of paper I had stuffed in my helmet, I read the dedication to Dad: "'We, the Class of 1966, feel honored to dedicate our annual to Army Second Lieutenant John Lance Geoghegan, Class of 1959.'"

"I think that's a very thoughtful gesture, and will mean a lot to his family."

"We are going to include the quotation, 'By their deeds do you know them.'"

"That's so true!"

"We have a quote he gave before he was killed and plan to use it under a picture of him as a cadet. It reads: 'Let us pray that the men who died here will not have died needlessly and that everyone who is trying to help this courageous little nation will see it rise above the devastation of war.'"

"I'll say that prayer as the lieutenant requests, son. Furthermore, I hope that my initial assessment is wrong, that he and the others didn't die needlessly, and that Vietnam rises above the devastation it is undergoing. But sadly, I must tell you that I don't think that'll be the case."

"I understand," I said with a sense of resignation.

As we approached the team bus, I told Dad I'd see him back at Cousin Dorothy's, my home away from home. I paused to reflect for a moment and take a backward glance as I boarded, for I would be going to a place Lieutenant Geoghegan no longer could go, home to celebrate Thanksgiving with my family. It would be a hard Thanksgiving for the Geoghegan family, and I said a silent prayer for them and their fallen son.

Then I saw Mary running toward the bus and leaned out the window to blow her a kiss as we pulled away. My teammates yelled to Brother Dunn, who stopped the yellow contraption long enough to let me say hello to her through the window before driving on. Mary and her parents had come up from the city to see the game and would be coming to Cousin Dorothy's house to have dinner with us.

And so it was in 1965, the year Vietnam invaded my consciousness.

thirty-two

If 1965 is the year that Vietnam first invaded my consciousness, 1966 is the year that Vietnam caught the nation's attention in earnest. Protests against the war became a commonplace occurrence on college campuses, in cities across the country, and on everyone's television screen.

It was the year of the great divide for my age group, a divide between those who would be deferred and heading off to college and those who would be graduating from high school and eligible for the draft. It was a time of soul searching for many of us.

In a year's time, some would be fighting in a place called Vietnam, of which they knew little. Some would be in the military and worried that they might be sent there to fight for reasons they were not sure they understood. Others would be savvy or have connections that enabled them to find refuge in the National Guard or the reserves.

Others still would choose to relinquish all and flee to Canada. Some would just acquiesce and go, hoping for the best, but expecting much less. A few, like Lieutenant Geoghegan before them, believed in the cause and joined willingly and with the conviction they were helping a courageous little nation survive the devastation of war and freeing that country's people from Communist oppression. All in one way or another would be making sacrifices that would forever alter the direction of their young lives. Lieutenant

Geoghegan and some others would be giving all in doing their nation's work.

It was in this setting that George Angelson and I graduated from Iona Prep in 1966. We went on to Boston College together. I was on a football scholarship and George would join the team the following year as a walk-on. We were filled with excitement and expectations, but we carried a tinge of guilt at knowing some of our friends would be heading into harm's way. George and Kelly Dougherty had broken up, but Mary had been accepted at Wellesley College, and would be going to school near me for the first time in our lives. This alone was cause for joy.

Paul White was off to the University of Scranton, Pete Huggins to Wisconsin, Nick Long to Notre Dame, and Chris Carter to Fordham, but others were being told to report to boot camp. We wouldn't see each other again until Thanksgiving when we would attend the Iona/New Rochelle Thanksgiving Day game as alumni for the first time. Some of our friends would be home on leave from the service and join us. None had been killed yet.

And so it was in 1966, the year my class went off to war.

1967 and Onward

thirty-three

I didn't have much time to think about the war, once I was into my routine at Boston College. Football and classes took up the lion's share of my time. Every free moment I could muster I spent visiting with Mary at Wellesley. One afternoon that changed, when it was announced that there would be an anti-war rally at Boston College. I was excused from football practice early because of a class I had to attend and was walking back to the locker room to shower, when I saw several yellow school buses pulling up. Their doors opened and out spilled faces, mostly female, that I'd never seen before. There were babies, real babies, being handed out for the young women to hold as they marched in a large oval procession. I didn't think the babies belonged to the young women, who were holding them. Soon the television crews showed up and began to film and interview them.

I watched quietly from a distance. Once the television crews left, the women handed the babies back to their handlers and boarded the buses that left soon thereafter. That evening I watched the news to see it reported that Boston College students, including young mothers, whose husbands were conscripted to fight in Vietnam, had protested the war. I honestly didn't think there were any Boston College students involved in the protest, let alone any mothers with children.

Later that night, I called Dad to tell him what I'd seen. He laughed and replied that all is fair in love and war. Well, it sure in hell was an education for me.

That fall semester George was busy running track and totally consumed with a project he was working on for his political science class. He'd made friends with a guy named Donny from the track team, and we didn't see much of each other. It wasn't because there were any problems between us. We were just both so busy.

In the spring, George got heavily involved with his theology class and we saw even less of each other. As part of that class he made a trip to Bridgehampton to attend an Episcopal Sunday service at St. Ann's with Wally Rather, a BC classmate who I grew up with out there. When he got back, he came bursting into my dorm room to tell me how fantastic Bridgehampton was, and how much he liked the place.

I smiled and said, "George, I know, I grew up out there, remember?"

However, I felt bad that in all our years together at the Prep, I'd never thought to invite him or the others out to Sagahawk for a visit. After all, George's family had invited me to their home for many a Sunday dinner.

I was enjoying my time with Mary at Wellesley. Her school was on a beautiful lake and the boat house for the crew team sat at the secluded end of it. We'd go for walks down the rustic path among the pines that led to the boathouse, and sit by the lake for hours. I told her that if we ever had any daughters, I wanted them to go to Wellesley. She smiled and told me it would have to be their decision, and not mine. I knew she was right, but secretly told myself that as their father, it was fair for me to lobby them early and often. They would all have a Wellesley College bib from the get go. As Dad said, all is fair in love and war, and this was a war for their hearts and minds.

In the fall of 1968, Christian Carter's father died unexpectedly and Christian dropped out of Fordham to join the marines. George and I drove down together to attend the wake. George was more involved than ever with his theology course professor, a Father Phillips. He told me on the car ride down in his new GTO that he was giving thought to becoming a priest. I was totally blindsided by the news, because I'd had no hint of it beforehand. I guess my shocked reaction may have left him unsettled, because he never discussed the subject with me again.

The 1968 football season brought with it a change in our head coach. Joe Yukica replaced Jim Miller, and gave George the chance to join the team as a "walk-on," or non-scholarship player. We opened at Navy on September 28, and hung a 49—15 pasting on them in Annapolis. We hadn't beat Navy in forty years, so it was sweet!

In the spring I was required to travel home often, because Dad hurt his back and needed help on the farm. I almost thought I'd have to take a leave from school, the way I'd done when I was younger. Fortunately I was able to work it out with help from my teachers, and didn't have to leave. However, it did make clear to me that there would be no graduate school in my future; I would have to take over for Dad, and start running the farm immediately following graduation the next year.

In the spring of 1970, George and I graduated from Boston College and Mary graduated from Wellesley; George and Mary with honors, me with a sigh of relief at having made it. George eventually went on to Law School; I returned to the farm in Sagahawk. We both were lucky to have avoided the draft and Vietnam with a lottery number of 228, when President Nixon froze the system at 195.

Dad thought he finally could rest easy about me being drafted to fight in Vietnam after the lottery was frozen at 195, and my number was higher. However there was something he didn't know because I was sworn to secrecy and couldn't tell him. A strange thing happened to me in March of 1970, shortly before I was scheduled to graduate in May.

Christian Carter called to see if I could meet him and another marine in downtown Boston, when they would be passing through. I agreed and met them as planned. They were attempting to recruit me for a special mission to Vietnam the following spring. They weren't at liberty to tell me very much, and I told them that I'd have to think about it and get back to them once I graduated.

A part of me very much wanted to do it, but after much anguish, including an ultimatum from Mary, I told them in July that I couldn't. The excuse I gave was Dad needed my help on the farm. While that was true, it was only part of the reason. More importantly, Mary emphatically threatened to leave me. Cold and firm, it was a side of her I'd not seen before and hoped to never see again.

I didn't hear anything more about the mission after that day in 1970. I suspect the reason is that Christian Carter was tragically killed in action a year later, on June 9, 1971, while rescuing a downed pilot.

George had deferred starting law school by a year, when he thought he might be drafted and before he knew the lottery would be frozen at 195. In the interim, he took a job with a local Ford dealer near his home while he waited to start school in September of 1971. In the spring of that year, George took a trip to Europe. While he was away, Mary and I got married in St. Ann's Episcopal Church in Bridgehampton. Luke was my best man.

At the reception afterward, I winked at Dad, for now there was no doubt that I'd done the right thing by that girl, when they introduced the woman for the first time as Mrs. Mary Bernadette Carr.

She went on to give us several beautiful children, some that lived and some that didn't so others could. And she helped me write this book in a magical place called Sagahawk, a place where we went searching through time for a reset—for an answer to our prayers—a chance to change history—a chance we had once in October of sixty-two, a chance we almost had twice in November of sixty-three.

—Joe Carr

Epilogue

Mary Bernadette Carr

My husband began this story by telling you that his little brother Luke was born with a birth defect that slowed his development. He also told you that his mother was religious and believed that God made Luke that way for a reason, but he didn't know what that reason might be. It's no accident that my husband Joe doesn't know that reason. However, I do and you should, too.

Recall that Joe shared his feelings about Luke with you when he wrote: "I just know that I love the little guy, and he follows me around like the tail on a dog." The night that my husband put the toy saucer down on the encrypted document on his desk so he could carry and tuck Luke into Luke's bed, there is something he didn't know. Luke awoke, followed him to the front door of the house, and went out on the porch. From that vantage point, Luke saw Joe investigate the bright light in the street coming from the direction of the village green. He also saw his brother disappear into that light.

As Joe told you, Luke might take a little longer than most to learn things, but once he did, there was no stopping him. He never forgot a thing. Locked in that head was a brilliant mind that was being held back by faulty pathways to learning. If, in time, science could find a cure for those shortcomings, his mind would shine.

Luke never forgot what he saw that night, nor did he ever forget what he saw the day he was allowed into Captain Harding's study. Besides the toy saucer, he kept the injection needle because it reminded him of a gun. And nobody noticed he'd done so. He hid the needle in the shed and would go there with Linus to play cowboys and Indians with it. His mother would have killed him if she'd known. But nobody missed it, not even Max Werner.

On July 7, 1970, shortly after Joe and I had graduated from college and were beginning to plan for our wedding the next year, I was sitting on the front porch of the Carrs' house, waiting for Joe, who was up taking a shower. Luke, who was now a teenager, came out with a needle in hand. He had filled it with water and sprayed me and himself with it.

I yelled, "What are you doing?"

"Saving your future husband!" he replied.

Before I could react, a bright light engulfed us, and I found myself with Luke in a clean, circular room with creatures that looked like the ones in the pictures in Captain Harding's study. The floor of the room was clear, and through it I saw the Carr gravestone at the cemetery in the village green, the one with the names of George and Brian Angel Carr. But this time there was another name and an inscription:

Joseph Christopher Carr, born June 2, 1946, died June 9, 1971, in action in Vietnam, serving his country. Posthumously awarded the Bronze Star and a Purple Heart

"No!" I screamed. "This has to be a bad dream!" But it wasn't. The creatures let me know that Joe was being recruited by friends for a secret CIA mission to Vietnam to capture a Russian advisor to the Vietcong who was the second gunman on the grassy knoll in Dallas, one of the assassins who shot President John F. Kennedy that day.

Luke looked at me and in a perfectly coherent and mature voice said, "If you want to marry him next spring, sis, you'll have to stop him from accepting the assignment. Otherwise you'll be burying him instead in 1971."

When I regained my composure enough to notice how differently Luke was conducting himself, I asked, "Luke what's happened to you?"

He smiled and answered, "It's the year 2061 where they come from, and science has found a cure for what ails me. In that world, I'm no different than you and Joe."

Perplexed, I asked Luke, "How did you know that putting water in the needle would work to envelop us in their atmosphere and allow them to communicate with us?"

"I witnessed Joe's experience the night he was in communication with them, the night he thought the toy saucer helped him translate the encrypted document. I also witnessed his concern at Mrs. Harding's house the night he got the liquid on him, and tried to wash it off. Then I remembered the needle in the shed, so I went to get it and tried to fill it with water. In my young mind, I wanted to get Joe back, and I thought it would work. It did. There was enough residue left in the vial that the water reactivated it. From there forward, they could make contact with me, but they didn't do so again until earlier today when I asked to return to bring you into the equation. I knew I would not be able to persuade Joe on my own and would need your help if we were to succeed in saving his life."

"Why didn't they just contact Joe and warn him directly?" I asked.

"They can't warn a person about his or her own specific future. It must be done by a contemporary. Someone has to self-select and then act as that person's emissary, as I did."

"Luke, are you going to want to stay in 2061 and not return to your 1970 ailment? I wouldn't blame you one bit if you did."

"Are you crazy? And miss being Joe's best man? No way am I going to do that!"

I leaned over and kissed Luke as I said, "You'll always be my best man, too, little bro!"

It took a lot to talk Joe out of wanting to join the mission that July. In a way it was the hardest thing I'd ever done. I knew it would mean so much to him to be able to help avenge the death of the president he couldn't save—by helping to capture one of his assassins. But in the end, when I gave him an ultimatum and made him choose between our futures together and his personal ambitions, he chose wisely. We had chased enough windmills for one lifetime, I told him. But it broke my heart to do it—to save my superhero and give him a chance to grow old with me and his family. But in the end, I'd rather have the man than the legend. I knew Mrs. Kennedy wouldn't fault me because she'd said much the same about her fallen husband.

I smile even today, so many years later, when I go by the village green and see the Carr gravestone unchanged. God has his reasons, even if we don't always understand them.